Praise for The Highlander's English Bride:

"As close to a perfect Scottish Regency romance as I've ever read." **Nicola Cornick, *NYT* bestselling author**

"Love a marriage of convenience? Love a romance that sparkles? Try Anna Campbell's *The Highlander's English Bride*. I was lucky to see an early edition of this latest in her Lairds Most Likely series and I'm wondering if it might be the best yet. I loved the glamour and tension of the London scenes, but things really heated up when the story moved to the highlands. Sexual tension galore and a really satisfying romance. Just perfect when you need a story that will satisfy and make you smile." **Annie West, *USA Today* bestselling author**

"My Star Rating: 5 stars x 100 Ugly cried AF. Major book hangover. Characters and storyline were freaken amazeballs. Made me wanna hug the author for writing a book that gave me all the feels!! Will definitely be reading this story over and over and over again!!" ***Estela Reads Romance***

"The Highlander's English Bride was an emotional romance that I truly enjoyed." ***Kathy's Review Corner***

"Deep sigh, this is how I feel when I finish one of Anna Campbell's stories, she never fails to makes me feel so good, I could melt in a puddle of happiness." ***5 stars Romance Book Haven***

"A lovely story involving two very admirable, passionate and likable people who you know belong together no matter how their marriage originated...a delightful reading experience." ***Blue Mood Café***

"I have read every one of her books. I have always had favorites and now I am adding this one to the top of my list. I absolutely loved this story from beginning to end! Hamish is now my favorite Highlander! Six Feet Five Inches of breathtaking masculinity, honor, and intelligence." ***The Reading Wench***

"My favorite of the series!" ***Roses Are Blue***

"This is my favourite book in the series." ***5 stars GoodReads Review***

"I love how Anna creates characters you fall in love with. I love how she writes stories that are descriptive and keep you hooked long after you've finished them!" ***5 stars GoodReads Review***

"I adored Hamish and Emily's story!! My emotions were all over the place with this book! The bantering between these two had me laughing out loud and other events had me crying!! OMG, it was so good!! This was a great addition to the Lairds Most Likely series and one you MUST pick up!!" ***Historical Romance Lover***

"Divine." ***5 stars Amazon Review***

"Perfect." ***5 stars GoodReads Review***

ALSO BY ANNA CAMPBELL

Claiming the Courtesan

Untouched

Tempt the Devil

Captive of Sin

My Reckless Surrender

Midnight's Wild Passion

The Sons of Sin Series:

Seven Nights in a Rogue's Bed

Days of Rakes and Roses

A Rake's Midnight Kiss

What a Duke Dares

A Scoundrel by Moonlight

Three Proposals and a Scandal

The Dashing Widows Series:

The Seduction of Lord Stone

Tempting Mr. Townsend

Winning Lord West

Pursuing Lord Pascal

Charming Sir Charles

Catching Captain Nash

Lord Garson's Bride

The Lairds Most Likely Series:

The Laird's Willful Lass

The Laird's Christmas Kiss

The Highlander's Lost Lady

The Highlander's Defiant Captive

The Highlander's Christmas Quest

The Highlander's English Bride

The Highlander's Forbidden Mistress

The Highlander's Christmas Countess

The Highlander's Rescued Maiden

The Highlander's Christmas Lassie

A Scandal in Mayfair Series:

One Wicked Wish

Two Secret Sins

Three Times Tempted

Christmas Stories:

The Winter Wife

Her Christmas Earl

A Pirate for Christmas

Mistletoe and the Major

A Match Made in Mistletoe

The Christmas Stranger

His Christmas Cinderella (in the anthology A
Grosvenor Square Christmas)

Other Books:

These Haunted Hearts

Stranded with the Scottish Earl

The Highlander's English Bride

The Lairds Most Likely Book 6

ANNA CAMPBELL

To my dear friend Cathryn Hein, who is always an
inspiration

PART ONE

CHAPTER ONE

Pascoe Place, near Greenwich, late October 1822

*E*mily Baylor was the most annoying girl in the entire world.

No, make that the entire solar system. And Hamish knew what he was talking about. He was an astronomer. And promising to become a deuced famous one, at that.

Or at least that was the plan.

But so far, the self-satisfaction he'd imagined – no, he deserved! – to feel at this defining moment of his career proved elusive. Not that he meant his advancement to stop at this level. He had his eye on the Astronomer Royal position, and all the honors thereto pertaining. Tonight was an important stepping stone toward achieving his ambitions.

If only a nagging voice in his ear didn't stop him basking in the knowledge of a job well done.

He wished to Hades he could say it was a strident, hectoring voice. But even at this instant, when the urge to pitch its owner down the steep hill into the Thames was nigh irresistible, he couldn't describe the voice as anything but a pleasant contralto.

Damn it, this wasn't fair.

Tonight was meant to be a major triumph for Hamish Douglas, Laird of Glen Lyon. Not that any of these ignorant Sassenachs gave a farthing for a man's Scottish titles.

They did, however, give a farthing if that same fellow had just discovered a new comet. Not to mention if he was the man likely to win the Royal Society's Copley Medal and who took up the post as assistant to the current Astronomer Royal, John Pond, in the new year.

But before Hamish could accept his well-earned acclaim, he needed to deal with the woman tugging at his sleeve and speaking in an urgent whisper. "Hamish, you have to withdraw the pamphlet. The calculations are faulty. I've checked them five times and got the same – wrong – answer every time."

"They're not faulty, blast you," Hamish growled, striving to keep his bass rumble of a voice so low that only Emily could hear him. They were standing in a corner of Lord Pascoe's beautiful ballroom, which was jammed with London's scientific elite, present to applaud the great discovery. Hamish didn't want the world and its wife to suspect that his findings might be in doubt. "Your father checked them."

"Papa is..." Emily trailed off and made a helpless gesture, when helplessness was a thousand miles from her usual condition.

To his sorrow, he knew why she had trouble finishing that sentence. Emily's father, Sir John Baylor, had been Hamish's mentor since he'd graduated from Cambridge. A tutor and a friend since Hamish had come to London to make a career in the field he'd loved from the moment he was old enough to understand what a star was. But over the last few years, Sir John's health failed, and with his health, his mind. Sir John was here tonight, sitting beside the lectern. The place of honor befitted the teacher who had shaped the new force in British astronomy.

Hamish was pleased to see Sir John looking better than he had in a long time. The old man hadn't been out in public since last year. Now his many friends and colleagues in the London Astronomical Society, the Royal Institution, and the Royal Society crowded around to pay court.

She tried again. "Papa is—"

"A great man."

"Inclined to be confused." Emily's bright hazel gaze, more green than brown in the light from the chandeliers, settled on her father with a frown of concern. Then she shifted her attention back to Hamish. "You can't make those calculations public. They will ruin you."

"They're not wrong," he said through his teeth.

"They are," she said, just as stubbornly.

"Damn you, Emily," he muttered and dragged her across to the long mahogany table where hundreds of copies of his paper about the comet awaited distribution once the speeches were done.

She hoisted her imperious little nose into the air. "I can't help it if you made a mistake."

He'd known Emily as long as he'd known her father. She'd annoyed him when she'd been a fourteen-year-old girl, partly because his masculine superiority hadn't overawed her as it should. He'd soon discovered that she possessed a brilliant, incisive mind. While he'd like to say her mind was unfeminine, he came from a family of clever women so he couldn't.

Nonetheless, she was far too ready to pit that mind against his. Even more annoying, on occasion her intellectual arrogance proved justified. On the very rare occasion, he wondered if, perhaps, her brain might surpass his.

Unacceptable.

Most people, even in England, rewarded him with immediate respect. After all, he came from a rich, powerful family. He owned a large and prosperous estate, and he was connected to a host of influential Scottish landowners. His late father had been a significant power in the War Office during the French wars, and his mother's passion for politics made her influence felt across the nation. Not to mention that he was the size of a mountain and he had a brain like a steel trap.

Yet Emily Baylor, even as a girl, treated Hamish like her slow-witted older brother. The sight of her turning up her nose at him was no novelty.

Hamish wasn't an overly vain main, but he was accustomed to female admiration. Emily most definitely didn't admire him. She never had. Which shouldn't niggle. After all, there was no accounting for taste. Most people loved strawberries. He couldn't stand the things. Perhaps he was to Emily what strawberries were to him.

Over the years, he'd learned to live with her ill-concealed disdain. Mostly. It was easier these days, when the fashionable and scientific worlds vied to praise him.

This uppity, frank, clever – much as he hated to admit it – snip of a girl didn't like him? So what? Everybody else did. In recent years, he and she had made an unspoken truce to stay out of each other's way as far as possible.

But when she set out to spoil his special night, the chit crossed a line. A tide of long-held irritation rose to clog his throat. He wanted to rage at her, tell her to find her own blasted comet, but both manners and the event's public nature meant he had to keep a lid on his exasperation.

"I didn't make a mistake," he said slowly and with commendable composure, given the provocation. "You did."

The long-suffering patience weighting her sigh made him want to push her out the window. "Let me show you."

He sucked in a deep breath and told himself he had too much at stake to inform this upstart what she could do with her interference. Hamish's temper could get the better of him, and right now he was angry. But he retained enough self-awareness to notice a couple of heads turning in their direction. Sometimes it was no gift to be six foot five and built like a marauding Viking.

Anyway, he was the guest of honor, and therefore the center of attention.

"Not here," he said, still in that unnaturally steady voice.

Emily's eyes narrowed. "I'm not going somewhere private, just so you can shout at me."

Offended, he drew himself up until he loomed over her. She wasn't a small woman, but compared to him, she was a mere scrap. "I do not shout," he said icily.

"Yes, you do," she said with equal coldness. "It's how you get your own way, when the practiced charm fails."

Bloody English witch. Most people found him a perfect gentleman.

Most people give you your own way, simply for the asking.

The nasty little voice in his head spoke with Emily Baylor's crisp consonants and ironic intonation. He ignored the jibe and tightened his grip on her arm. "I promise I won't shout."

The angle of her fine dark brown eyebrows indicated skepticism, but after a pause, she nodded. "All right, I'll meet you there. But the moment you raise your voice, I'm leaving."

He ground his teeth to restrain a blistering response. "There's an anteroom down the corridor." Those curious glances worried him. He didn't want to continue this discussion in public. "I'll meet you there in five minutes."

"Very well," she said in a clipped tone.

She didn't ask for more directions than that, reminding him that she belonged to the London scientific establishment in a way he never had. She'd been born to this world. He'd had to fight his way into it. Emily had been a regular visitor to this luxurious house since she was a toddler. Lord Pascoe's estate was only a few miles from the Royal Observatory, and he often hosted intellectual gatherings.

She paused to pick up a pamphlet from the table. As if he chose a dueling pistol, Hamish did, too.

It took him slightly longer than five minutes to find her in the side room. A couple of his friends came over to congratulate him, and he needed to extricate himself from their good wishes.

He wasn't sure she'd still be waiting, but she was there. She was a remarkably headstrong lass, inclined to go her own way. She was so headstrong, she could almost be Scottish. Most well-bred English girls were brought up to do what they were told.

It was no surprise that Emily Baylor was still on the shelf at twenty-four. What man would want to take on such a hellcat? She'd be more likely to argue philosophy with him over breakfast than smile sweetly and wish him good morrow as she refilled his coffee cup.

Except...

Except the most annoying aspect out of Emily's multitude of annoying aspects was that she was so damned pretty.

For years, her shining, changeable eyes and her fine-boned face with its pointed chin had inspired a host of forbidden dreams that had Hamish waking hard and ready. In the dark, Emily wasn't annoying because she tried to put him in his place. No, she was annoying because she was a mere figment of his fevered imagination, instead of real and warm and lying in his arms.

Even now, when she was even more annoying than usual, he couldn't help admiring the way she looked, standing under the small chandelier. His gaze fixed on the luxuriant sable hair caught up in loose curls. What man wouldn't burn to sink his hands into that glossy tumble? Nor could any red-blooded male ignore how her deep blue gown clung to her magnificent bosom and lissome figure.

When she turned a hostile gaze in his direction, he battled to ignore what a diamond she was. As usual, he didn't quite succeed. Even though he told himself that diamonds didn't just glitter, they cut.

"You should have got me to check the calculations."

Definitely annoying. His lips tightened as he stepped into the room. "You have a high opinion of yourself, miss."

"I'm good at the details. You know that."

He did. Despite their combative relationship, he'd always felt sorry that Emily was born a woman. If she'd been a man, a brilliant scientific career would have beckoned.

He bristled with awareness of the risks that he and Emily took, sneaking away like this. The corridor behind him was empty. He couldn't be sure it was going to stay that way. There was no reason for any of the guests to venture into this small room, but if they heard voices, they just might. "Come out to the garden and tell me what you think is the problem," he said wearily.

She stiffened. "It's freezing out there."

It was. Winter had come early this year. "We can't stay in here. If anyone finds us, there will be gossip."

She greeted that with a scornful snort. "Nobody in their right mind would imagine you and I are carrying on a flirtation."

Hamish closed the door to the corridor and marched across to stand in front of the doors leading onto the dark terrace. "Nevertheless, I'd rather have a little more privacy." He took off his coat and held it out between his hands. "Emily?"

She didn't shift. "Do we have time before the presentation?"

"I think so."

He could see she wanted to argue. Arguing with him was natural to her. But with another of those sighs that always made him bristle, she let him help her into his coat.

Hamish stepped back. She should look silly with his evening coat draped over that spectacular gown with its filmy midnight blue skirts and pretty pattern of spangles. The dress reminded him of the night sky.

Even when Emily was annoying him, which was most of the time, he couldn't deny her effortless elegance. Topping her stylish ensemble with a masculine coat did nothing to lessen that. The coat was miles too big, of course. It fell to past her knees, and the shoulder seams drooped down her arms.

As they stepped outside, she clutched the coat around her throat. "Won't you be cold?"

"I'll manage," he said gruffly, as the chill air struck him like a blow.

He paused to look up at the stars, but flying clouds masked the sky. All his life, it had been his habit to wonder at the night's beauty. It was second nature to note the name and position of the few pinpricks of light he saw.

At his side, Emily did the same thing. The fleeting moment of common ground between them eased his crankiness. As he drew her down to the garden, the hand he curled around her arm wasn't quite as insistent as it had been. With another woman, he might even call his touch tender.

"Now tell me what you think you found," he said, as they entered a bedraggled garden, all bare sticks with the coming winter. The light from the house saved him from stumbling around in the pitch black.

When she raised her face, he caught the glint of her eyes. "I *found*..." She placed a slight emphasis on the word. "...an error in your figures for the velocity. You've transposed sine for cosine three lines down on page three. Why on earth didn't you ask me to check it before you published?"

His lips turned down, although somewhere in the back of his mind, he couldn't help wondering if Emily might be right. She sounded so certain, and her mathematics were usually reliable. His pride insisted that he stifled the unwelcome niggle of doubt. He'd been over those calculations a hundred times. "I don't need your supervision, Emily."

"Apparently you do," she retorted, and he was immediately back to wanting to lift her high over his head and hurl her into the river. "Anyway, it's pointless talking about it out here in the dark. Take me back inside, and I'll show you."

"You're set on ruining my success tonight," he said grimly. "I'd thought better of you."

"Oh, for heaven's sake, Hamish, I'm not doing this out of spite. Anything but. I don't want to see you make a fool of yourself."

"Because it reflects on your father as my mentor?"

"There's that, but for your own sake as well. I bear you no ill will."

"Right now, I have difficulty believing that," he said, his temper rising to a dangerous pitch. He reminded himself again that he had too much to lose to unleash his anger. "You could have approached me privately about this."

"I only saw the paper tonight," she responded just as hotly. "These last months, I've had my hands full with Papa. It never occurred to me that you'd make such an elementary mistake."

The superior little baggage. "Elementary?" he asked on a rising note.

She faltered back into the spindly bushes and that displeased him, too. As if he'd descend to violence.

"Yes, elementary." At least she didn't sound frightened.

His burgeoning anger made him say something he didn't mean, but that he knew would rankle. "Everybody says there's nothing but trouble in store, when a female dabbles in higher learning."

"Then everybody is a dimwitted ass."

"I suppose that means me."

"If the cap fits."

His hands fisted at his sides as he battled for calm. He and Emily had often squabbled before, but this threatened to disintegrate into a juvenile quarrel that would show neither of them in a good light. "There's no point in continuing this discussion."

She didn't budge. He should have known she wouldn't. She was as stubborn as a mule. "So are you going to withdraw that paper and make corrections?"

"I believe it's unnecessary," he said coldly, although he was desperate to check the equation that she'd singled out. He wouldn't admit that to Emily, though, even under torture. Hamish held out his hand. "Allow me to escort you back inside, Miss Baylor."

They'd known each other for ten years and been on first name terms for most of that time. He intended the formal address to wound. By God, after tonight he'd be happy never to see her again.

"Now you're acting like a child."

"If I am, it's of no concern to you."

"Oh, Hamish, don't be like this."

The world of disappointment in the words made him grit his teeth until his jaw ached. "There's nothing more we can achieve out here."

She made a soft exhalation, redolent of irritation. "We haven't achieved anything out here."

"Emily, stop playing games," he said in a rush, and only realized he'd used her Christian name after he'd spoken. So much for staying on his high horse. He shivered and to make matters worse, it started to rain. "It's as cold as a witch's tit. If you mean to berate me, at least do it inside in the warm."

"It was your idea to come into the garden." She still sounded sulky.

It had been. Because he'd feared a scandal if anyone caught him alone in a side room with his mentor's bonny daughter. Now if they both went back into the house, wet as herrings, questions would arise anyway. "Well, now it's my idea to go inside. Are you coming?"

There was a silence while he wondered what in blazes fretted the pestilential girl now.

"I can't," she said in a small voice.

"Emily," he growled, hunching his shoulders against the wet. "I told you to stop playing games."

"I'm not playing games. I'm stuck."

CHAPTER TWO

"What?" Hamish bit out.

"When you shoved me into this bush, my dress got caught."

"I did not shove you," he retorted, even as he shifted around Emily to try and see where she was attached to the branches. It was dark in this corner of the garden. And muddy. Damp seeped into his shoes and chilled his feet. His evening pumps weren't designed for anything but a dance floor. "Hold still and I'll set you free."

"Try not to rip my dress."

Hamish ignored her habit of giving orders. He usually did. He dropped the pamphlet to the ground so he had two free hands. Bending down, he tried to use his fingers to work out where dress and thorns made contact. Devil if he could see a damned thing. And Emily's smoky, alluring scent, all honey and jasmine, teased his nostrils and made it almost impossible to think. "Plague take you, stay still."

"Well, that's charming."

He tugged at his coat and loosened it with what he hoped was minimal damage. "See if you can get out of my coat."

"I'll tear it."

"I don't give a fig if you do. You'll freeze to death if you stay out here."

So would he. He'd intended taking a few unobserved moments to put this impudent miss in her place, but they'd been out here for over a quarter of an hour now, and his shirt offered precious little protection from the elements.

"If you say so."

With some trouble, she wriggled out of the fine black coat, and he heard fabric ripping. He ground his teeth in irritation. When he stood up on the podium to give his speech, he wasn't going to make much of a show, by God.

He shrugged on the coat, immediately welcoming the warmth. But now Emily only had that damned becoming gown to cover her, and it was as unsuited to the outdoors as his pumps.

"Why the devil do women wear these ridiculous rags?" he muttered, trying to make sense of a million layers of petticoats tangled around the thorny bush. "Hell."

"What is it?"

Those thorns meant business. "Nothing. Can you move now?" he asked, striving not to bark at her.

"My skirt's still caught."

Of course it was. Could this night get any worse? He muffled a sigh and went down on his haunches to see what else he could do to free her. "Keep still."

He could smell rain and cold fresh air. But as he kneeled at Emily's side, mostly he just smelled her. Crushed flowers. And beneath that, a warm, alluring scent that he'd long ago identified as essence of

Emily. By God, if he was a chemist, he'd work out how to bottle that. He'd make a fortune.

That scent turned his usually deft hands into ten thumbs. While here and now he'd like to consign this interfering besom to perdition, tonight that scent would twine its way through his dreams. It would make him hot and frustrated, and angry with himself for the depraved things he did to his mentor's daughter in his fantasies.

"Hamish, I'm freezing." She didn't sound nearly as full of herself. He wasn't the only one who knew they'd been out here far too long.

"I know." Even with his coat on, he was cold. He was close enough to hear her teeth chatter. He reined in a lunatic offer to sweep her into his arms and warm her up. It didn't help that he crouched mere inches from graceful hips and a nicely rounded rump. "Forgive me, I'm going to have to tear your dress."

"Do it."

His shoulders tensed as a cold dribble of water ran down the back of his neck. "People might notice."

"I'll make repairs in the retiring room before I return to the reception." She paused. "Or go back outside and wait in the carriage."

"Very well."

In the silent garden, the sound of shredding fabric was loud. Loud and too damned evocative to a man who might resent the girl's effrontery, but who couldn't help wanting the woman.

As if they had a chance of getting together. What a disaster that would be. If he did manage to inveigle his way into her bed, she'd take notes on his performance. Once they were done, she'd give him chapter and verse on where he went wrong.

The minute she was free, she staggered. As Hamish rose, he reached out to catch her. For one dizzying moment, he clasped Emily Baylor to his chest, and she wasn't bossy or prickly or difficult. She was soft and supple, and she smelled sweeter than a flower garden in high summer.

"Oh…" she gasped, lifting her face in surprise.

The light from inside revealed shining eyes and lush red lips parted on a breath. As she struggled to find her balance, her hands tightened on his brawny arms.

Then after too short a time – too long a time, rather, he should say if he had an ounce of sense – she let him go.

"Thank you for releasing me." Her gratitude sounded grudging.

"Emily…" He remained lost in the extraordinary moment when he'd held her.

She stepped away, and her tone became all business. "You still have to withdraw your paper."

His enchantment dissolved into the much more familiar and much more comfortable irritation. "Because Queen Emily of the Royal Society decrees it?"

She made a growl of annoyance deep in her throat. "Because it's flawed."

He caught her hand and hauled her back toward the French doors. The urge to kiss her retreated. The rain was getting heavier, the wind whipped about them, and the ground under his feet was slick and muddy.

"All right, show me the calculation. I'll prove you wrong, then we can go back to the party, and you can eat humble pie while everyone showers me with congratulations."

Another of those growls. After ten years, the sound was familiar. "You're so full of yourself."

"This is my night. And you're doing your best to ruin it."

They were back inside the anteroom now. "I'm doing my best to save your worthless hide, you great conceited clodpoll," she snapped back.

She lifted the now soggy pamphlet detailing the discovery that would make his reputation. He snatched the paper from her and turned to the calculation. Out of the corner of his eye, he was aware that she folded her arms over that very nice bosom. Less nice was the brazen superiority in her regard. That expression always made him want to kiss her into trembling acquiescence.

Perhaps he hadn't abandoned all thought of kissing her after all, God rot him.

It took him a few seconds to control his temper long enough to make sense of the rows of figures.

When he did, humiliation crawled through his belly like a slug through a lettuce patch. Humiliation and chagrin and disbelief.

Hot color flooded his cheeks, and he raised his eyes to his bugbear. "Damn it, Emily..."

"I'm right, aren't I?"

He sucked an audible breath in through his nose. "Yes, you're right, devil take you. Feel free to crow all you like."

"It could happen to anyone, Hamish. You still discovered the comet. You just have to adjust your figures."

Hamish was so mortified, he hardly noticed that this time, she sounded neither triumphant nor belligerent. She sounded relieved, as if she really cared that he didn't go out there tonight and make a fool of himself. "I have to destroy that pamphlet."

"Yes."

He should thank her, he supposed, but the words stuck in his throat. He scrunched up the paper and tossed it into the unlit fireplace. The only place fit for it, to his chagrin. "Let's go and get them off the table before anybody picks one up."

He stepped forward and caught her arm and only then noticed the damage rain, mud, his fumbling, and Lord Pascoe's shrubbery had done to her appearance. "Emily…"

"Yes?"

"To blazes with you, you can't go out there looking like that. I'll have to escort you to your carriage after all."

"The retiring room—"

"This is more than a few pins and a handkerchief can put right. You look like you've been with Wellington, following the drum across Spain. Through an earthquake and a thunderstorm."

When she glanced down at her gown, dismay flooded her expression. "Oh, for pity's sake, you're right."

"We need to get you out of here before anyone sees you."

"What about Papa?"

"I'll make sure he gets home safely. You can't hang about. You'll catch pneumonia." Time was getting short, and he was due to make his speech in a few minutes. After he got her safely into her carriage, he'd need to come back in and tidy himself up. He wasn't in much better state than Emily. "I'll take you along the terrace, then down to your carriage. That way, there's a bit of shelter from the upper floors. It's raining cats and dogs out there now."

He waited for an argument. With Emily, there was *always* an argument. But to his relief, she nodded.

Once more, he removed his coat. He could see her shivering from here. "Take this, or you'll catch your death. Not to mention it will help you fade into the shadows."

"Thank you." This time, she responded with suitable gratitude, although she looked sad and put upon.

Unwilling pity pierced him. He could imagine the evening hadn't worked out the way she'd wished either. Since her father's illness had worsened, she hadn't been out and about very much. Tonight had been a chance for her to see her friends and sample a little high life.

While she pulled his coat over her shoulders, he checked to make sure the terrace was empty. Although who in their right mind would choose to be outside in this tempest? He turned back to her. "Ready?"

"Yes." She didn't look like a harridan right now. He wished to heaven she did. Instead with her wet tangle of hair and her oversized covering, she looked like a winsome urchin.

Winsome? That would be the day.

"Let's run," he said.

As they dashed out into the blustery night, he somehow ended up holding her hand. It felt small and cold and fragile in his grasp, and a surge of unaccustomed protectiveness caught him unawares.

With the wind blowing and cold rain lashing them, they darted between the squares of light shining from inside the house. They slipped on the cold, wet marble and a couple of times he nearly fell to his knees, but they kept going. He could see the top of the steps ahead. He just needed to get Emily down to the road and into her carriage and they were safe.

Hamish began to hope that they'd make it without being seen.

He shouldn't have.

As they scurried past the ballroom, one of the French doors swung open. Before Hamish could drag Emily into the shadows, a plump blonde girl appeared in the gap and released an ear-splitting scream.

Startled, Hamish slammed to an abrupt stop. Emily stumbled and crashed into his back with an audible *oof*.

In one calamitous instant, the whole damned world collapsed around his ears.

CHAPTER THREE

he high-pitched female shriek sliced through the buzz of conversation filling the ballroom. Silence crashed down, and every eye in the room arrowed in on Hamish and Emily poised between the open doors like actors in limelight.

"Oh, my goodness, Emily Baylor!" Matilda Conley exclaimed on top note, although at least now she'd stopped screaming. "I thought I saw someone sneaking around outside. Now I find it's just you and Mr. Douglas. But look at you! What on earth have you two been up to? Your dress is in absolute tatters."

Wrenching her hand free of Hamish's, Emily stifled a curse. Of course the silliest girl in Christendom had to catch her slinking away from the reception, not to mention notice her *dishabille*. And noticing, had to announce it to the world.

"N-nothing, Matilda." She hated the betraying stutter in her voice. She also hated the telltale heat flooding her cheeks.

She could imagine what a spectacle she must make. She recalled Hamish's appalled expression when he saw her in the anteroom. Not to mention, she was wearing his coat, and he was in his shirtsleeves. Any transfer of clothing between a well-bred young lady and a rakish young man reeked of scandal.

"You look like you've been crawling around a muddy shrubbery," Matilda said, still speaking in a piercing soprano. People crowded in behind Matilda, craning their necks to see what was happening.

"What a ridiculous idea," Emily muttered, consigning the younger Miss Conley to Hades. Her father was a brilliant man who edited a respected scientific journal. His three daughters didn't have a brain between them.

"It's not ridiculous. You've got twigs in your hair, and your dress is torn and wet, and your hem is all muddy."

"Miss Matilda, there's no need for concern." Hamish's deep rumble of a voice emerged from too close behind Emily. She heard the ironic weight he put on the word "concern," but she doubted Matilda did. "I was merely showing Miss Baylor a constellation we were discussing earlier."

"On your knees in the dirt obviously," Matilda said, and she didn't sound hysterical at all. She wasn't shocked at Emily's breach of propriety. She was gloating at this public fall from grace.

As Emily met the girl's sharp little eyes, she had cause to regret her former behavior to the Conley girls. She hadn't hidden her dismissive attitude as well as she might.

Emily edged into the ballroom, further away from Hamish. Mortification and an utterly futile wish to turn the clock back created a sour mixture in her stomach. "I...I tripped," she said, with no hope at all that anyone would believe her.

"Into Mr. Douglas's embrace, I'm assuming," Matilda said snidely.

Shut up, Matilda. What Emily would give to scratch the silly widgeon's eyes out. The girl was clearly set on causing trouble.

As she observed the sea of faces turned in her direction, she saw trouble was exactly the result. Some expressions were concerned, some expressions were shocked. The majority were brimming with salacious curiosity.

People outside the rarefied world of science imagined that its denizens devoted their time to higher matters. From long experience, Emily knew that wasn't the case. An interest in learning didn't preclude an equally powerful interest in scandal. Catching the man of the moment skulking around in the dark with Sir John Baylor's spinster daughter provided a tasty tidbit.

"The weather worsened while we were outside," Hamish said, stepping up beside her, plague take him.

Emily closed her eyes and prayed for control. Couldn't Hamish see he only made things worse? She wished to heaven that she'd thrown him to the wolves when she found that error in his calculations. What did she care if he faced professional criticism? It wasn't as if they'd ever been friends.

"Why would you go stargazing when it's raining?" This from Matilda's older sister Cassie, who now hovered at Matilda's side.

"Just how long were you out there, young man?" Lord Pascoe asked, and Emily cringed when the question drew forth a muffled snicker. "Long enough to be grubbing around on your hands and knees, if the state of your clothes is any indication."

"Miss Baylor's honor is untarnished," Hamish said, then spoiled everything by taking her arm. She stiffened under his touch and only just stopped herself from jerking free.

This whole disaster was all Hamish's fault. Damn him.

Except it wasn't. She knew better than to go out into a dark garden alone with a young man. His arrogant dismissal of her concerns had made her so cross that she'd given no thought to how all this would reflect on her reputation. It was so unfair, the restrictions the world placed on a woman of brains and spirit.

Except right now, she could lay no special claim to possessing brains. She might call Matilda Conley a nitwit, but Matilda wasn't the one facing a wall of disapproval and nasty curiosity. Matilda Conley wasn't the one feeling sick with humiliation and self-hatred. No, it was that intellectual prodigy, Emily Baylor.

Then the worst thing of all happened.

"Emily?" The crowd parted as her father tottered up to her. "What's all this fuss?"

"Nothing, Papa." She broke away from Hamish and rushed forward to take his arm. She'd been too angry to cry before, but the bewilderment in her father's voice had her blinking away tears. "It's time we went home."

He'd been so good this evening, almost like his old self. Seeing his friends and hearing praise for his protégé's brilliance had sparked some of his former fire.

Now he frowned in incomprehension. "But Hamish hasn't made his speech. I'd dearly like to stay for the presentation."

"My speech has been delayed," Hamish said, taking her father's other arm.

Emily cast Hamish a killing look that he ignored. No matter how she tried, she couldn't escape him, it seemed.

"Delayed? Why delayed?" As her father glanced around the packed room, she watched him retreat into the mists of confusion.

Hamish faced the crowd, and his voice rang with effortless authority. "I believe Sir John needs quiet and privacy. Under the circumstances, I won't be making my presentation. It's also been brought to my attention that the pamphlets contain a printing error. So all round, we must delay our celebration of the new comet for a few weeks. I apologize for your disappointment, and I thank you for coming tonight."

Emily regarded him in amazement and unwilling admiration. She'd forgotten he was a lord up in his wild Scottish hills. His air of command and his clear-eyed gaze had quite a few of the guests shuffling in embarrassment. She also had to give him credit for his quick thinking when it came to the pamphlets. A printing error indeed.

The guests started to shuffle toward the doors, however reluctantly. To her surprise, that lordly dictate achieved its purpose, despite Hamish being younger than nearly every man here and the room heaving with London's great and good. Not to mention that this wasn't his house, so he had no right to order visitors on their way.

On the other hand, Hamish was big and strong enough to toss any naysayers out on their ear if they dared to dawdle. When Emily first met him, his size as much as his intellectual self-confidence had daunted her. He was a huge, yellow-haired bear of a man. Handsome, she supposed, if one wanted a great lump of potent masculinity overshadowing one. She had more refined tastes. Although few of her female friends had ever found all that raw muscle and Scottish vigor off-putting.

"We must expect some high spirits from the young people. A storm in a teacup. Speaking of storms, given the weather, it would be prudent to make our way home." Sir Humphry Davy, President of the Royal Society for the last two years, threw his considerable influence into clearing the room. He hadn't been well lately and walked with a stick which he deployed with complete lack of ceremony to usher the guests out. After the previous president, the urbane Sir Joseph Banks, Sir Humphry's bluff manners had come as a jolt to the gentleman scientists. "I'll arrange for Mr. Douglas to present his findings at the next meeting. No harm done. No harm done."

Except Emily could see that great harm had been done. The crowd might disburse as requested, but she caught the speculative glances leveled at her and Hamish. With difficulty, she kept herself from cringing away from the knowing looks. She knew just what the scientists of London and their wives would talk about over their toast and marmalade tomorrow morning. That shameless hussy Emily Baylor and that rogue Hamish Douglas.

Nausea churned in her stomach, and her hand tightened on her father's skeletal arm. Once upon a time, he'd been fit and alert. Once upon a time, he'd be the first to defend his daughter's honor. Now he was old and frail and lost to what went on around him most of the time. That was the cruelest cut of all. Because in his more lucid moments, he'd understand the spiteful things that people said after tonight's farrago.

Sir Humphry bustled toward them. She read concern and apprehension beneath his air of bonhomie. "John, Emily, I'm so sorry the evening has come to an early end. John, we haven't seen enough of you these past months. I hope you'll come to the society's meeting, when this young Apollo finally gets his chance to report on his discovery."

With a vague air of recognition, her father peered at the man who had been one of his closest friends. Emily mustered a shaky smile for her godfather. "Uncle Humphry, I'm sorry for causing all this trouble. I swear nothing untoward happened. My frock got caught in a shrub."

Uncle Humphry's round, blunt-featured face flushed with embarrassment. "I trust your word." His voice lowered, although Emily could have told him her father was too tired to follow the conversation. "Perhaps not the wisest—"

"My fault entirely, Sir Humphry. Please accept my apologies," Hamish said. "Such a pity that my request for a few moments of private conversation should cause this brouhaha."

Sir Humphry directed a disapproving stare at Hamish. "Yes, well, this room might be packed to the gills with the biggest brains in England. That doesn't stop them enjoying a good gossip. They lap up scandal as avidly as any empty-headed old maid in Tunbridge Wells."

A warning that Emily didn't need. Her stomach heaved, and she feared she might actually be sick. By tomorrow morning, the tale of her lapse with the young Laird of Glen Lyon would be all over Town.

CHAPTER FOUR

*E*mily was in the library at the Bloomsbury house, struggling to focus on the household accounts. That task was always a trial, even when she felt vigorous and alert. But her father had had a bad night, and she'd been up to him several times. Eventually just before dawn, he'd fallen into a restless doze. This was his second interrupted night in a row, and it was all Hamish Douglas's fault. Papa had come back from Greenwich in a state, despite her best efforts to reassure him that everything was as it should be.

The problem was that she was a terrible liar, especially when she was in a state herself. While her father drifted in and out of reality with bewildering swiftness, enough of his native brilliance remained for him to note a room's emotional temperature. Not only that, he knew her too well to believe her comforting falsehoods. Since her mamma's death eleven years ago, Emily had worked in close partnership with him. He knew she was upset, he knew something untoward had happened at Pascoe Place, and he knew nobody had yet told him the full story.

No wonder he fretted.

Now on this rainy morning, Emily fretted, too, as eyes scratchy with sleeplessness studied the neat rows of figures in the ledger. There was enough money – just – but it was clear that she needed to make more economies. In recognition of his distinguished scientific work, the Crown had granted her father a modest pension. But the next payment wasn't due for another six weeks.

She struggled not to think of the grim future awaiting, once her father passed away and the pension ceased. Aside from her inevitable grief, she'd have to find some way of supporting herself in a world that didn't favor overeducated females with a high opinion of their capabilities.

Groaning, she covered her face as she recalled those vile moments in Greenwich. The queasy feeling returned with a vengeance, although it had never really gone away. Thanks to the night before last, she wasn't just an overeducated female with a high opinion of her capabilities. She also had a scandal hanging over her head.

Emily was so lost in misery, it took her a moment to realize that someone knocked at the door. With a heartfelt sigh, she lowered her hands and squared her shoulders. No doubt, given how gossip spread, the staff already knew about her disgrace, but she intended to put a brave face on things for as long as she could. "Come."

Polly the housemaid opened the door and curtsied. "Begging your pardon for interrupting, miss, but Mr. Douglas is here."

Mr. Douglas? Outrage twisted Emily's stomach. The author of her current troubles was the last person she wanted to see. How she wished to heaven she'd left Hamish to stew. "I'm not at home to visitors this morning, Polly."

The maid cast a quick look behind her. "He's very set on seeing you."

She could imagine. No wonder Polly looked flustered. Hamish in full flight could take on Napoleon and win. A mere housemaid would have no chance against him.

Nonetheless after about three hours' sleep in the last two days, Emily was in no mood to hear his apologies. If apologies were indeed what he came for.

"Well, he can be set somewhere else," she said. "I'm busy."

"Not too busy to see me, I'm sure," a rumbling bass voice said from the corridor. Hamish brushed past a fluttery Polly to stand large and vivid and so cursed self-satisfied in the middle of the floor.

Emily ground her teeth and narrowed her eyes on the almost ridiculously virile male adorning her library. How she wished that he wasn't such a supreme example of masculinity. His self-confidence had always stuck in her craw, and she hated having to admit that there might be some justification for his swagger.

Perhaps it was because he was Scottish – even if he sounded as London-bred as she did – that Hamish always brought the suggestion of a wilder, more exciting world with him. He was huge, taller than any other man she knew, and built like a Viking raider. Broad shoulders, beefy arms, a chest that should be covered in chainmail instead of the perfect Savile Row tailoring he wore.

He was fair like a Viking, too. With wheat-blond hair, and golden skin that never faded to a London pallor, and bright blue eyes that didn't miss a thing. On first meeting him, people sometimes assumed that Mr. Douglas's overwhelming physical presence must equate to a dull mind. They didn't assume that for long.

Emily had grown up surrounded by clever men. Hamish Douglas was the cleverest man she'd ever met. Or at least he was when his volatile emotions didn't get the better of him.

The way they'd got the better of him two nights ago.

The recollection of the disaster he'd caused lent her voice a hard edge. "My father may have let you run tame over this house, Hamish. But right now I'm in charge, and I don't have time for your nonsense this morning. In fact, after what happened at Greenwich, I doubt I'll ever have time for you again."

Since leaving Lord Pascoe's, her main concern had been calming her father's agitation. Her secondary concern had been how on earth she could come around from the wreck of her reputation.

No one had called at the house yesterday, which was indication enough that the world was busy elsewhere, dragging her name through the mud. Her pride shied away from the thought. Even without fearing how this scandal would affect her future, she cringed from being the target of vicious gossip. With her odd intellectual interests and outspoken manner, she'd never been the ideal of womanhood. But in all her twenty-four years, nobody had ever questioned her virtue.

Which was why right now she'd happily slap the cheerful smile from Hamish Douglas's face. If only he'd acted like a reasonable man in Greenwich and accepted her conclusions, she wouldn't be in trouble.

"That would be a pity when we're such old friends," Hamish said, which was a blatant lie. They'd never been friends. He cast a meaningful glance at Polly. "I'd like a word alone with your mistress."

"Polly, please show Mr. Douglas out," Emily said over the girl's quick, "As you wish, Mr. Douglas."

"Polly!"

Hamish smiled at the maid with the flashing charm Emily had always acknowledged, however reluctantly. "Someone's in a ticklish mood today."

"Miss Baylor was up all night to the master, sir. I'm not surprised she's a bit grumpy."

"Polly, that's enough," Emily snapped.

"Yes, miss. I'm sorry, miss." The girl blushed and avoided her eye. "I'll go now."

"Not before you show Mr. Douglas to…"

But the maid had already scuttled out of the room and closed the door behind her. If Emily had a shred of reputation left to lose, she might worry about the propriety of staying behind a closed door with Hamish. She was too furious to be worried.

Surging to her feet, she clenched her hands at her sides. She told herself that she couldn't punch him. She was a lady. But by God, she'd like to, even if he was too lumbering and brawny to notice her flimsy attempts to harm him.

"Hamish, this isn't your house," she said through stiff lips. "You no longer live here. You have no special rights. I've been polite and asked you to leave. I'll thank you to cooperate."

One dark gold eyebrow quirked in her direction. "Polite?"

Her lips tightened. "At least as polite as you've been, barging your way in here, when you must know you're the last person I want to see."

The spark of teasing amusement faded from his eyes, although he didn't show any sign of leaving, damn him. As if to confirm that, he placed his high-crowned beaver hat on a chair. "I'm sorry to hear that."

"But surely not surprised," she retorted.

He shrugged. "Not entirely. I'm also sorry to hear your father isn't well."

"He hasn't been well for two years."

Hamish frowned, and she shrank from the compassion that softened his eyes. That unwelcome sensitivity was one of the most grating things about him. She'd dearly love to dismiss him as nothing but a mountain of puffed-up male conceit, but Hamish was among the few of her father's protégés who had made a real effort to help Sir John in his decline. "I know. But I was shocked to see him at the reception."

Since her father's health started to fade, anxiety and grief underlay everything Emily did. Now that sorrow threatened to rise and shatter her shaky control. Frantic not to break down, she chased after her anger and caught it in a firm grip.

Her anger with Hamish made her feel strong. Dissolving into a storm of tears in front of him would not.

"Your actions the other night didn't help."

She waited for him to defend himself, but instead he leveled his shoulders and subjected her to an unwavering stare. She'd never seen him look so serious. "That's what I'm here to talk about."

Oh, dear Lord. What was the point of going over the finer points of that shambles? "It's too late for an apology."

"Yes, it is. Nonetheless, I apologize unreservedly. I wronged you, Emily."

Surprised, she met his eyes. He still looked somber and troubled. And damn him, far too handsome for his own good. Or hers.

His ready shouldering of the blame forced her to a grudging confession. "It wasn't all your fault. I knew better than to go outside with you."

Grim humor turned down that expressive mouth. "When I build up a head of steam, I'm hard to gainsay."

That was something else she liked about Hamish – once his temper subsided, he was willing to own up to being in the wrong. Even in Greenwich, after he checked the offending calculation, he'd admitted his mistake. But by then, faulty mathematics had been the least of their problems.

Her belligerence became more and more difficult to maintain. She sighed and despite everything, the taut, high line of her shoulders relaxed. "You are. And we were unlucky, too. I wanted to throttle that blasted henwit Matilda Conley."

"Bad luck was only an issue because of my bad judgment."

She gestured for him to sit, accepting that she wasn't going to throw him out. Raising her chin, she injected false cheerfulness into her tone. "It will all blow over."

Hamish didn't shift from where he stood. "No. I don't think it will."

Nor did she. Not really.

Feeling cornered, she backed away and curled one hand over the back of the chair she'd been sitting in. "We didn't do anything wrong."

No trace of his usual smile lit the deep blue eyes he leveled on her. Nor did he sit down, which meant he still loomed over her like a mighty cliffside. "The world sees it differently."

She sliced the air with a dismissive hand. "I'm a spinster lady past marriageable age and up until this point, I've had a spotless reputation. Outside the scientific community, nobody even knows I'm alive."

She hid a wince as more of that dratted compassion softened his gaze. Hamish Douglas would not feel sorry for her. She would not permit him to.

"The scientific community includes many of society's darlings. Only the great and the good have the money to dabble in arcane matters like the discovery of comets."

A realization struck her, and not a particularly pleasant one at that. "You're worried for your own reputation."

He didn't even flinch. "I am indeed. I hope one day to be Astronomer Royal. At the very least, I plan to spend the rest of my life working with the men who witnessed our downfall."

She wanted to object to his use of the word "men," but they both knew how few women carved out a scientific career. Influence in London's intellectual circles was a masculine prerogative.

"I'm sorry your ambition has suffered a minor setback," she said with a hint of sarcasm.

"Hardly minor. A man with a dishonored name is unlikely to reach the peak of acclaim. Don't mistake me. I also care about the damage to your name. These things are always worse for the lady, however much I wish that wasn't the case. But nor am I blind to the harm all this talk will do to my hopes."

Emily hid another wince. She felt small for mocking him.

As a woman, she'd always be an outsider in the scientific community, however clever she was. Hamish had started with a disadvantage that was almost as fatal. He was Scottish, and he'd arrived in London with no connections in the world he aspired to dominate. But because he was a man and because he had an exceptional brain, he'd made his way so successfully that when he spoke of becoming Astronomer Royal, it didn't sound like hubris.

"I'm sure they'll forgive you in time. You just need to keep your nose clean from here on in."

With visible regret, he shook his head. "They'll forgive me after I make amends for my sins."

She frowned. "Are you going away until it all dies down?"

"That would be something."

"So you're here to say goodbye to Papa?" Both of them knew that if Hamish went into extended exile, Sir John Baylor wouldn't live to see his return.

She felt a pang at the idea of him going. Which was mad when he'd caused her so much trouble.

Hamish's chiseled jaw set in a determined line, and a muscle flickered in his lean cheek. "No."

"I'm sure he wouldn't mind if I woke him. He always loves to see you. Although I'm not sure how alert he'll be."

One large, capable hand made a sweeping gesture. "Yes, I'll need to talk to him. But, Emily...Miss Baylor, you misunderstand me. I'm not here to say goodbye. I'm here to ask you to become a permanent part of my life."

Oh, no... Not this. Not this.

Her knees turned to water, and she gripped the back of the chair so tightly that her knuckles went white. Icy dread trickled down her backbone. Surely he couldn't mean what she feared he did. "Hamish, I..."

He rushed on before she could finish. Nor did he sound any happier to say what he did than she was to hear it. "Miss Baylor, I'd count myself the luckiest man in England if you will consent to become my wife."

CHAPTER FIVE

*D*evil take it, his proposal left Emily looking even more devastated than she had after they were caught out. She was pale as paper, and her great hazel eyes were wide and dark with distress. Hamish watched her delicate throat move as she swallowed. He might as well have delivered a death sentence, instead of an offer of marriage.

The silence, as sharp as a honed blade, continued.

And continued.

Since that fraught night at Pascoe Place, Hamish's gut had been tied up in knots. Right now, he felt like he'd swallowed a coiling cobra. It was bad enough having to make up for his unacceptable behavior. It was worse when his proposal made the lady to whom he made amends react with unconcealed horror.

Eventually he couldn't bear the wait. "Emily? What do you think?"

She swallowed again, but this time she managed to speak. Her voice was hoarse and unsteady. "Of course the answer is no."

His lips firmed, but he placed a short rein on his temper. Her immediate, unthinking refusal shouldn't hurt. Now wasn't the time to harangue her. After all, his temper had got them into this deplorable situation in the first place. "That's not good enough."

Still with that awful frozen expression, she sank into the chair that she'd been clutching like her dearest friend.

"You're overreacting." She linked shaking hands in her lap, as she stared up at him as if afraid he meant to run mad. He supposed he couldn't blame her.

If only she knew how he'd already raged through his luxurious rooms in the Albany, cursing chance and society and his own bloody stupidity. But all the fury in the world couldn't alter the fact that he was trapped.

So was Miss Emily Baylor, however she might rail against their inevitable fate.

"The sooner we sort this out, the better. If we delay, the scandal will only deepen."

"You didn't come yesterday," she pointed out.

Her sharp mind was recovering from the shock, he was grateful to see. She started to sound more like her clever, capable self. Someone so smart would soon see that neither of them had any choice in what happened next.

"No." He'd spent yesterday desperately trying to come up with some other way of salvaging his reputation – and Emily's. The unpalatable truth was that he was no more reconciled to the future looming ahead than she was. He'd just had more time to come to terms with the fact that marriage was the only thing that would save them.

When he'd entered the room, he'd been appalled to see how tired she looked. Tired and hounded and defeated. Defeated was a word that he'd never before associated with indomitable Emily Baylor.

She didn't look indomitable now. She looked young and defenseless and lost.

Hamish had often indulged in forbidden fantasies where he took his mentor's prickly daughter into his arms and taught her about passion. This was the first time he'd ever wanted to hold her purely to provide comfort.

The girl who sat before him wasn't his razor-tongued bugbear. In her shabby green merino gown and with her luxuriant hair confined in a knot that looked ready to fall down, she seemed vulnerable and fragile. He felt a ridiculous urge to protect her, when his protection was the last thing she wanted. As proof of that, he only needed to recall her discourteous response to his proposal.

"But you don't like me," she said in the tone that told him her conclusion was inarguable.

He shook his head. "Circumstances dictate that my feelings – our feelings – are irrelevant." He watched her eyes widen, and realized that perhaps she wasn't the only one guilty of discourtesy. Heat rose to his cheeks. "Anyway, I do like you."

Her glare was disbelieving. "No, you don't. You think I'm far too big for my boots and I show an unfeminine interest in areas where no woman should presume to intrude."

It was true. Mostly. "But that doesn't mean I dislike you."

"Yes, it does. Name one thing about me you like."

Your bosom.

He retained enough grip on strategy to keep that to himself. "I like your loyal heart. I like how good you are with your father. I like your mind. If you'd been born a man, you'd make a name for yourself in science."

"Thank you," she said, looking dazed.

"That's three things. I could list more." He took a chance as he continued, although what he said might scupper his plans forever. "I also like how you look. You're a dashed pretty girl, Emily. When you take the trouble, like you did for the reception at Pascoe Place, you're beautiful."

She looked even more astounded. And disgruntled. It was clear the compliment didn't please her.

"Are you saying you're...attracted to me?" She asked the question as if she needed to wash her hands afterward.

Hamish controlled the childish impulse to tell her that if she didn't find him appealing, plenty of other girls did. "I'm saying I've noticed that you're a pleasure to look at."

When your mouth is closed.

That wasn't entirely true either. When she wasn't set on puncturing his conceit, she was clever and interesting.

"That's not enough to build a life on."

It wasn't. But it would have to be. "Emily, we must wed."

"So you can become Astronomer Royal." She sounded sour, although he couldn't see why she should scorn his ambitions. She knew what it took to pursue a scientific career.

He kept his voice steady. "So your life doesn't become impossible."

Her chin jerked up. "I can survive a bit of gossip."

She must know it was worse than that. "You and I were caught in an assignation, Emily. The world and its wife will talk of nothing else. If we don't wed, you'll be ruined. No respectable household will allow you across the threshold."

"I've always been considered an original."

"But a chaste one." He made an impatient sound. "For God's sake, can I sit down? I feel like a bully, standing over you while you cower away."

That made her sit up straight and glare at him. "You don't scare me."

Her defiance made Hamish feel better. This combative relationship was what he was used to. He crushed the memory of that strange moment when her vulnerability had made him want to pledge himself to her service. Jammed it deep down inside him, where he'd never have to look at it again.

"That's a good start if we're going to get married."

She stared at him, and he saw her mind whirring behind those hazel eyes. With a sigh, she waved to the chair opposite the desk. "Oh, sit down, for pity's sake. I invited you before."

The impatience in her voice was also familiar. Feeling on firmer ground, he took the chair. Although he hadn't yet convinced her of the stark necessity for a wedding, he could see. "Thank you."

She studied him as if she'd never seen him before. When she finally spoke, she sounded less overwhelmed. "Why should we marry? We didn't do anything wrong. Anyone who knows us will understand that you and I sneaking off to enjoy a romantic interlude is as likely as the Thames flowing west instead of east."

Bleak humor turned down his lips. "That makes the scandal even more delicious."

Her pointed chin set in a stubborn line. "I can weather a passing scandal. If I marry you, it's forever."

In other circumstances, he might laugh at her bluntness. But the situation was too dire for amusement. "Yes."

Emily continued to regard him with that searching look that usually ended with a trenchant critique of one of his scientific theories. "You can't want this."

With a heavy sigh, he raked his hand through his hair. "It's not about what I want. It's about damage control."

"The damage will be you and I tied together for life. We'll end up killing each other."

Highly likely.

Hamish couldn't fault her unflattering assessment of their chances of marital happiness. Through two sleepless nights and a wretched day, he'd said most of the same things to himself.

"Still we must marry." He paused, playing what he hoped might be his trump card. "Emily, forgive me if I intrude on private matters, but the demands of caring for your father must stop you accepting any work of your own. I know he hasn't taken on any students in years. I assume household income has shrunk."

Pink tinged her slanted cheekbones. "You're right."

"About the hardship?"

Her hands clenched on the arms of the chair. "No, that you intrude."

His gesture was dismissive. "Polly didn't answer the door last time I visited. Hoskins did. I'm guessing you've dispensed with your butler. I also noticed that the Reynolds no longer hangs in the hall, and the two blue Chinese vases have gone from the mantel behind you."

"You have no right," she said tightly, her color flaring hotter.

He hated doing this to her. She was a proud creature.

"I'm a rich man." He kept his voice low and reasonable, praying with not much optimism that she'd acknowledge the practical good sense of what he said. "If we marry, your life will change. So will your father's. I'll arrange a nurse. I'll ensure his every comfort. You've already got his health to worry about. Wouldn't it be nice not to have to worry about money as well?"

She looked at him down her neat little nose. "Are you trying to buy me, Hamish?"

Again he took firm hold of his temper. "I'm pointing out that a match between us has more advantages than just the restoration of your good name."

"And what do you get out of it?"

"The chance to fulfill my ambitions, however much you deride them."

She sighed. "I don't deride them. I suspect if I was a man, I'd aim to be top of the tree as well."

Hamish permitted himself a faint smile. "If you were a man, I doubt I'd have a shot at becoming Astronomer Royal."

She didn't smile back. "Don't try and charm your way into my good graces."

"Perish the thought," he said. "I'm happy to go away and let you consider my proposal. Just don't take too long."

"You speak as if I'm sure to say yes," she said, bristling up again. For a few seconds there, he'd wondered if she softened toward him. He should have known better.

"When you've had a chance to think, you'll see this is the only way."

Emily shook her head, more in bafflement than denial, he thought. "But I don't want to marry you."

He didn't want to marry her either, although if he were a different man in a different universe, he'd gladly take her into his bed. Emily Baylor had a flash and a fire that had always drawn him. "I hope you'll come to terms with the idea."

She frowned as if at last she put the pieces of the puzzle together – and she didn't like the picture she saw. "I rarely go out in society, especially now with Papa..."

It was mere weeks since he'd called on Sir John. The deterioration in that time was shocking. "Don't think you can come through this, just by holding your head up and spitting in society's eye."

She shrugged. "Why not?"

"Because we were caught in public. Because the story is too spicy to fade away." He paused. "Forgive me for asking, but have you any thoughts about what you'll do, once Sir John is no longer with us?"

Grief flickered in her eyes, but she answered in a firm voice. He'd gladly add courage to that list of the qualities he commended in her. "I've had a fine education, better than most women receive. Surely that means I'll find employment. I already copy scientific papers for some of Papa's colleagues. Perhaps someone will take me on as a secretary."

"Secretaries are generally male."

"If that doesn't work, I'll find a post as a governess."

The thought of brilliant, pretty Emily Baylor becoming a drudge in someone's household made his gut clench in denial. Although the bleak truth was that she was unlikely to find employment, even without taking the other night's hullabaloo into consideration. No sensible lady would take on such an attractive girl, if there were any virile males in the vicinity.

"A governess needs a spotless reputation, Emily," he said quietly.

He saw the second the full horror of her changed circumstances hit her. Her eyes rounded, and her mouth dropped open. "But we're innocent of anything but stupidity."

"The world doesn't believe that." Aching regret weighted his voice. "And the world has the last word on this matter."

He rose and bowed to her. He knew her well enough to see that all he could do now was leave her to stew on their predicament. "I'll call tomorrow to hear your answer."

Emily went back to looking hunted. "Tomorrow?"

"Yes. And if we're proceeding with this match, I'll call on your father on Friday morning so you can prepare him for my visit." He picked up his hat and turned to go, but paused at the door. "I'm sorry, Emily. This is all my fault. My damned temper got the better of me."

When she didn't respond, Hamish glanced back. As unmoving as a marble statue, she stared after him. He could guess the thoughts whirling through her mind, and he couldn't help but pity her. She'd soon understand the inescapable price of their recklessness.

His shoulders slumped as he left the room and the woman who was to become his bride. However much she might wish to evade that fate.

CHAPTER SIX

*H*amish stood outside the tall white house in the heart of Bloomsbury and knocked.

Polly opened the door to him as if she'd been waiting in the hall.

She probably had.

Yesterday he'd turned up uninvited on the Baylor doorstep. Last night, he'd received a brief note from Emily asking him to call at eleven in the morning. She hadn't said anything else, so he remained unsure whether she meant to agree to marry him or send him on his way with a resounding refusal.

He hoped to the devil she intended to accept him. As he'd gone about yesterday, he'd resented the curious glances cast in his direction, and conversations cut short the moment he came into earshot. The longer he and Emily delayed announcing their engagement, the worse the talk would get. As he'd said to her, he'd meet with some disapproval and official support for his activities would evaporate, but he'd be able to continue his life as a young buck about town. Emily, on the other hand, would become an outcast. It wasn't fair, especially when the fault was his. But it was the way of the world.

If common sense prevailed, he'd leave this house to see Emily's vicar, then arrange the betrothal announcement in the *Morning Post*. He'd decided to proceed as if scandal hadn't precipitated this engagement. Having the banns called and pretending that wedding Sir John Baylor's daughter was his dearest wish would combat the nasty rumors.

At the thought of how his life was about to change, his gut clenched with useless denial. He didn't want to marry Emily. He didn't want to marry anyone, not under duress.

If Emily had let her resentment get the better of her – and he wasn't the only one in this partnership who could build up a head of steam – he'd have to abide by her decision, however unwillingly. It was up to her if she wished to accept his offer later, once she realized how the scandal was going to destroy her life. He'd seen enough of the world to know that if they did nothing to scotch the talk, life was going to turn very unpleasant indeed for her. Whichever way he looked at it, a wedding loomed in his future.

"Mr. Douglas has called, Miss Baylor," Polly said, ushering him into the library.

Even the usually irrepressible housemaid seemed to know that something momentous happened here today. This morning, there had been no indiscreet chatter.

Looking composed and pale, Emily rose from behind the desk as Polly left. "Good morning, Hamish."

She'd dressed for his visit in a dark blue gown that lent her an austere air. Her lovely hair was confined in a tight knot that made him want to wince. She looked like a nun.

Hamish searched her wan face for some sign of emotion, but her eyes were opaque and her lips didn't curve in a smile. He began to suspect she'd called him here to reject him. "Good morning, Emily."

She indicated two chairs in the center of the room, clearly placed ready for this interview. He noted the more than tactful distance between them. "Please sit down."

He waited for her to take her place, then sat down. "How is your father this morning?"

Now Hamish was closer, he noticed that she looked even wearier than she had yesterday. There were shadows beneath her fine eyes, and he guessed some of her pallor must be due to sleeplessness. Had she lain awake worrying about her future? Or had she nursed her father through another troubled night?

Whatever happened today, Hamish had decided to pay for a qualified woman to assist with Sir John's care. He owed it to his mentor, although right now he was more interested in restoring the bloom to Emily's pretty face.

With more of that studied calmness, she folded her hands in her lap. "He had a better night, thank you."

"I'm glad."

So Hamish must blame his proposal for robbing her of sleep. He wished it was otherwise. But then he'd wished things were otherwise since he'd faced that wall of avid faces in Greenwich.

"The party at Lord Pascoe's was good for him, but it took him out of his routine. He needed a few days to settle."

The door behind Emily opened, and Polly brought in a laden tea tray. Apparently the plan was to treat this visit like a conventional call and not a matter of life and death.

Hamish had no objections, especially as he could see Emily drew strength from the social rituals and the fact that as hostess, she was in charge of proceedings.

They managed a few more minutes of polite conversation, including an enquiry as to how he took his tea, when Emily had known that since he'd moved into this house as a raw and eager assistant to her father.

A silence fell. An awkward, heavy silence.

Hamish grabbed his courage in both hands. He set his half-empty teacup on a side table. Strange how the subject of marriage felt more forbidden in these formal circumstances than it had yesterday. "Have you thought any further about what I said?"

It was an inane question. She'd hardly have put his proposal from her mind.

Her huff of grim amusement told him she also considered the question asinine. "I've thought about little else."

He leaned forward, resting his elbows on his thighs. He'd dressed with care, too, in a bottle green coat and biscuit breeches. The shine on his hessians was dazzling, and the arrangement of his neck cloth would do Beau Brummel proud.

The hands on Emily's lap twined around each other as she bit her lip. These were the first signs of uncertainty she'd shown.

Another thorny silence descended.

Patience wasn't Hamish's specialty. He bore the wait as long as he could, but after a couple of moments, he said, "And that decision is?"

She swallowed. Another sign of nerves. But she met his gaze squarely, and her voice emerged with admirable steadiness, if with a lowering lack of enthusiasm. "I will marry you, Hamish."

Relief rushed through him. In a perfect world, this marriage wouldn't be his choice. But in the world they lived in, this was by far the best outcome.

He rose to his feet and stepped toward her. "Emily…"

Her jaw tightened as she waved him back. "Please sit down. I haven't finished."

Hamish subsided into his chair. "Oh?"

Dear Lord, what the devil did she intend? Whatever it was, it couldn't be good.

"I have several conditions." She sat as straight as a wooden ruler and determination settled on her face, making her look more like a gorgeous mother superior than ever. "Once you've heard them, you may wish to withdraw your offer."

"I doubt it," he said. "Nothing is liable to change my reasons for proposing."

That didn't reassure her, he noticed. "Listen to what I have to say, then see what you want to do."

"Very well, then." He leaned back in his chair, stretched his legs out before him, and folded his arms over his chest. "I'm all ears."

She swallowed again, as if she had trouble forcing the words out of her throat. "I have to stay in this house as long as Papa is…alive. Change upsets him, and he finds comfort in his memories of life here with Mamma and with all his students over the years."

Hamish frowned as he sifted what she said. "If we don't live together after the ceremony, we'll create even more gossip."

She sent him a direct look. "I think you should move in here, at least for the present moment."

More relief. This was a perfectly reasonable request. If she imagined living in Bloomsbury was a major stumbling block to their match, her other conditions weren't likely to be too onerous.

"I'm more than happy to do that. In fact, it's a capital idea. You need help with your father, and he and I have always got on. I meant what I said about getting some nursing staff."

"I don't want your charity," she said sharply.

He smiled at her. "It won't be charity if I'm your husband. If this goes ahead, I'll endow thee with all my worldly goods in front of God and society."

"Bloomsbury isn't the most fashionable quarter of London. You're used to Mayfair."

He shrugged. "I'm sure my dignity will survive a return to this house. After all, I lived here when I left Cambridge."

"That's a long time ago now."

"I promise not to cause difficulties, Emily. Or no more than I can help. A husband joining the household will mean a few adjustments, I'm sure."

As they spoke, she started to appear a little more cheerful. Thank God. When he came in, she looked like she awaited a hanging. "That's another thing. I've run this house for years. I would like to remain in charge."

He gave a dismissive grunt. "What the deuce do I know about housekeeping? I'll leave domestic matters to you. I'll make you a generous allowance, so you don't have to run to me every time you want to buy a pound of tea." He paused. "As Lady Glen Lyon, you'll need to take some role in society. I'll make sure you have plenty of pin money, too. If you want a few folderols, you shall have them."

This speech left her looking uncomfortable. "You're very generous."

He shrugged. "Not really. You'll be my wife." He paused. "And a woman I take pride in, however this match has come about. The only way we can rise above the scandal is to behave in high style and act as if we have nothing to be ashamed of."

"We don't."

"I know that, and you know that, but it's a secret from the rest of London."

"Very well," she said with a nod. "Thank you."

Another silence. Not quite so thorny as the previous one. As before, Hamish broke it. "Is there more?"

"Yes." She sucked in a shaky breath and surveyed him warily as if expecting him to start rampaging about like an enraged elephant. "I'd like to continue my father's scientific work and follow up a few projects of my own. I refuse to dwindle to a society wife, merely because I've agreed to marry you."

He regarded her with interest. He'd be devilish interested to hear about her projects, although perhaps not right now. "Shall I build you an observatory in the back garden?"

"You can if you like," she said with surprising sangfroid. "If that's a serious offer."

"It is. I told you – I'm a rich man. We both have things to gain from this match."

"The light in London isn't good for stargazing."

"Then I'll find us a place in the country where nothing will interfere with your investigations."

Emily eyed him uncertainly. He had a feeling that his cooperation unsettled her, although he couldn't for the life of him imagine why. So far, her requests had been nothing out of the ordinary. "You won't mind having a bluestocking wife?"

He shrugged again. "I assumed you'd undertake some scholarly activity after we married. I'm not expecting the weight of a wedding ring on your finger to grind your brains to dust. Perhaps we can work on something together."

"We'd fight like cat and dog," she said on a discouraging note.

Hamish wasn't going to start a quarrel. Not now when he was so close to getting her agreement. "Perhaps. And perhaps we'd make a great team."

Her expression told him that suggestion was beyond the realms of possibility. "Will you put all this in writing?"

"Yes, willingly." Although her lack of faith in his word galled him.

Another silence. She looked uncomfortable, before she raised her chin and stared at him with a hint of defiance. "As you so gallantly pointed out, money is tight here these days. I'll come to you with a small legacy from Mamma, and...later, the rights to Papa's books, and the lease on this house. It's not much of a dowry."

He gave a dismissive laugh. "Fie, Miss Baylor, for shame, when you led me on to believe you're an heiress."

To his relief, a smile tugged at her lips. A small smile and a reluctant one, but better than nothing. She'd been deathly serious so far, outlining her modest demands.

"All jokes aside, it seems an unequal match."

"In worldly terms, perhaps it is, but I have plenty of money for both of us and I meant it when I called you a prize."

"You really are trying to charm me."

"If we're to spend a lifetime together, it won't hurt to have you on my side." He paused. "Are we to spend a lifetime together?"

"You agree to my requests?"

"Of course."

"There's more." She avoided his eyes. "I doubt you'll agree to my last condition."

He frowned. "Another condition?"

"Just one." She was visibly nervous, which was a pity when he'd just coaxed her into a friendlier frame of mind. What on earth was troubling her? Something was. She was back to biting her lip and wringing her hands.

"Is it so unreasonable?"

His attempt to coax another smile from her didn't succeed. "I expect you'll think it is."

He watched her, but didn't speak. After a long while, she raised her chin and met his eyes. "I won't share your bed, Hamish. I want a chaste marriage."

CHAPTER SEVEN

$\mathcal{E}$mily watched shock flood Hamish's expression. Then a flash of fierce displeasure.

She gripped the arms of her chair and braced for a blast of his temper. Not that she could blame him for being angry. It was an unfair condition to place on any man, and even though he didn't want her, her decision to sleep alone would gall his vanity.

But after that betraying moment when he'd looked ready to explode, his gaze turned watchful. "I...see."

She swallowed to moisten a mouth dry with nerves. "I imagine you want to withdraw your proposal now."

"Do you?" He spoke slowly and that intent blue stare didn't shift from her. He looked utterly relaxed, but she knew better.

She rushed into speech, although she'd promised herself that she'd be calm and reasonable and above all understanding, when he decided he couldn't wed her after all. "No man would want to marry under these circumstances. And it's even worse for you."

Something like surprise flickered in his eyes before he went back to looking enigmatic. She was used to Hamish wearing his heart on his sleeve. As her father's protégé, he'd been a turbulent presence in the house before he'd moved out six years ago. It suddenly occurred to her that perhaps she didn't know this man as well as she thought she did. If they really were to marry, that was a disturbing thought.

Of course she'd just put that outcome out of reach. No man with an ounce of pride would accept such a bargain. And Hamish was the proudest man she knew.

"How so?"

She made a helpless gesture. Her cheeks felt so hot that she feared they must catch fire. The possibility of carnal relations wasn't something she'd ever expected to have to talk about. And never with such an extraordinarily...male creature as Hamish Douglas.

One of the reasons they clashed so often was that some essentially feminine part of her resented his easy dominance. Everything female in her revolted against his overt masculinity. In general, her father's students were a lily-livered lot, terrified of their own shadows, even more terrified of women. Hamish had arrived from Cambridge looking ready to conquer a nearby nation, and she'd heard enough talk over the years to know that he liked the girls and the girls liked him.

"You're...very virile." Her awkward answer made her blush even hotter.

One dark gold eyebrow twitched, but he didn't laugh at her. If he had, she'd tell him he could stick his marriage proposal up the nearest chimney – or some other place.

"Thank you." He paused. "I think."

It hadn't been a compliment, and she suspected he knew that as well as she did. "Not to mention you need an heir for Glen Leven."

He'd gone back to studying her. "Glen Lyon."

To avoid that perceptive stare, she rose and crossed to the window. "The name hardly matters," she said, looking out on the gray day outside.

As a scientist, she shouldn't see the dismal weather as a portent. As a woman, she couldn't help feeling that the bleak outlook signaled things to come, when she was alone and trying to make her way in a world that despised her as spoiled goods.

"It does, if you're going to be its lady."

Confusion made her turn to face him. "Don't tell me you're still thinking of marrying me."

"If I don't marry you, we remain in an impossible situation. You more than me. Respectable society will shun you."

"I know." Her lips turned down, as she recalled what had happened when she went out yesterday afternoon. Hamish had told her that now she was considered a fallen woman, she'd be a pariah. She hadn't quite believed it, until she faced it in person. "None of the neighbors will look at me, let alone talk to me. Yesterday on the street, Mrs. Carew rushed her daughters away as if I had the plague."

Hamish's eyes darkened to sapphire. "Spiteful, self-righteous cat."

"Yes." His pity was never welcome, but right now, she felt better to know he took her part. She'd started to feel like nobody else did.

He came to his feet and moved to stand a couple of feet away. "Is it the physical act itself that repulses you?" The question was gentle. "Or is it me in particular?"

She studied him, as she struggled to come up with an answer he'd understand. Hamish was highly annoying and far too full of himself, but he didn't repulse her. "It's not you in particular."

"That's something." He didn't sound gratified. "If it's the act itself, how did you imagine you'd manage to marry?"

Oh, dear, she didn't want to talk about this. She really didn't. Her stomach clenched with embarrassment.

When she'd lain awake all night, wondering what on earth she could do, she'd assumed that her ridiculous demand would set off one of Hamish's tantrums. He'd storm out and leave her to muddle through on her own.

Perhaps his temper at Greenwich had been an aberration. Perhaps the man of thirty had learned a self-control that the pretty, spoiled boy of twenty had lacked.

Of course he has, you brainless widgeon. He's been out making his way in the world – and very successfully, too. He doesn't have to settle for a dedicated spinster past first youth.

Emily told the snide voice to shut up. Since the incident at Greenwich, that snide voice had become a constant companion. "I'm twenty-four and haven't yet met a gentleman for whom I'd sacrifice my independence."

Except her independence relied on her place as John Baylor's daughter. Without her father's protection, her independence became frailer than rice paper. Hamish knew that as well as she did.

"I'm sure you've had offers."

She shrugged. "A couple. Men hoping my work would assist them to a scientific reputation, even as they deplore God wasting a good brain on a mere female. Older gentlemen seeking a capable housekeeper and an unpaid secretary. Nobody I could—"

"Love."

The word crashed down between them the way a boulder toppled from a cliff onto a mountain path.

"Yes," she said gravely. "I suppose you disdain the idea."

To her bewilderment, he smiled. And not one of his lofty "I'm a man and better than you, and don't you forget it" smiles. This smile was sincere and held a touch of sweetness. Her heart started to behave very oddly, as though Hamish Douglas caught it and squeezed it tight in his big hand.

"Not a bit of it. I've seen too many successful love matches to doubt love's power."

Well, for heaven's sake, that wasn't what she'd expected him to say.

Astonishment thundered through her. So far this interview had been uncomfortable and full of unwelcome discoveries. One of the most unwelcome discoveries was that Hamish Douglas wasn't nearly as easy to understand as she'd thought.

She tangled her hands in her skirts, and to her surprise – yet another surprise – she found herself speaking from the heart. "I don't want to share my bed with a man I don't love."

When Hamish didn't respond, she went on in a dull voice, because the neighbors' snubs had given her a foretaste of a grim future. "So you see a match between us is impossible."

"If I give you time, might you change your mind about marital relations?"

Go to Hamish's bed where his big body would invade hers and when there was no genuine fondness between them at all? No, she didn't want that. She couldn't imagine she ever would. "No."

He eyed her as if she was a constellation he set out to map. "You forgo the chance of children."

"I had no firm plans to marry anyway." His focused attention made her feel uncomfortable, and she shifted under his searching gaze. "I told you I like my independence too well to sacrifice it to a man's convenience. Most men don't want wives who go their own way. You're the one who needs children. You owe a duty to your title and ancestral lands."

He shrugged. "I have nieces and nephews and cousins aplenty. Glen Lyon can go to someone in the family. It's not entailed."

Her mouth dropped open in shock. She'd always assumed that Hamish would be determined on having a son to continue his line. It was all part of his king of the beasts personality.

He left her at a loss. She'd been sure he'd march out in high dudgeon, the moment she said she wouldn't share her body with him. "Don't you mind?"

A grunt of bitter laughter. "That my wife can't bring herself to tolerate my attentions? Of course I mind. But that doesn't change the facts. A marriage still works to both our advantage."

Emily squared her shoulders and told herself to be brave. "Under the circumstances, if you agree to my request, you have my permission to seek your pleasure elsewhere. Discreetly."

He settled a discontented gaze on her. "It still seems a rum sort of bargain."

"I suspect it is." She paused, then spoke hesitantly. "Perhaps in time we can become friends."

His eyes darkened with what looked like hurt, when she'd never thought she had any power over his emotions at all. "Don't you think of me as a friend already, Emily?"

She made a baffled gesture. She wasn't sure what he was to her, although right now it looked like he'd soon be her betrothed, then in a few weeks, her husband.

He sighed as if her lack of response was answer enough. It probably was. "Are we going to do this thing?"

Emily told herself that what couldn't be mended must be endured. Since her father's brilliant mind started to fail him, she'd had to be strong. Surely she could dredge up an ounce more courage to face this marriage.

But embarking on a future she'd never choose for herself, she didn't feel nearly as staunch as she wished. Her voice emerged as a glum murmur. "I think you could do better."

Hamish smiled, but this one seemed forced. She wasn't surprised. He knew he could do better than marrying her, too. He was a rich man with a title and a reputation with the ladies. She was an eccentric bluestocking from the middle class, however many accolades her father had amassed. Even aside from worldly considerations, most marriages started with the promise of passion and affection. Or at least they should. This one began as a cold contract between two people who didn't even like each other.

Emily's insides felt as if they were made of ice. She'd never wasted much time contemplating the pleasures of the flesh. The pleasures of the mind had taken all her attention. Now physical satisfaction was to be forever denied to her. She wouldn't be human if she didn't wonder what she was missing out on.

She studied this big, clever, handsome man who was likely to become her husband. She'd wager her back teeth that he knew exactly how nice it was to lie down with someone he desired. She'd also wager that if he didn't find satisfaction at home, he'd soon seek it elsewhere.

Given she banned Hamish from her bed, she was hardly fair to resent him for finding relief in another woman's arms. But lack of fairness didn't stop her from resenting the prospect with every cell in her body.

Emily didn't like the idea of the world knowing that her husband was unfaithful. Because of course the world always found out. She'd heard enough *on dits* to understand how fast gossip spread. Today the talk was about her, and she hated it. She'd hate it, too, when London tittered over Hamish Douglas's conquests and how his wife couldn't keep her roving spouse at home. Even worse, while she mightn't want Hamish touching her, something deep inside her didn't want him touching anyone else either.

"Emily?" His voice was kind.

"Think about what we're doing, Hamish." She sounded desperate, but whether desperate for him to walk away, or stay and bring this mad plan to fruition, she couldn't have said. "If we marry, there's no escape."

Bleak humor quirked his lips. "No escape for you either."

"I know," she said with such dourness that he laughed, although with a hint of chagrin.

"I'm sure I'm not nearly as bad as you think I am. I was a barbarian at twenty, but that was a lifetime ago. Since then, I've become almost civilized."

She didn't smile. "Your temper can still get the better of you."

His brief amusement faded, and he frowned as he stepped back from her. "By God, you're not afraid of me, are you?"

"You're big."

He gave a self-derisory grunt. "That I am. But I swear I'd never hit a woman."

Actually despite his size, she'd never considered him a violent man. "I believe you."

"Thank you." He looked relieved. "And I come down from the heights pretty quickly."

Her lips compressed. "But by then, the damage is usually done."

"This trouble we're in is a case in point, isn't it?"

"Yes," she said, because really what else was there to say?

Looking for all the world like a reasonable man, he spread his hands in appeal. But with Hamish Douglas, she knew better than to rely on appearances. "I'm sorry I didn't believe you when you told me about the mistake. If I had, none of this would have happened."

"I suppose your masculine superiority couldn't countenance a mere woman pointing out your error."

He subjected her to another of those piercing gazes that always breached her defenses. "You know, you've said something like that before."

"Like what?"

"That I think you're a lesser creation because you're a woman. As if being female makes you weak and foolish and incapable."

"Don't you think that?" she asked, astonished. "Most men do."

"Not any men with a scrap of intelligence." He gave a wry laugh. "I might have made a few unfortunate remarks to that effect, but that was only to needle you. I grew up with formidable women. Damn it, my mother pretty much runs the government, whoever the newspapers might say is in charge."

Lady Glen Lyon, a vaunted beauty in her youth, was now a famous political hostess. Emily had met her a couple of times and found her absolutely terrifying. Charming but daunting.

"Then why do you always try to cut me down to size?"

He responded with another of those amused grunts. "That's not because you're a woman. That's because you're...you."

"I don't understand."

He ran his hand through his thick mane of golden hair. In private, Emily admitted that his mother wasn't the only Douglas who could be charming. He'd arrived this morning dressed fit for a royal audience, and she'd wondered in despair how such a common creature as Emily Baylor could aspire to marry him. Now with his hair ruffled and with a gilded lock falling over his high forehead, he looked disarmingly approachable.

"Do you really want to talk about this?"

She folded her arms, wondering why he looked shifty all of a sudden. "I'd like us to understand each other better."

He sighed and tilted his head back so he could stare at the plaster ceiling.

"Seeking heavenly guidance?" she asked in the sweet voice that she knew drove him to the edge.

His eyebrows arched as he shifted to survey her. "You always treat me like a blundering hound that someone had the bad manners to release in the drawing room. You act as if you're not sure if I'm housetrained."

"That's not fair," she said, although to her regret, it really was.

He shrugged. "You asked. When I arrived here ten years ago, you stuck that perfect little nose in the air. Since then, it hasn't lowered an inch. Every time

I opened my mouth, you delivered a crushing response. What else is a man to do but fight back?"

"That doesn't paint a very flattering picture." She swung away, trying to evade his accusations.

Although looking back, he was right. From the first, she'd set out to puncture what she saw as Hamish's arrogance. Which now seemed silly, given that he was considerably less arrogant than most of her father's cronies. At least Hamish always acknowledged her existence.

"Is it Scotsmen you don't like?"

She came to a stop near the fire and curled one hand over the corner of the mantelpiece, which as Hamish had pointed out, now lacked two Chinese vases. "You never sound like a Scotsman."

His features froze. She must have hit a nerve. Goodness knew why. It seemed a less controversial comment than some of the other things she'd said to him today.

"My father lived in London all through the war, so I was brought up with a crowd of useless Sassenachs." He sounded defensive, although she hadn't meant to insult him. "I can't help it if I talk like them."

"Sassenachs?"

"The English. North of the border, it's no favor to sound like the enemy, believe me."

Startled, she stared at him. "Surely you don't think of the English as your enemy."

He sighed again. "No, not really." As she noted the revealing "really," he went on. "Old hatreds die hard in my homeland."

She hadn't factored his nationality into the barriers to their marriage. Perhaps she should. "Now you're marrying an Englishwoman."

He stepped closer. "Emily, let's just admit that in an ideal world, neither of us would contemplate this marriage. Yes, I'd always hoped to marry a Scotswoman and raise my children as good little Highlanders. That isn't going to happen, just as if you marry me, you won't have the love match you wanted. But right now, we need to work out the best way to proceed in the world we live in. The world we live in will punish both of us for breaking its rules."

"Perhaps this marriage is our punishment," she said in a low voice, burying shaking hands in her dark blue skirts and staring blindly down into the flames.

"Perhaps it is." His voice held no trace of humor. "Do you want more time to think?"

If she thought any longer, she'd go mad. Hamish was right. He'd always been right. They were trapped.

"No. I've made up my mind." She raised her chin until she met his eyes, and she tried very hard to keep her voice steady. "I'll marry you, Hamish."

"That's a bonny decision." He didn't smile. Why would he? He was as much a victim of a malicious fate as she was. "Thank you. I swear I won't let you down."

His promise, while patently sincere, offered no reassurance. Feeling as if she was drowning, she made a despairing gesture. "What happens now?"

"I'll go ahead and make the arrangements. You've got enough on your plate looking after your father." His tone hardened. "But there's one thing I want to make clear, Emily."

She braced for some added proviso, something unbearable that she couldn't refuse because she'd already given him her consent. So far, he'd placed no conditions on their nuptials at all. "What's that?"

His jaw firmed, and that muscle danced in his cheek. His answer emerged sharp as the flick of a whip. "We won't be putting any of these private arrangements in writing."

CHAPTER EIGHT

"What a lovely day for a wedding," Emily's father said. He sat opposite her in the luxurious closed carriage that Hamish had bought last week.

"Yes, Papa," Emily said, because what was the point of saying that while the sun might shine with a brightness exceptional for November, in her heart it rained fit to flood the Midlands?

Wearing his best coat, her father looked well and happy. One might almost imagine he was still the brilliant, self-assured man who had dazzled London's intellectual elite. He'd get tired later, she knew. She'd made arrangements for him to leave the wedding breakfast in the care of Miss McCorquodale, the nurse who now ran the sickroom like a well-oiled machine. And somehow did it with such tact that Emily didn't hate her.

Miss McCorquodale worked at the house, courtesy of Hamish's generosity, too. These days Emily began to feel that every breath she took was courtesy of Hamish's generosity.

Which wasn't fair, when life was so much easier since he'd opened his coffers to help her and her father.

It was doubly unfair when she thought how much better Papa had been since his protégé, the young Laird of Glen Lyon, had called to request permission to marry his daughter. The daughter who now sat ten minutes away from St George's in Hanover Square and wished herself on the dark side of the moon.

As she'd expected, her father had been in alt about the engagement. When Emily saw how the news lifted his spirits, she verged as close to being glad about the marriage as she'd come before or since. Only at that moment did she realize that her father had also fretted about what was to become of her. Now she was to marry a rich man with close connections to the scientific community among whom she'd grown up, an oppressive weight had lifted from Papa's spirit.

That was one of the most upsetting things about her father's decline. She was never sure how much of a grip he kept on what happened around him.

True to his word, Hamish had carried off this betrothal in high style. He'd placed a notice in the *Morning Post*. He hadn't rushed to get a special license. Instead, he'd had the banns called on three successive Sundays.

He'd escorted Emily around town as gallantly as if he really wanted to marry her. They'd been to the theater and the opera, four lectures, and two balls. What a pity that she missed the one event she'd have liked to attend, Hamish's presentation about his comet, this time with correct calculations. But women were barred from the Royal Society's meetings.

Now instead of a hole-in-the-corner affair cobbled together to hush up a scandal, she and Hamish were marrying under the full glare of society's gaze.

Up to a point, his bravado had succeeded. She wasn't fool enough to think her fall from grace forgotten. But nobody at their outings had snubbed her, and the neighbors were back talking to her.

Emily supposed she should be grateful that she was too busy feeling scared to have room left for other emotions. For most of her life, she'd been in control of her life – too much so, according to her father's more conservative colleagues. But after today, she stopped being Emily Baylor and became Emily Douglas, Lady Glen Lyon. She had no idea what that would mean. She had a horrid feeling that she'd stop being Emily Baylor in more ways than just her name.

"You and Hamish make an excellent pairing. Stop stewing, kitten."

Surprised out of her miasma of doubt and despair, Emily stared at her father. She'd clearly underestimated quite how much he did notice. He looked more alert than she'd seen him in months. "Yes, Papa."

The love in her father's smile had her blinking away tears. Because while restoring her reputation was an important consideration, it was a recent one. Her fears for her father's health had dogged her for nearly two years.

"Don't say 'yes, Papa,' to keep me quiet. I know you're frightened and uncertain, but you and Hamish will both find your way."

"Because he's plump in the pocket." She couldn't conceal a hint of bitterness. The carriage turned a corner, and she looked out the window at tall rows of pristine white houses as they proceeded through Mayfair.

"I won't pretend I'm not relieved that your material future is secure. But that's the least of the reasons this match pleases me. You're an unusual person, Emily. You're a particularly unusual woman. I've long wanted you to set your heart on a man who appreciates you for the treasure you are."

"Papa..." she said, shocked and moved and cringing with guilt, because it was clear her father believed that this was a love match.

Her father went on before she could clarify her arrangement with Hamish, which was fortunate. Far better that Papa believed she followed her personal inclinations, rather than just doing her best to keep her name out of the gutter.

"I'm happy that you've found a man who won't seek to crush your spirit, just because you're a girl. I'm happy you're marrying someone who is your equal in intelligence and heart. You're an exceptional woman, Emily, and I'm proud to call you my daughter. Hamish is a good man, and he knows how lucky he is to win you."

Her father's generous praise left her floundering. He sounded like he was in full possession of his wits, and she couldn't mistake how sincerely he meant what he said. "Does he?" she asked before she could stop herself.

"He told me so when he asked for your hand."

She should be grateful that Hamish had put a gloss of false affection on his proposal when he spoke to her father, but she was too busy digesting what her father told her to be tactful. "We've always clashed."

Her father smiled. "You've studied enough chemistry to know that when two volatile substances combine, there's always an explosion. A bit of excitement is good for a marriage, kitten."

A bit of excitement? She was likely to strangle Hamish, if he didn't strangle her first. The problem with explosive combinations was that there were *explosions*. "He's a stubborn brute."

Her father leaned forward and took her gloved hand. "Yes, he is. But you're stubborn, too. I long feared that you'd give yourself to someone who wasn't strong enough to stand up to you."

"Hamish stands up to me."

"Yes, he does, and you stand up to him. I've known for a long time that you two are meant to be together. I'm just thankful that I lived to see this day."

Emily struggled to banish the mist in front of her eyes, and when she did, she saw the sheen in her father's eyes. He was so happy she was marrying Hamish. She couldn't destroy his illusion that she only suffered bridal nerves, instead of the conviction that this was the stupidest thing she'd ever done. "I'm glad you're here, too, Papa."

At least that wasn't a lie.

"I love you, Emily. I just wish your mamma was with us. She'd be so proud of you. You remind me of her so much. I just hope that you and Hamish are half as happy as we were."

A jagged lump of emotion clogged Emily's throat. She always missed her mother, never more than in these last two years. Her determination to marry only for a great love was born in witnessing the bond between her parents. She betrayed that today by wedding Hamish Douglas.

But that was yet another insight she couldn't share with Papa. So she lifted his hand to her lips and kissed it with a reverence she saw he noted. "I love you, too, Papa. And I know Mamma is looking down from heaven and wishing us well."

She wanted to say more, tell him what a wonderful father he'd been and how grateful she was that he'd valued and nurtured her talents, despite her being a girl. But the carriage was drawing to a stop. "Too soon, too soon," she wanted to cry. When she looked out the window, she saw the imposing columns of St George's portico.

"I wish you and Hamish all the luck in the world, Emily," her father said, as the footman opened the door and held out a hand to assist her to the pavement.

"Thank you, Papa," Emily forced out, her nerves threatening to snap.

She didn't want to do this, she really didn't. But it was too late to back out. She raised her chin and straightened her spine. Summoning a smile, she emerged from the carriage to a ragged cheer from the crowd of onlookers gathered around the church.

Hamish stood at the altar beside his cousin Diarmid Mactavish, who had come down from Scotland to be his groomsman. Diarmid's lovely wife Fiona sat in the congregation. The profound love his cousin had found with the pretty blonde provided a cruel contrast to the barren bargain Hamish made in wedding Emily.

"Stop acting as if you're afraid she willnae show up," Diarmid hissed at him. His intense features were rigid with impatience at Hamish's constant fidgeting.

"I *am* afraid she won't show up," Hamish said, glancing behind him for what must be the hundredth time. But the wide doors to the big, ornate church remained empty.

The pews however were packed. All Hamish's numerous family attended, most of them having crossed the border for the ceremony. His scientific colleagues were here, as were his society friends. It turned out Emily had very little family, but given she'd lived her whole life in London, she had plenty of people to fill her half of the church. It was a large enough crowd to witness his humiliation, if his intended decided to jilt him.

His original idea was that a splashy wedding would give his bride countenance, prove to the world that he and Emily had nothing to hide. Right now, he was rethinking that particular flash of brilliance.

The church was infested with massed hothouse flowers. The sickly sweet smell of lilies weighted the air and made Hamish feel nauseous. He resisted the urge to tug at his elaborately arranged neck cloth. It felt too tight, but he knew that was only because he was nervous and uncomfortable. He really wasn't strangling, even if that was how he felt.

"She sounds like a lassie who kens her own mind. If she said she'll marry ye, I suspect she means to. Especially as leaving ye flat will only add to the gossip."

Diarmid and Emily were yet to meet, although Hamish had an odd feeling they'd like each other when they did. Emily's cleverness and lack of artifice would appeal to his cousin.

Last night, he and Diarmid had sat up late with a bottle of Bruce Mackenzie's finest whisky as Hamish struggled to lend a favorable tone to the story of his engagement. He didn't manage as well as he'd like. It didn't take Diarmid long to winkle out most of the facts behind the scandal.

By God, it had been a treat to drink good whisky after months of French brandy, the tipple of choice in London. The conversation, however, hadn't been nearly so agreeable.

Diarmid had been scathing in placing the blame for this shambles firmly upon Hamish's shoulders. Hamish supposed that was what family was for – to tell a person the unpalatable truth when nobody else would. Although Emily was never slow to point out his failings. Dear God, he faced a lifetime of criticism, and he had nobody to blame but himself.

That was if the bride deigned to turn up at all.

"She doesn't see me as any great prize."

"Given the trouble your temper has caused her, I cannae blame her," Diarmid said grimly.

"You haven't told Fergus and Marina or Brody and Elspeth, have you?"

"Damn it, man, I sat up with ye until the wee small hours. After ye went home, all I did was tumble into bed at your mother's house, grab a couple of hours' sleep, and scramble into my clothes to be fit to stand up for an eleven o'clock wedding. I havenae had a chance to share your tale of woe with anyone."

"Well, don't. I don't want my idiocy broadcast all across the Highlands."

Actually Diarmid had scrubbed up well, given how little sleep he'd had. Not to mention that he and his family – Diarmid had a son called Richard now, along with his stepdaughter Christina – had just made the long journey down from the north of Scotland.

Nobody looking at the cousins would see any family resemblance, apart from a certain arrogance of bearing. Diarmid was as dark as a gypsy and built on long, lean, dangerous lines. While he was a tall man, Hamish topped him by several inches.

Diarmid's dark blue coat fitted perfectly, outlining shoulders as straight as a ruler, and his linen was so white it dazzled. Hamish was similarly attired in Savile Row's best. Now Hamish wondered if all this dressing up had been a waste of time.

By God, he hoped some of Bruce Mackenzie's whisky was left. He might need it.

Another glance behind him. Another disappointed dip of his heart because Emily wasn't here yet. Surely she wouldn't let him down. She mightn't like him, but she wasn't spiteful, and this marriage was as much for her benefit as his.

He just hoped to hell she saw it that way.

"She's no' that late." Diarmid's reasonable tone made Hamish want to clout him.

"Not yet," Hamish said gloomily, wondering how much of the murmuring behind him related to the scandal in Greenwich a month ago.

During the engagement, he'd done his best to give the impression that Emily and he were April and May, head over heels in love. He wasn't convinced he'd succeeded. At least the delay between betrothal and wedding told the world that no baby would arrive less than nine months after the ceremony.

Given this devil's bargain he'd made with Emily, there wouldn't be a baby in nine months or nine years or ninety. More was the sodding pity.

The awful truth was that ever since she'd declared that she'd never sleep with him, Hamish had thought of little else but getting Emily Baylor into bed. He knew it was the lure of the forbidden, but somehow over the last four weeks, his mentor's uppity daughter had become the most desirable woman in London. It was a character flaw with him that the minute someone told him no, he set out to make the answer yes.

His dilemma was made even more painful because as Emily's chosen escort, he inevitably had to touch her. Often. None of the contact overstepped propriety – which only worsened his torment – but by God, he must have held her arm a thousand times, taken her hand in a hundred dances, brushed her skin when like a devoted fiancé, he placed a pelisse or a shawl over those slender shoulders.

He remained woefully aware that to her, he was nothing more than an annoyance. It was a joke that she'd told him he was too virile for her tastes. As far as he could see, she didn't think of him as a man at all. Yet every time he touched her, his heart crashed to a standstill and the rush of blood to his ears muffled her polite thanks.

It was enough to drive a hot-blooded Scot to madness.

Even a hot-blooded Scot who sounded like a blasted Sassenach.

He'd never kiss that prim pink mouth. He'd never run his hand through that wealth of shiny hair. He'd never cup that lovely round bosom in his large hands. He'd never possess that slim, graceful body.

With a sigh, he glanced toward the vicar and caught the old man's eyes. And had the grace to feel a qualm for his lascivious thoughts in this holy place.

Hamish was in the process of yet again shifting from one large foot to the other when he heard a rustle from the congregation. The organ started to play Handel's Largo.

Relief flooded him – he wasn't a coward, but the prospect of fresh gossip made him quail – and he turned. His bride poised at the church door, her father beside her.

The breath jammed in his lungs, and his usually doughty knees wobbled. His heart began to race with an excitement that this wedding didn't justify, not when a solitary night awaited.

But he couldn't help it. She was just so damned beautiful.

"You didnae tell me," Diarmid said in a voice quiet as a breath.

Hamish had to swallow twice before he could speak. "Tell you what?"

"That she's exquisite."

To Hamish's despair, she was.

With dazzled eyes, he drank in every detail of Emily's appearance. She wore a rose pink silk gown that might appear modest on a woman with a less spectacular figure. On Emily, the soft fabric clung to every sinuous line and whispered seduction. Her lovely hair was caught up in a mass of loose waves and threaded through with pearls. More pearls encircled her graceful neck and one wrist. She wore white lace gloves and carried a bouquet of white roses. A lace veil was pinned to her crown and draped down her back.

She stood straight and proud. After her attendant straightened her short train, she took her father's arm. With a confidence Hamish couldn't help but admire, she started down the aisle.

Especially as he knew her well enough to see the nerves raging beneath the regal air.

By heaven, she was a cracker of a girl. Her bravery made his heart swell. Any fellow would be privileged to wed her. The anger at himself, at fate, at society, that had been his constant companion for a month faded to nothing.

"She was worth waiting for," he said to Diarmid, and he meant every word.

Hamish turned to the front as his bride took her place beside him and the vicar began the service.

CHAPTER NINE

When Emily returned to the Bloomsbury house with her new husband, it was evening and the staff had lined up on the front steps to greet them. An augmented staff, thanks to Hamish's generosity over the last weeks.

The new butler Roberts stepped forward with a bow. "On behalf of everyone downstairs, my lord and lady, I'd like to offer our warmest congratulations and best wishes for many happy years together."

Emily made herself smile, even as she was startled to hear herself called "my lady." She kept forgetting that Hamish was a lord in his remote northern fastness of Glen Lyon. A few people at the wedding breakfast had addressed her as Lady Glen Lyon, but it was only now on the threshold to her own home that she registered the radical change this marriage made to her life in worldly terms.

Hamish must be used to it, although his title cut little mustard in the scientific circles they inhabited. He went as plain Mr. Douglas in London, even if nobody who met him could doubt that he came from society's upper levels.

Now it seemed she did, too.

"Thank you, Roberts." With a proprietary air that she had no right to resent, Hamish took her arm. In the eyes of the law, he owned her and all her chattels. Not that her meager assets bore any comparison to his. "Thank you, Miss McCorquodale, Mrs. Roberts, Mrs. Brown, Polly and Mary and Florrie and Elsa. And Edward, too."

Edward was the new footman. The Baylors had never been grand enough to need a footman before. Emily wasn't convinced she needed one now. Edward was a handsome devil who sent the maids silly. Perhaps she might talk to Hamish about dispensing with his services.

Emily wasn't surprised that her husband knew the name of everyone who worked in the house. While he might be aristocratic, he'd never been high in the instep. When he'd lodged here as a young man, he'd been a general favorite with the household. Now she noted genuine pleasure on every face as the staff welcomed her new husband.

She drew away from Hamish to climb the steps and express her gratitude to everyone there. Behind her Hamish was busy shaking hands.

"Cor, miss, you do look lovely and all," Polly said, dipping into a curtsy.

"Polly," Mrs. Roberts, the new housekeeper, said in a stern voice, "remember your place."

"It's all right, Mrs. Roberts. I think today of all days, we don't need to be too strict." Emily smiled at the maid who had come to the house as a twelve-year-old girl.

Polly was the only servant here who remembered her mother. Again, Emily felt a painful pang of longing. How she'd missed the late Mrs. Baylor's quiet strength and unfailing love today, when she felt so appallingly alone.

Emily preceded Hamish into the house, aware that now he had a right to be here beyond the welcome of an honored guest, and tonight they'd sleep under the same roof. She tried to tell herself that he'd done that before, but he'd left the house for his lodgings at the Albany when he was twenty-four. She'd been a mere eighteen. A boarder studying with her father wasn't at all the same thing as a husband.

"Miss McCorquodale, how is Papa?" she asked the nurse who had followed them inside.

The wedding breakfast had been a crowded affair, held in Hamish's mother's elegant house in Fitzroy Square. Emily's father had lasted only half an hour, before Hamish arranged for his return home in the care of Miss McCorquodale and one of the innumerable Scots.

"He's sleeping, my lady. He was very tired when he came back. Tired and unsettled. I needed to give him a sleeping draft." The woman curtsied. Emily had never been the recipient of so many curtsies in her life. "If you'll excuse me, I'll go back to him."

"I'll look in, once I've changed." She still wore her wedding finery.

Most couples left on a honeymoon after their nuptials, but she and Hamish had used her father's health to explain their continued presence in London. Hamish had asked if she wanted to go anywhere, but it would be difficult enough to get used to his presence in familiar surroundings. The thought of going somewhere romantic where they were alone and endlessly awkward with each other made her queasy. He'd cooperated, as he had so often during their betrothal.

He was handling her with kid gloves. That shouldn't irk, but it did. His behavior smacked a little too much of humoring her.

After she waited in the hall for Roberts to remove the paisley silk shawl from her shoulders, she prowled through to the library. She and Hamish hadn't been together in this room since the day he proposed. She stood in the center of the floor, while her husband – she still couldn't quite believe that was now true – strode across to stare into the blazing fire with a brooding expression.

Within minutes, Roberts carried in a tray of tea and sandwiches and cakes. "I took the liberty of arranging refreshments. I remember when I married Mrs. Roberts, neither of us took a morsel of food at the wedding breakfast. I thought you might have been in a similar case, my lady."

He was right. Emily had nibbled on a lobster patty, but her throat had closed against swallowing. Hamish hadn't managed to eat much more. She knew. Ever since the wedding service, they'd stood side by side, presenting a united façade.

"Thank you, Roberts," she said, although she didn't feel much more like eating now than she had in Fitzroy Square.

"Please set up the brandy on the sideboard," Hamish said, looking up from the fire.

"I have a bottle of champagne on ice, sir, if you'd prefer that."

"Emily?" Hamish asked.

She shook her head. Right now, she'd choose hemlock over champagne. The grim line of Hamish's lips told her he guessed her wish to end this ruse of celebration.

"Just the brandy," he said to Roberts. "We'll have dinner at eight."

Emily bit back a protest. She was ready to scream for a little privacy, although she supposed if she ate alone on her wedding night, it would cause comment below stairs.

Again Hamish seemed to read her thoughts. "Or perhaps, after this long day, Emily, you might prefer a tray in your room. After all, we have a lifetime of dinners ahead."

Oh, dear, didn't that make her want to run away to Timbuctoo and stay there?

"Yes, I am a little tired," she murmured. "Perhaps that would be best."

That was a vast understatement. Since agreeing to marry Hamish, she'd hardly slept a wink, and her face ached from a day of forcing a smile. She felt about ready to drop.

"Very well, my lady," Roberts said, as Hamish returned to contemplating the fire.

After he left, a heavy silence descended. When Roberts returned to set up the decanters on the sideboard, Emily and Hamish were standing exactly where they'd been when he left. The tray of food remained untouched. Repeating his good wishes for their happiness, the butler left them alone.

"Can I help with your veil?" Hamish raised his gaze from the flames. "You look like you have a headache."

She knew enough from talking to her married friends that having a headache was often code to tell a husband that sexual congress wouldn't take place. In Emily's cold marriage, no such code was necessary.

The powerful, handsome man she'd married stood before her in the home where she'd lived all her life. As she surveyed him, she wondered what most women felt at this moment. Not this dreadful grim numbness, she was sure.

"My head is jangling like untuned bells," she admitted, raising one unsteady hand to a throbbing temple.

When he walked toward her, his smile was gentle as it rarely was. She turned her back to give him access to her veil.

His touch was gentle, too, as he began to dismantle the arrangement of pins that had kept her elaborate hairstyle in place through the long day. Stupidly she trembled, as if the unveiling was the prelude to further incursions. When she knew better. He was a man of honor, and she trusted his word that he'd forgo his conjugal rights.

Hamish was only touching her hair, but that big, heavily muscled body felt too close. She picked up the drift of his scent. Citrus soap and clean skin, and something warm and spicy that belonged to him. With an unpleasant shock, she realized somewhere during the last four weeks, that scent had become part of the fabric of her life.

"We'll need to get you a lady's maid," he murmured, his deep voice making the hairs stand up on her skin. Or perhaps that was the sensation of his fingers moving in her hair. This was the most intimate they'd ever been physically. When he'd kissed her in the church, he'd given her a brief peck on the cheek, the sort of kiss he'd give an aunt. It didn't compare with the sensuality humming between them now.

"I don't need one. I never have before." Even if her father had been able to afford it.

"You will now." With a care she could feel, Hamish lifted her veil away. "We'll have social obligations, and you'll want to look your best."

"You mean you want me to look my best," she responded with an edge.

"That, too," he said easily as he draped the veil over a chair, then returned and began to untwine the strings of pearls twisted through her hair. "Did I tell you how lovely you look? When you arrived at the church, I was quite overcome."

"Hamish..." She started to retreat then winced as the movement tugged on her hair.

"No, stay there. I haven't finished." His hand brushed her shoulder and damn her if she didn't stop shuffling around. He touched her the way he'd settle a restless horse. The odious truth was that she suspected Hamish was fonder of his horses than he was of his wife. "You're a beautiful bride, Emily."

"Thank you," she said grudgingly and hated that she sounded like a sulky child. Hamish turned his attention to the pearl pins that held up her coiffure. She struggled to sound more gracious. "Thank you for my wedding gift. They're very pretty."

Yesterday a velvet case had arrived from Rundle and Bridge. Inside she'd discovered the pins and ropes of pearls, with a note from Hamish asking her to wear them for the wedding. Another example of Hamish's largesse, another occasion for her to feel like her new life overpowered the woman she used to be.

"The second I saw them, I imagined them in your hair, like moons in a dark sky."

"You picked them out?" she asked, surprised and dismayed at the way his poetic description sent warmth pulsing through her veins.

"Of course I did, you silly widgeon." The unexpected note of affection in his voice stifled her protest about the way he touched her hair. "How else did you imagine they came to you? The fairies?"

She shifted from one foot to the other as one long curl of dark hair slipped down to dangle over her shoulder. "I thought you might just tell them to find something nice and send it over with your compliments. To date, my life hasn't been full of dealings with the royal jewelers."

"That's going to change."

Why did that sound like a threat? "Oh," she said in a small voice, as another lock of hair unraveled.

"I thought you'd like the pins better than a parure."

"A parure…" she echoed.

"Yes, a tiara and a necklace and bracelet and—"

"I know what a parure is. I just never imagined I'd be wearing one."

"You're Lady Glen Lyon. Of course you'll wear a parure."

"You've already given me a ring."

"Two rings."

"Well, yes, but I'm talking about the engagement ring." Unable to resist, she lifted a left hand now weighed down with a simple gold band and a magnificent ruby. "That's extravagant enough to be going on with."

With little fanfare, Hamish had produced the engagement ring a few days after his proposal. Both rings symbolized the vast changes she'd faced, and the even vaster changes ahead. The wedding ring branded her as Hamish Douglas's wife until the day she died. The ruby announced her new status as Lady Glen Lyon.

Briefly, Emily wondered about her husband's Highland estates, so far away on the west coast of Scotland. He rarely talked about them. Just as he rarely talked about his family. She'd been surprised at the number of relatives who traveled down for his wedding. Surprised and envious. It was all too clear that his family adored Hamish, whereas apart from her close relationship with her father, she had no strong family ties at all.

Even worse, most of Hamish's friends and relatives seemed to be happily married. Their joy in one another had been palpable, even to a stranger like Emily. The contrast with this empty union she entered into had been painful.

She shivered as the weight of her hair slithered down her neck. "You don't have to undo my hair. I thought you were just taking off my veil."

"You know me. When I do something, I like to do it properly."

Surely only this intimate atmosphere building between them made his remark sound like an invitation to sin. It was an innocent enough comment.

"You can stop touching me now." She cursed how quivery her voice sounded.

He made a soft hum under his breath, and those clever, insinuating hands began to massage her skull. "I'm helping to get rid of your headache."

Emily wanted to tell him that he was her headache, but the sensations emanating from his hands were too delicious for her to summon the words.

"You've never touched me like this before." How could that sound like another invitation?

"I wouldn't dare," he responded with the wry humor she'd always liked.

Right from the first, Hamish had set her hackles up, even when he wasn't doing anything overly objectionable. But on those rare occasions when she didn't want to cosh him with the nearest blunt instrument, he also had the knack for making her laugh.

"I don't think you should touch me like this now." In concert with that lovely rubbing across her poor, tortured scalp, her heart pounded hard and deep. She should be more insistent. She should shift away. When Hamish took down her hair, it felt disturbingly bridal.

"Do you feel better?"

Better? Plague take him, she felt like melting into a puddle at his feet. Far from her hackles rising, her shoulders felt ready to slide off her neck and drop down to the floor. As he changed the pressure, she made a soft growl of pleasure. "I suppose so."

"You're a bonny fighter, Emily," he murmured. "And you have lovely hair. For years, I've wondered how you'd look when you let it down."

There was something wrong with what he said, but she was too lost in weariness and the haze of pleasure to work out what it was. Her legs felt so rubbery, they were likely to collapse under her.

When her back met something large and warm, she realized with a distant shock that she leaned into him. Somehow his attention to the tight muscles of her head had loosened every other muscle in her body.

He made a soft sound of satisfaction, and she noticed that he'd stopped massaging her skull and had started stroking her hair. He ran his fingers through it, until it cascaded around her in long waves.

Since he'd started touching her, Emily's vision had grown mistier and mistier. Now she closed her eyes and sighed with a mixture of physical wellbeing and exhaustion. For so long, she'd battled to stop everything caving in on her. Now for a miraculous instant, someone else held up the sky when her strength threatened to fail.

She had to move. She would move. If only because the man who propped her up was Hamish Douglas, and she wasn't even sure she liked him.

But how she longed for one small moment's rest. How she longed to take a breath that was free of fear and grief and worry.

Emily hardly noticed when he slid his arms around her, bringing her closer into his body. She was warm and safe and drifting in a world rich with the smell of citrus soap. She felt a ridiculous desire to cry. For months, she'd held herself as tight as a drum. Now all she felt was relaxed and unencumbered.

"Emily, my lovely wife…" A soft bass voice rumbled in her ear before lips brushed the sensitive skin of her neck.

The forbidden thrill that ripped through her jolted her out of her languor. With a gasp of horror, she wrenched away from Hamish.

"Let me go." On unsteady legs, Emily whirled to face him. "You're trying to seduce me, you devil."

Despite everything, when he smiled, she needed to steel herself against the onslaught of charm. Her accusation didn't prompt a scrap of guilt from the cad. "You can't blame a fellow for trying, darling."

Her shoulders tightening, she scowled at him. "Don't call me that. It doesn't mean anything."

He arched those expressive eyebrows. "Do you want it to mean something?"

No, no, no. This wasn't what she planned when she said she'd marry him.

"I want you to stick to the bargain we made." She meant her voice to cut like a knife, but it emerged wobbly and uncertain. She wished to glory he'd left her hair alone, however badly her head ached. With her hair flowing around her, it was impossible to maintain her dignity. Curse him, she must look like a wanton dairymaid.

"Are you sure?" When Hamish spread his hands, she hardened herself against the appealing picture he made. "It seems a dashed lonely way for us to go on."

He was right. Emily only had to recall all those smug, happy Scots making sheeps' eyes at one another to understand that her marriage locked her inside an invisible cage. Inside her cage, she was safe. Outside her cage, she wasn't. She just had to look back on these last few minutes to understand how dangerous Hamish could be.

But while a retreat to safety was her only choice, it still left her trapped in a cage.

"I'm sure." This time, she managed to sound more convincing.

Disappointment shadowed his eyes, and she tried not to feel guilty. He'd behaved so well during the last month. She couldn't have asked for a better betrothed. And he was right. Their marriage was going to be lonely.

"You knew our arrangement when I agreed to marry you, Hamish." She shouldn't sound defensive. After all, she'd set out her conditions before their engagement and he'd agreed to abide by them.

As he lowered his hands, an uncharacteristically desolate expression settled on his face. "I knew, but it seems a waste when we could have so much more."

"Physical pleasure, you mean," she said in a snide tone.

"Don't knock what you haven't tried, my dear."

The insincere endearment struck her on the raw. "How do you know I haven't tried it?" she asked, before she could question the wisdom of challenging him.

She saw straightaway that she didn't fool him. He tilted one sardonic brow, and his reply was a sarcastic drawl. "You shock me, my lady."

"No, I don't," she said, too tired to have this argument. "I'm going upstairs. I'll see you in the morning."

"Really?" he said with a hint of bafflement. "That's where you mean to leave things?"

"That's where I mean to leave you," she said curtly, marching toward the door. "Good evening, Hamish."

When she paused to look back, he was still watching her. She'd wondered if her refusal might anger him, but his expression was enigmatic.

"My offer remains open, should you change your mind," he said, as though he asked her if she'd like a biscuit with her tea.

The scoundrel! Emily growled deep in her throat and stormed out, slamming the door behind her.

CHAPTER TEN

*H*amish set down the half-empty brandy decanter and stood to make his way to bed. Damn it, he was still stirred up from all that blasted touching when he'd taken down Emily's hair. So stirred up that he only now realized that he had no idea where his room was.

When he'd lodged with the Baylors, the scholars had slept in the attic. It was a big room divided into cubicles, with a staircase up to the roof, in case anyone wanted to do some extra stargazing. He couldn't imagine Emily would put her new husband there, no matter how much she resented his presence.

It was late, well after midnight. He should have gone upstairs before this to change out of his wedding clothes. But after getting a curtailed taste of the pleasures his wife meant to deny him, he'd been too grumpy to leave the library.

A taste? Not even that. He'd had lovers before, and he knew the sweet tug of carnal hunger. But nothing had rivaled those sensual moments, when he'd taken down that wealth of sable hair and buried his hands in its lustrous thickness.

He'd soon wanted more. Emily had been so soft, lying against him, he couldn't imagine she'd resist. But resist she had. As a result, he suffered an agonizing case of blue balls. Since then, he'd picked at his dinner and drunk too much. But nothing he did shifted the alluring scent of Emily's skin from his nostrils.

He sighed, bleakly aware that his troubles were just beginning, and rang for Edward who had stayed up to look after him. He didn't expect to sleep a wink, but it was time he retired and let the household do the same.

The young man appeared at the door. "My lord?"

"It's Mr. Douglas," he said.

Edward frowned. "Mr. Roberts says you're a lord up in Scotland."

"A laird. There's a difference."

"So does that mean my lady is Mrs. Douglas?"

Not in any real sense of the word, plague take her. And there was no bloody sign of that changing before the dawn of doomsday. "No, she's Lady Glen Lyon."

"But..."

A grunt of reluctant amusement escaped Hamish. "It all makes no sense, I know, but I'd appreciate it if you don't 'my lord' me."

Edward nodded, although it was clear he remained confused. On the other hand, he was paid a generous wage to take orders without question. "As you wish, my...Mr. Douglas."

"Well done, lad. You'll get into your stride in no time. Now I'd like you to show me where I'm sleeping."

"Very good, sir."

Feeling like his head was stuffed with lead, Hamish followed Edward upstairs and along a lamplit corridor until they stopped in front of a closed door. "Sir John sleeps in there. And you're here." Edward opened the door across the hall. "Shall I stay and help you undress, sir?"

"No, thank you. I'll manage." The way he was feeling now, he was likely to collapse fully clothed on his bed.

Edward lit him a candle and waited outside while Hamish entered the shadowy dressing room. Once he was alone, he flung off his clothes and stood at the washstand to splash himself with warm water.

He looked around for his nightshirt but couldn't find it. None of his kit seemed to be in here. The shelves surrounding him were half empty and what was stored on them seemed to be sheets and pillowcases.

This morning, he'd had all his belongings transferred over from the Albany. He would have thought the servants had had plenty of time to unpack for him. Excitement over the wedding must have led to some slackness in the household.

Hamish pushed open the bedroom door. Beyond the small circle of light his candle cast, the room was pitch dark. He'd have thought the servants would light a fire for him. It was late November, after all. Something else to talk to the housekeeper about.

He made out the dark shapes of furniture, including a large bed set off in a corner alcove. He placed the candle on a table near the door and blew it out. Barefoot, naked and shivering in the cold, he padded across the floor to slide between the sheets. As his body subsided into the thick mattress, he stretched out with a long, weary groan.

By God, he was tired. Perhaps he would sleep after all. If he could just banish Emily's haunting scent from his dreams. Lying here in this empty room, it was more invasive than ever.

What a rum wedding night. Dinner on his own, followed by equally solitary slumber, if he managed to slumber at all. Good God, if his friends could see him, they'd laugh their heads off.

He released a depressed sigh and wriggled onto his side, straightening his arm. His hand landed on something soft and warm.

What the devil...

His thick head struggled to interpret what his senses told him. After all that brandy, his thoughts were confounded sluggish. "Emily?"

She made a drowsy sound and shifted under his hand, rolling onto her back. His fingers automatically curled to shape one round breast. Still far from alert, he squeezed the lush flesh and felt a sweet little nipple harden against his palm.

A sleepy growl of pleasure escaped him, and he went as hard as a flagpole. He didn't know what the deuce she was doing in his bed, but he wasn't going to ask too many questions. As his thumb teased that flannel-covered peak, he edged closer.

Emily went as rigid as a plank under his touch. "Hamish, what on earth are you doing?"

"Doing?" What in Hades did she think he was doing?

Frantic hands shoved at him, and she landed a couple of resounding blows to his jaw and chest before she managed to push him away. "Get your hands off me."

Brandy, tiredness, and a raging cock-stand stopped the blood flowing to his brain. He was still befuddled. Befuddled enough to hope this endless, miserable day might yet see a happy ending.

"What's wrong with you, girl?" His eyes had adjusted to the darkness enough that he caught her flailing hands. "Settle down, damn you."

"What's wrong with me?" she asked in affront. One might almost say she shrieked. One would be right. "What's wrong with *you*?"

She started to kick which, given his unclothed state, could result in some serious damage. In an attempt to calm her, he rolled on top of her. "Stop it, Emily. I'm not going to hurt you."

The rolling didn't help. For one quivering instant, she lay trembling beneath him, before she started to struggle again. "You're...you're naked, you filthy beast."

Her wriggling wasn't doing much for his self-control, and every breath he snatched was alive with her bewitching scent.

Hamish flattened her hands on either side of her head. He was having trouble putting words together. "Couldn't find my nightshirt," he finally managed.

She was panting, and her movements grew choppy as she ran out of puff. "A likely story!"

"What right have you to call me a filthy beast when you came to my bed of your own free will?" He was feeling aggrieved. He'd spent the whole bloody night playing the gentleman, and what had he got in return for his exemplary behavior, apart from a rampant erection and a headache? "For God's sake, woman, will you lie still?"

"I'm not going to just let you..." She paused and spoke in a completely different tone. "*Your* bed?"

"Yes, my bed. And how the dickens did you think I'd react to finding you beside me? By the way, I might point out this is our wedding night."

"Your bed." She wasn't wriggling anymore, but somehow during their epic struggle, Hamish had insinuated himself between her legs. Her knees rose on either side of his hips and only a layer of flannel barred his access to her body. All the while, that damned perfume, warmer and earthier than the everyday, tantalized him.

He set his jaw until it was like rock and told himself that he would not brush aside the frail barrier of her nightdress and touch her there. The fog of drink and drowsiness had evaporated from his mind. He wasn't as sharp as he was in the full light of day, but a few things became clear.

Dismally so.

Striving to rein himself in, he gulped for a breath. When he spoke, his voice was flat. "You didn't change your mind about sleeping with me?"

"No, I did not," she said with an emphasis he couldn't help but feel was uncalled for. "Why on earth would I?"

Piqued, Hamish spoke with more heat than perhaps he should. "Maybe because you like me. Maybe because you saw sense and realized that this is a mad arrangement. Maybe because you had an itch to discover what it's like to take a lover. How the bloody hell do I know what goes through that gorgeous, muddled head of yours?"

He sounded cranky. He couldn't help it. Four weeks ago, his life had been exactly as he wished. He'd been poised on the brink of a brilliant career. He'd been as free as a bird, and as happy as a spring lamb at Glen Lyon.

Since then, he'd endured a month of putting a good face on an engagement that he didn't want. He'd borne Emily's barely hidden disdain, the snickering of his friends and colleagues, the prospect of professional ruin. And all without a tip-top swiving of his new bride to look forward to as compensation for his trouble.

Good God, a saint would be disgruntled.

"But I left you downstairs, saying I didn't want to see you."

What was new? She never wanted to see him. "People can change their mind."

"Only a lunatic could undergo such a change in mere hours."

"Is that so?" he asked on a rising intonation.

He would not lose his temper. He wouldn't. His pestilential temper never helped matters. Look at the disaster he'd sparked the last time that he got angry. But his good intentions grew shakier by the minute.

"Yes, it is."

She squirmed again, which given the circumstances wasn't wise. He closed his eyes and did long division in his head as her supple body slid and shifted around his. It turned out even long division couldn't distract him from what he burned to do to his wife.

"You're turning me into a lunatic," he muttered.

Wisely she didn't respond to that. "For pity's sake, will you get off? You're crushing me."

"With pleasure," he bit out, although disentangling himself from yards of flannel and piles of winter bedding proved more of a task than he'd like.

All this wriggling around wasn't conducive to sticking to the straight and narrow. Although one part of him was very straight indeed. The rest of him might be vastly displeased with his bride, but his dick liked her very much and had ambitions to get much closer.

He rolled off her, which didn't put him nearly far enough away from temptation. So he left the bed and marched into the middle of the room. Behind him, he heard rustling bedclothes. Such an evocative sound. After a few seconds, light flickered.

He swallowed a groan and closed his eyes. His jaw ached from all the gritting of teeth. "No, don't light the candle..."

It was too late.

Sitting propped up against the pile of pillows, Emily stared at him wide-eyed. "Dear heaven."

Her appalled gaze roamed every inch of his body. His bare and massively aroused body.

If his presence was a genuine mistake, he couldn't blame her for her reaction. Even decently clad, he was a huge bugger. In a virginal lady's bedroom in the middle of the night, he must seem as unnatural and terrifying as a naked giant.

In the uncertain light, he saw her turn as red as a beetroot. He blushed, too, when her gaze inevitably dropped to where his cock rose in brazen demand. "That's not what they look like on the statues in the British Museum."

"For pity's sake..." With fumbling hands, he grabbed for the bedcover and hauled it around his waist.

Still she stared at him...*there*. He suffered the horrid sensation that those clever hazel eyes pierced the rumpled swathe of material to where he was hard and heavy and ready. After far too long, she raised her gaze to his.

With a shock, he realized that she no longer looked appalled. Instead she looked curious. The expression was familiar. This was how she looked when a new scientific theory caught her attention. He wasn't sure whether he preferred this clinical interest to having his wife despise him as a ravisher of innocent maidens.

"I didn't think you were interested," she said in wonder.

Battling for control, he ground his teeth together. "Well, it's bloody obvious that I am."

When she licked her lips, his cock twitched. He smothered another groan.

"That's so like you, Hamish. Just because you can't have me, you want me."

"You do me an injustice. I've wanted you for years," he snapped. The night had been a trial for his already limited tolerance. He'd give her the truth, whether it disgusted her or not. "I might be stupid, but I'm not shallow."

With an alarmed squeak, she pressed back against the bedhead. It was the reaction he should have expected, but it still stung.

Despite his throbbing erection, his vision cleared enough to take in the details of her appearance. How he wished he damn well couldn't see her. Tonight had provided quite enough new information about his wife to torture him, thank you very much. He knew how it felt to stroke her hair, and touch her breast, and lie on top of her, and drink in air tinged with her scent. He knew what she wore to bed.

Confound it, she wasn't dressed to seduce. The billowing white flannel could have come out of his grandmother's armoire.

But she hadn't plaited her hair after she'd come upstairs. Now it tumbled about her shoulders, begging him to snatch it up in silky handfuls. The frail candlelight lent mystery to her features, made her hazel eyes smoky, turned her soft lips to kissable red.

"You're not stupid," she said, sounding more like herself. "Although sometimes you do stupid things. I had no idea you'd noticed me that way."

Hamish sighed and ran a shaking hand through his hair. Then hurriedly lowered his hand to catch the sagging coverlet. This evening, he'd spent more than enough time with his tackle waving in the breeze. "I'm a man. Of course I noticed."

"But you don't like me."

"You're always saying that, and it's not true," he growled. "Anyway, liking has nothing to do with it. It's a natural reaction when a fellow sees a pretty girl."

She frowned. "You've never said I'm pretty."

"Yes, I have. I told you when I proposed."

"That was only to get your own way."

"That, too, but it doesn't mean I was lying." He gave an exasperated hiss. "If you don't want me to act on those natural impulses, we should change the subject."

She clutched the blankets to her breasts, although he could have told her that monstrosity of a nightdress already did an excellent job of preserving her modesty. The problem was that during that short, furious interval in the bed, his hands had learned too much about the delectable shape beneath the flannel. His powerful imagination had no trouble translating what he'd learned into picturing her naked.

Or perhaps she pulled up the blankets because it was colder than a polar bear's toenail in here.

"Why the hell don't you have a fire? There's no need to stint on coal now. I'm paying the bill."

"Don't boast about your wealth," she snapped. "It's laid, but I told Polly to leave it until the morning. Since Papa fell ill and money's been tight, I've got used to doing without a fire."

Hamish ground his teeth again. At this rate, he'd soon have no teeth left.

Gathering the voluminous bedcover around him, he stomped around the bed to grab the candle. "I won't have my wife freezing to death because she's trying to save a few pennies."

He stalked across to the hearth. It was a relief to turn his back on Emily and hunker down in front of the fireplace. If he kept looking at her, he was likely to move from looking to touching, and she wouldn't like that. She'd go back to calling him a brute and a beast, and he'd have to slink out of the room like a beaten hound. He didn't want to go through all that. He'd already been humiliated enough for one night.

After tucking the coverlet around his waist so he had two hands free, he set to lighting the fire. She remained mercifully quiet while he fiddled with the kindling and got the flames going. Getting up presented a challenge, but he managed it with only a few flashes of thigh.

"You didn't come here to force yourself on me?" she asked, once he was standing.

He reined in a blistering response. "If you don't trust my word, you shouldn't have married me."

"I did trust you." After he shot her a narrow-eyed look, she spread her hands in silent apology. "I *do* trust you."

"Doesn't seem like it."

Impatience flattened that delectable mouth. "What are you doing here, Hamish?"

He ran his hand through his hair again. "I think it might be a misunderstanding. I asked Edward to show me to my room. As this is our wedding night, I imagine by my room, he thought I meant your room. He brought me to the dressing room next door. You know what happened after that."

"Oh." He waited for her to call him a self-serving liar, but she seemed to give his answer due consideration.

"I only realized my mistake when..."

When he'd put his hand on her breast. Once again, her cheeks tuned pink with embarrassment. They both knew how that sentence ended.

"I put you along the corridor, so the servants will at least think—"

"That we have a real marriage? They won't, you know. It's impossible to keep secrets from the staff." He hitched up his makeshift covering, wishing he presented a more dignified picture. This hadn't been a great night for his self-esteem. "So once I'm out in the hallway, I turn left?"

"Yes, the next door down leads to another dressing room which is where I asked Roberts to put your belongings. The door after that is your bedroom. I'm sorry I didn't tell you before."

At least she didn't sound angry anymore. "You had other things to think about."

After bouncing around on top of her, he had more than enough to think about, too.

"No harm done."

He wasn't so sure about that either, damn it.

"I'm sorry I jumped to conclusions," she said softly. Her eyes shone gold in the firelight and seemed to send him messages that he knew couldn't be true. The nascent desire in her face was nothing but wishful thinking on his part.

She didn't want him. She'd made that more than clear.

"I should go." He didn't shift from where he stood. "You're tired."

Her attention dropped to his bare chest, and she licked her lips again. Was that admiration? Despite everything he knew, he started to get excited.

Careful, Hamish, remember who she is. Remember you made promises.

"Yes, you should." That murmur didn't sound at all like forthright, opinionated Emily Baylor. Those great hazel eyes ate him up, like he was a pot of brandy custard and she had a very sweet tooth.

Again he told himself to go. But his feet didn't heed his brain's command. As he stepped toward her, the heavy brocade cover slipped. "Emily..."

A rapid knock at the door smashed through his confusion. Without waiting for an answer, Miss McCorquodale stood at the entrance to the room. "Miss Baylor... I mean, my lady, your father is having a bad spell. He's calling for you."

The dazed look vanished from Emily's eyes, and her head snapped around in the nurse's direction. "I'll come straightaway."

Miss McCorquodale sent Hamish a blushing glance. "I'm so sorry to burst in like this, Mr. Douglas."

He hauled the coverlet back into place. It must be obvious he was naked beneath his unconventional garb. He supposed that at least now the staff would believe that he and Emily had consummated their marriage.

He wasn't sure whether the interruption left him disappointed or relieved. Common sense insisted that if he'd followed up on Emily's encouraging manner, she'd only slap him down again. Something addled in his mind whispered that she'd been edging around to the idea of saying yes just as the nurse barged in.

It hardly mattered now. The moment was lost.

Emily scrambled out of bed and flung a knitted shawl over her shoulders. "It's all been too much for him."

Without a backward glance at Hamish, she followed Miss McCorquodale out into the hallway.

CHAPTER ELEVEN

"*B*ut I have to go to the Astronomical Society," Emily's father said in a querulous voice from where he stood clinging to the mantelpiece with both hands. "They're expecting me. I'm presenting my paper on the moons of Jupiter."

"No, Papa. It's night time. You need to sleep." Emily kept her voice even, although her father had been saying the same thing for the last fifteen minutes. When she tried to catch his arm, he wrenched away hard enough to hurt her. The strength in his wasted body always surprised her.

The man who had spoken to her with such moving sincerity before her wedding was no longer in evidence. The abrupt changes that afflicted him were enough to break her heart.

"The wedding was too much for him," Miss McCorquodale said from his other side. "He got overexcited. And the recent disruption in the household has upset him."

"Who is this lady?" Papa fastened a hostile stare on the nurse, who looked as tired as Emily felt. "I don't believe we've been introduced."

"I'm your attendant, Hilda McCorquodale." Her composure remained unruffled. "I'm here to put you to bed, Sir John."

"I don't want to go to bed. I want to present my paper," he said fretfully. "I have some interesting observations on the Medici Moons. I told you all about them, Emily, my dear. Don't you remember? Where are my notes?"

Ten years ago, his findings had been published in a well-received monograph. The paper had been one of the triumphs of his career. "Papa, it's not time to leave. If you lie down for a moment, I'll go and check that everything is ready."

"Yes, Sir John, they're expecting you at the Astronomical Society, but not just yet," a deep voice said from behind her.

Startled, Emily glanced away from her father to see that Hamish had joined them. She'd been so preoccupied with Papa that she hadn't noticed her husband arrive. He was in shirtsleeves and trousers. Hardly formal attire, but an improvement on the bedspread.

Briefly the magnificent image of a huge, naked and aroused Scot flooded her mind. The sight had made her feel like swooning. She'd almost asked him to stay there and let her examine him. In her whole life, she'd never seen anything so interesting as Hamish wearing nothing at all.

Her father took advantage of her distraction to approach Hamish where he stood in the doorway. "At last, someone sensible. I have to go to the Astronomical Society this morning, Hamish. Will you come with me?"

"Don't let him out of the bedroom," Emily said urgently. "He'll head straight for the front door. Once he's on the street, he's almost impossible to catch."

Hamish cast her a quick unreadable glance, before he stepped forward to take Sir John's arm. "The lecture has been postponed. There's a problem with the drains."

Her father stared blankly at Hamish. "You married my daughter today."

Hamish smiled. "I did indeed."

Emily watched fleeting awareness animate her father's features. "I'm glad. You're the son I never had."

Hamish was still smiling. Ridiculously Emily couldn't help noting the open affection in his manner. He never treated her like that. He always acted as if he expected her to bite him.

With some justice, she supposed.

"And I think of you as a father. We're both lucky that Emily decided to make me the happiest of men."

"She's a good girl. I hope you mean to look after her."

"Nothing but the best for my wife. And for my wife's father." He edged the old man back toward his bed, where Miss McCorquodale was restoring order to the chaotic bedclothes.

"What are you doing here?" Papa asked. "Shouldn't you be alone with your bride?"

Hamish didn't glance at Emily, but she saw the way his lips compressed. "We came to ask your blessing, Sir John."

Hamish lowered the old man until he sat on the edge of the mattress. Suffering and ill health had turned her father's face gaunt and pale, and his nightshirt hung loose from his bony shoulders. Only a year ago, he'd addressed the Royal Society to great acclaim, although not about the moons of Jupiter. How his world had shrunk over these months.

Emily stared at her father, trembling and uncertain in the care of her strong, vital husband, and recognized that he wouldn't be with her for much longer. She'd known this rationally for weeks, but only now in the middle of this shipwreck of a wedding night did her heart accept the unavoidable truth.

Some sound of distress must have escaped her, because Hamish shot her another glance. For once, he didn't look superior. Instead he looked as devastated as she did. He, too, must see that Sir John's health reached a critical point.

"My blessing..." Papa looked around him and plucked at the nightshirt as if checking for pockets.

"Yes, sir. If you're willing to give it."

"Where the deuce are my spectacles?"

Miss McCorquodale picked them up from the bedside table and held them out to him. "Here, Sir John."

"What on earth do I want those for, you nitwitted woman? It's the middle of the night."

"Oh, I see," Miss McCorquodale said with admirable calmness and put them back. "I do beg your pardon."

"Emily, come and stand beside Hamish. It does my heart good to see you two together."

"Yes, Papa," she said meekly and stepped up next to the man she'd married against her deepest inclinations. Although seeing him so gentle and patient with her father, especially when by nature he was neither gentle nor patient, she could almost imagine loving him.

Hamish took her hand. She knew it was all for show, just as everything today had been for show, but reviving strength flowed from his firm clasp. Right now, she dearly needed that strength.

"I promise to cherish your daughter and do my best to make her happy," Hamish said in his deep voice. If Emily didn't know better, she'd almost think he meant it.

There was a pause, and Emily realized it was her turn to speak. The truth was too unacceptable. How could she tell Papa that she'd married Hamish to quash a scandal and that she and her husband would never live as man and wife? Her father would have no grandchildren to carry his line into the next generation.

She licked dry lips, and her voice sounded scratchy when it emerged. "I promise to honor Hamish and care for him through all the vicissitudes of life."

As a statement of lifelong intentions, it was weak, but she already felt enough of a hypocrite. Lying declarations of eternal devotion stretched her too far.

To her relief, the lukewarm vow seemed to satisfy her father. With difficulty, he rose from the bed and placed his hand on her head. He even laughed as Hamish had to bend to allow him to reach his crown. "I bless this union. I bless both of you, my dear children. Knowing you go forward into life hand in hand eases my heart and makes me thank heaven that you found each other. I loved your mother very much, Emily, and I know she's looking down on you now and wishing you and Hamish a long and happy life together."

As her father's hand rested a moment longer on her head, Emily blinked back tears. How she wished she did love the man she'd married, so her father's beautiful words didn't make her feel like a fraud.

"Thank you, Papa," she said thickly, when he lowered his hands.

"Thank you, Sir John," Hamish said, straightening.

Emily glanced at him. He sounded as choked up as she did. She was touched to see tears brightening those blue eyes, but she wasn't surprised. Hamish had always worn his heart on his sleeve. She supposed there was some advantage in marrying a man who could never tell a convincing lie.

Then with a pang, she realized that there were disadvantages, too. When he sought his physical pleasure elsewhere as he inevitably would, she'd know the minute he strayed. She shouldn't care that he went to another woman's bed, especially as the only thing she could do about that was to take him into hers. She wasn't just a fraud, she was a dog in the manger as well. Sometimes she didn't like herself very much.

The crisis with her father had pushed tonight's revelations into the background. But Emily suddenly recalled Hamish saying that he'd always wanted her. She mightn't want to believe it, but Hamish didn't lie. It shouldn't change things between them – she was no more eager to yield to him than she'd been before. But somehow it did, leaving her curious, unsettled, and filled with a forbidden excitement that made no sense.

Hamish released her hand – ridiculous, too, to miss that link – and stepped forward to take her father's elbow. "Time for bed, I think."

Her father scowled at the bed as if it was an instrument of torture. "Yes," he said without enthusiasm.

Miss McCorquodale held out a small glass. "Here's a drink to settle you down, Sir John."

Emily braced for some act of rebellion, but it seemed that Papa was exhausted at last. With help, the old man swallowed the sleeping draft, then with a docility in stark contrast to his earlier peevishness, he slid between the covers and closed his eyes.

Hamish stood up from where he'd been stoking the fire, although the room wasn't cold. "Go to bed, Miss McCorquodale. You've been with him all day, and you look wrung out. Emily and I will take over from here."

"But it's your wedding night."

"My bride and I have a lifetime ahead of us. This is only one night," he said with the sudden flashing charm that hadn't lost its power to make Emily's knees wobble. It had been making her knees wobble since their first meeting. Now inevitably it made her remember quite how breathtaking he'd looked standing before her without a stitch to cover that superb body.

"I'll sit with him," Emily said, cramming those troubling insights into a remote corner of her mind where she hoped they'd never again see the light of day.

"No, I will." Hamish set a chair at the bedside. "Tomorrow we'll see what we can do about getting both of you some more help. I had no idea Sir John's health had reached this pass."

Miss McCorquodale curtsied. "Thank you, my lord."

Hamish's smile was weary as he sat down. "Mr. Douglas is perfectly fine."

Emily struggled to remind herself that this man who treated her father and the nurse with such consideration was overbearing, irritating Hamish Douglas. Her antagonist for the last ten years. The man whose every remark made her snipe and snarl like a cat with its fur rubbed the wrong way.

Now, watching him settle down beside her father's bed with every sign of good grace, she couldn't summon her usual animosity. Which was as troubling in its way as her odd response to his touch.

She accepted his explanation of the mistake about his room. When he'd found himself lying beside her, his shock had been unambiguous. Anyway, he wasn't a man given to sneaking around and dissembling to achieve his ends.

Which didn't mean she was at ease with what had happened.

She had a nasty suspicion that tonight she and Hamish had crossed a barrier that until now had kept them decorously apart. She'd wake up tomorrow as virginal as she'd ever been, but not nearly so innocent.

Now she knew that her husband wanted her, had wanted her for years. She knew what he looked like naked. As the unforgettable picture swamped her mind once more, she swallowed to moisten a dry throat. Even worse, she knew how it felt when a large masculine hand cupped her breast and a big masculine body pressed her down into a bed.

Yesterday she'd been convinced those acts would frighten her. She had been frightened, at least for a moment. But along with the fear had come an extraordinary thrill that turned her blood to lava. It was a little like her shivery reaction when he'd taken down her hair.

When he fondled her nipple, there had been an undeniable spark of...*something*. For one insane instant, she hadn't wanted him to stop.

She'd imagined that after their wedding, she and Hamish would remain virtual strangers. But already it became clear that sharing a house with her new husband posed challenges she'd never foreseen.

They'd been married little more than half a day, and already her plans to lead a separate life were in ruins.

What other disagreeable revelations awaited?

She squared her shoulders and told herself to stop fretting. This bleak self-reflection just proved how tired and on edge she was. Hamish's visit to her bedroom had upset her, even before Miss McCorquodale called for her help.

Yes, upset. That was how she chose to define those bizarre tingling sensations when Hamish caressed her. She'd stick to that definition until the crack of doom, by heaven.

He wouldn't come to her bed again, not now he knew where his room was. Not now he'd discovered the cold welcome he'd receive in her chamber.

That sudden weight in her empty stomach was not disappointment. She wouldn't let it be disappointment.

She and Hamish were a disastrous mixture. They always had been. Flame and touch paper. Gunpowder lit with a fuse. Their only chance of finding contentment was to avoid each other as much as possible.

If right now the future seemed to stretch ahead of her like a vast and barren desert, that was only because she was worried about her father and exhausted and...*upset.*

Yes, upset.

It had been a day of upheavals, and Emily wasn't herself. So she kept her voice calm and practical as she wrapped her shawl tighter around her shoulders. "Miss McCorquodale, Hamish is right. You need your rest. Papa is in safe hands tonight."

Hamish glanced up with a hint of a smile, and Emily struggled not to notice how handsome he looked when laughter lines formed creases around his blue eyes. "Go to bed, too, Emily. You look ready to collapse where you stand." The smile deepened. How she wished it didn't. That strange heavy feeling in her stomach grew more acute. "I'll come and get you if I need you."

She suppressed a sour laugh. He didn't need her. He never had, and he never would. He might express a yen to have her, but she had no illusions that meant anything beyond the male urge to claim and possess a nubile female.

She turned to go. "Good night, Hamish," she said, and told herself that the emotion tinging her tone wasn't wistfulness.

CHAPTER TWELVE

On Emily's second night as a married woman, if not in any real sense a wife, she and Hamish were to dine at the home of Hamish's intimidating mother. Emily was sickly aware that she would be the center of attention and an object of curiosity. Right now as she dressed for the event, she almost wished she'd taken a wedding trip, despite the thought of being alone with Hamish bringing her out in a cold sweat.

"Smile, my lady," Polly said with her usual cheerfulness, as she placed the last pearl hairpin in Emily's elaborate coiffure. "It might never happen."

As a lady's maid, Polly had proven a mixed blessing. It turned out she was a devotee of the fashion magazines and knew to the inch how to dress Emily for her newly elevated status. She was also unfailingly jolly. On the other hand, she carried the old familiarity forward. At times, Emily found herself longing for someone who treated her like a stern mistress, instead of a middle-class girl she'd known most of her life.

Now Emily met her troubled hazel gaze in the mirror and obeyed Polly's command to smile. Her reflection informed her that the attempt lacked conviction. "I just hope Papa will be all right while we're out."

After she left Hamish in charge of her father, she'd slept late and more soundly than she had in weeks. Some part of her must have known that Papa was safe. She'd woken to Polly telling her that Hamish and Miss McCorquodale were already interviewing nursing staff. By lunchtime, they'd employed two assistants for the sickroom and another footman fully dedicated to Papa's service.

Over the last months, Emily had found it harder and harder to juggle caring for her father and running the house. She should be grateful that Hamish lightened her burden, but she couldn't help feeling he was taking over her life.

Of course he was. He'd married her, hadn't he?

Resentment at her loss of independence came too late. If she complained that her new husband splashed his money around on presents for his wife and extra servants, anyone who heard her would think she belonged in Bedlam.

Hamish hadn't restricted his latest round of generosity to the household. This morning, a *modiste* had arrived to ensure that the new Lady Glen Lyon looked the part. A couple of the gowns Madame Lisette brought had only needed small alterations. Emily wore one now, an emerald green sarcenet that was the most spectacular dress she'd ever owned. How she wished it didn't feel like yet another link in the chain tethering her to the bars of her cage.

There was a soft knock on the door. Without surprise, she watched it open to reveal the man she'd married.

Hamish stepped forward. He was so large, he made her spacious chamber seem small and unfamiliar, although she'd slept here all her life. In a dark blue coat that fitted him like a second skin and deepened the already extraordinary color of his eyes, he looked magnificent. "How is the dress?"

"See for yourself." She hated how ungracious she sounded. Pushing away from the dressing table, she stood.

If he noticed her moodiness, he gave no sign of it. Instead his eyes glittered with appreciation, as they devoured the sight of her. "Lovely. I thought it would be."

"Our young lady do look pretty, don't she, my lord?" Polly said with a proud smile.

Emily saw Hamish consider correcting Polly's use of the title, then dismiss it. He hadn't had much success convincing the servants to address her as Lady Glen Lyon, while calling him plain Mr. Douglas. There were times when she knew exactly what ran through that handsome head.

"Thank you, Polly," she said.

"My pleasure, miss... I mean, my lady."

Hamish's lips twitched, as Emily sent Polly a straight look. "As in 'Thank you, Polly. That will be all.'"

"Oh. Right. As you wish, my lady." She bobbed into a curtsy and with barely concealed reluctance, left the room.

"I asked Madame Lisette to put you in bright colors. I'm glad she took me at my word."

"You're too extravagant," Emily said.

One eyebrow tilted in her direction, and he smiled as if they shared a private joke. "After what happened at Pascoe Place, I owe you a new dress or two."

Taken aback, she regarded him with wide eyes. "You can laugh about that?"

"You can't?"

"The memory is still too raw," she said somberly and saw him grimace. She still hardly credited that she had the power to hurt his feelings. "I'm sorry."

His smile returned, but she saw it took more effort now. He stepped closer. "Let me try and make up for my crimes by giving you the occasional present."

That was so far from the actuality of what he did that she gave a snort of laughter. "This is not the occasional present. You're overwhelming me with your largesse. I feel like you're King Cophetua and I'm the beggar maid."

"So you'll call me Your Majesty?"

"Not on your life."

"Pity."

This teasing exchange left her unsettled. It made her wonder if she and Hamish could be friends, rather than wary adversaries. She wasn't sure if getting any closer – in all senses – to her handsome husband was a good idea. A sudden and disturbing memory of his hand on her breast assailed her, and her heart skipped a beat.

His touch had made her feel like a different person. She didn't want to be a different person. She wanted her world to stay as it was.

Except that wasn't entirely true either. She wanted her father well, and she wanted the house properly staffed. These last months, she'd lost sleep over how to pay the bills. At least Hamish's bounty saved her that worry.

Oh, you're absurd, Emily. You want your independence, and you want your husband's financial support. You've got a galloping case of having your cake and eating it, too.

But one thing was clear, and she needed to mention it. Her voice lowered into seriousness.

"Hamish, you can't spend the rest of your life using your wealth as a sop to a guilty conscience. That will blight every day we spend together."

"But I have got a guilty conscience." She was relieved to see the humor drain from his remarkable eyes. With amusement lighting his features, he was far too attractive.

"I've forgiven you," she mumbled, sitting at her dressing table again.

She chanced a glance in the mirror and caught Hamish's expression. His skepticism was clear. "Have you indeed?"

Her traitorous heart crashed hard against her ribs, and the breath jammed in her throat. It turned out he was just as dangerous to her composure when he was serious, curse him.

Blindly she fumbled with the pretty jeweled reticule that matched her dress. "I'm doing my best. I can't spend my days, crushed under the burdens of anger and resentment and disappointment."

A muscle flickered in his cheek. "By God, that's a stark assessment of your feelings."

A remorseful smile twisted her lips. "You know I'm not the most tactful creature. My lack of tact got us into this mess. If I'd approached you in Greenwich with a bit more humility, you might have listened, instead of hauling me out into the night for a scolding."

His grunt was dismissive. "I doubt it would have made much difference. I'm inclined to fly off the handle."

"I know," she said glumly. "We're a terrible mixture. We always have been."

"Yes, we are."

Another of those awkward silences descended. Eventually she broke it. "We have to find a way to go on."

"We do." He spoke the words as if pronouncing a death sentence. It was her turn to feel a sting, although how else would he sound? Without the scandal and despite his improbable claim that he desired her, he'd never have chosen Emily Baylor as his wife.

"Your every second word can't be an apology."

"Perhaps only once a week?"

She didn't smile, in part because she didn't trust his charm. He charmed people as easily as a robin perched on a holly branch. It would be so easy to fall under his spell.

While this marriage promised to be a disaster on so many levels, she refused to let him make her wretched. She'd seen so many girls go completely silly over him, and most of the time, he didn't even notice. She'd always believed she was made of stronger stuff – but that was before she'd seen him naked.

"Perhaps save the apologies for some new infringement."

A faint smile returned. He smiled a lot. People were fooled into seeing that and not the razor-sharp mind operating behind those glittering eyes. Emily had learned long ago not to underestimate him.

"You're so sure there will be one?"

"I'd wager my lavish pin money on the possibility."

She had a sick feeling that those infringements would include women in his bed. Although given their arrangement, would he feel he owed her an apology for infidelity? Even before she'd seen his magnificent body in a state of sexual readiness, she'd known her husband was a virile, sensual man. He'd never swear eternal chastity just because his wife preferred to remain untouched.

"Let's cross that bridge when we come to it." He paused "We've strayed a long way from what I came in here to talk about."

"Oh?"

He looked uncomfortable. "I know you hate to lie."

Startled she turned on the stool to face him. "So do you."

The unshakeable confidence he'd possessed even at twenty looked shaken. He brushed his hand through his hair, making one golden lock flop forward over his forehead. "You held your head up at the wedding. But tonight it's only my family and closest friends."

"I know," she said grimly, her nerves reviving to set a plague of grasshoppers leaping around inside her stomach.

"Do you think...do you think you could pretend to be happy with the match?"

"What?"

"It's only for one night. I don't want the people who care for me to know that we share no affection. Especially when happy marriages abound in my circle."

She tried not to flinch at the no affection remark, although she supposed she deserved it after what she'd said about anger, resentment and disappointment. "You'd like to save your pride."

"And yours."

And hers.

She didn't want Hamish's nearest and dearest taking a dislike to her – or worse, feeling sorry for the laird's unloved bride. "They must have heard about what happened at Pascoe Place."

"My mother has. Which means my sisters, too."

She cringed. None of his relatives knew her well enough to understand that she was a million miles away from a scarlet woman. "Don't you think people who know you well will guess we married out of necessity rather than...love?"

It shouldn't be difficult to say that last word, but it stuck in her throat like a chicken bone. Perhaps because when she looked ahead, not one scrap of love awaited her. No love of a husband. No love of a child. The only person in the world who loved her now was her father, and she couldn't pretend he'd be with her for much longer.

Emily leveled her shoulders. No more self-pity. She wouldn't yield to maudlin weakness. As Hamish had pointed out, she had her pride. She might face a lonely, unhappy future, but she refused to be pathetic as well.

He looked uncomfortable. "I'm not expecting the impossible, Emily, but I'd like my family to think that we're compatible at least. Don't jump like a scalded cat when I take your hand. Stop pokering up like I'm about to rob you every time I come near."

"I don't," she said in outrage.

A sardonic arching of gold brows. "You do."

She sagged in swift surrender. She did. "I'm sorry."

"No apologies."

"No, no apologies." She frowned. "They'll still think our wedding was very sudden."

"My Scottish relatives know little of my day-to-day life in London. My mother probably could find out what I'm up to, but she's too busy nagging the prime minister to pay much attention. They remember that I was your father's student. Our marriage isn't as much of a surprise to the world as you might think."

"It is to anyone who knows us," she retorted.

He spread his hands in appeal. "Won't you help?"

"And carry on as if I'm giddy with triumph at capturing such a prince?"

Her sarcasm fell flat. The problem was that most girls would consider Hamish a prince. He was rich and charming and generous, and he had no heinous vices. Heaven help the susceptible females of the world, he even looked like a prince.

His smile was wry. "There's no need to go overboard. But perhaps when we're in public, avoid ordering me around as if I'm a thick-witted pug."

He was trying to make her laugh, but it didn't work. She slumped on the stool. "You make me sound like such a witch."

"A very pretty witch."

More charm. She supposed he couldn't help it, even when his compliments fell on such stony ground as Emily Baylor's soul. "They'll hate me. For a start, I'm English."

"They'll love you – especially if you give them a chance and don't make them pay for my sins. You made a good impression at the wedding."

Goodness knew how. She'd been caught up in a fog of misery, and worried sick over her father as well. She'd been so lost in her own unhappiness that she hadn't even registered who any of the exuberant Scots at the wedding breakfast were. "You'll have to help me with names."

"I won't leave your side."

That wasn't as reassuring as he might want it to be. Especially now she'd promised to feign a modicum of contentment in this marriage.

To her surprise, Hamish reached out to tilt her face up. "Stop fretting. I'm almost sure that no Douglas has killed an Englishman – or woman – in at least twenty years."

Emily made herself smile, although it was difficult when she was far too conscious of the heat of his fingers on her skin. If she hoped to convince an eagle-eyed band of sisters and cousins and childhood friends that she was happy as Hamish's wife, she needed to become accustomed to his touch. "I'll do my best."

"It's only for one night. Not even a night. A couple of hours."

"They're all going back to Scotland tomorrow?"

Her unconcealed relief made him laugh as he released her. For pity's sake, what was wrong with her? She missed his touch the moment it was gone.

"Most of them. Fergus and Marina are staying behind to talk to some art dealers and meet with the committee of the Royal Academy."

She frowned. "She's the striking Italian lady, and he's your cousin with red hair?"

"She's a famous artist. You've heard of her, I'm sure. Marina Lucchetti."

Her eyes rounded. "Lord above, I had no idea." The night ahead sounded more alarming by the minute. She started pleating her shiny green skirts, even though she knew that would crease the silk.

"And he's not my cousin, but the brother of my soul. Diarmid is my cousin."

"The tall, dark-haired one who looks like a poet. He was your groomsman."

"That's him. Diarmid and Fiona and their children are staying a few more days, too. Fiona's never been to London before."

Emily didn't recall Fiona at all. Panic fluttered inside her like a trapped bird. She was sure to make a complete fool of herself.

"You'll get them straight in your mind soon enough." Hamish shifted away. "A lass who can cope with calculus can cope with sorting out my family connections."

Emily breathed more easily now Hamish had stepped away. It was odd how her lungs stopped working when he was close. When he touched her, her breath stopped altogether. "I think...I think I'd rather stay home."

"And waste that gorgeous dress? Perish the thought." He reached into his coat and drew out a narrow velvet case. "Which reminds me – I came in to give you your wedding present."

She sat up straighter on her stool and made herself stop fidgeting with her dress. "You already gave me a wedding present."

"That dress doesn't count."

"I wasn't thinking of that. I was thinking of handfuls of pearls, three housemaids, two footmen, and a bevy of nurses."

"I don't like to live in an inadequately staffed house. I do have some standards, you know."

"I see." If not for the nurses, she might almost believe he'd put on the new staff for purely selfish reasons. Because while she spent half her life wanting to clout him, she wasn't blind to the wide streak of kindness that ran through him. She'd benefited from it last night when he sat up with her father. He'd been tired, too. Their wedding day had been no easier for him than it had been for her.

"See what you think of this." He held the slim case out and without thinking, she accepted it. "It's only a small token, but I hope you like it. There are the family jewels, too, of course."

Of course, she thought with bleak humor. Didn't everyone have family jewels?

He was still talking. "They're in the bank in Edinburgh. I can have them sent down, if you have a yen to see them."

"Perhaps later," she said faintly, feeling overwhelmed again.

When she opened the case, overwhelmed didn't come close to describing her reaction. Bewildered, she looked up from the sparkle of diamonds. "Hamish, it's too much. I can't accept this."

He smiled. "Yes, you can. You're my wife, and I'm proud of you. I want the world to see how much I value you."

Her stomach sank in misery as she shut the case with a snap. "You don't mean that."

Hamish sent her a straight look. "Yes, I do. I don't want anyone whispering that we made a shabby bargain." He paused and subjected her to a thorough inspection that had her heart hopping and skipping in a most provoking way. Perhaps she was coming down with something. "Anyway you were born to wear diamonds."

"I wouldn't know. I don't own any." One nervous hand rose to play with her mother's gold locket. The necklace was pretty, but even Emily acknowledge that its modest sweetness didn't match the splendid gown.

"You do now." Unfamiliar tenderness tinged his smile. "Shall I put the necklace on for you, or should I call Polly back? We ought to leave soon. My mother expects us at eight."

Calling Polly was the wiser choice, but even sensible bluestocking Emily wasn't proof against the idea of a handsome man draping her in jewels. She held out the case. "Please, you do it."

And told herself she was stupid to thrill at the pleasure warming his eyes as he took the case. Two days married, and she discovered that she was in danger of developing a lamebrained, completely unrequited *tendre* for her husband. She'd expected these first days as a wife to be fraught with conflict. Compared to the gamboling of her dimwitted heart, conflict seemed preferable.

Be careful, Emily.

Because while she knew now that Hamish would gladly make this a real marriage, she was under no illusions that she remained anything but an inconvenient bride. Since the occasion when he'd behaved so badly, he'd behaved well. But they both knew that he merely put a good face on a disaster.

Nor did she imagine he'd stay as charming or attentive as he was now. He wouldn't be cruel, or at least not deliberately. Under all that gilded magnificence, he had a good heart. If he hadn't, she'd never have married him, scandal or no scandal. But if she allowed herself to care for him, she invited an ocean of trouble.

She turned on the stool to present him with her back. In the mirror, she watched him open the case and take out what looked like a fistful of diamonds. He set the empty case on the dressing table and leaned forward. He was close enough for her to catch his scent. Citrus and clean healthy male.

For one giddy second, she was back in bed with him, while his hand played forbidden – glorious – music on her body. Her breath caught in an audible gulp, and she told herself to settle down.

"Are you all right?" he murmured.

How on earth could that sound like a promise of pleasure? If only they were downstairs in one of the more workaday rooms, not here in her bedroom.

"Perfectly." She heard the wobble in her voice.

"Stay still."

With a deftness that spoke volumes for his familiarity with feminine gewgaws, he released the clasp on her locket and drew it from around her neck. "Pretty."

"It was my mother's." She hoped he'd put her husky tone down to grief.

Emily lifted one hand to take the delicate necklace, then watched Hamish loop the diamonds around her throat. The emerald silk dress was more décolleté than her usual gowns. Madame Lisette had insisted that a married woman needed to stop dressing like a nun.

As the glittering necklace settled across what already seemed a shocking expanse of bare bosom, Emily swallowed to moisten a dry mouth. In the mirror, Hamish appeared large and dominating behind her. As he fiddled with the clasp, his face was almost stern.

"You're...you're taking a long time over that," she said unsteadily, cursing diamonds, and overgenerous husbands, and her own unfortunate impulses.

"The clasp is tricky." His fingers brushed the sensitive skin of her nape. The nipples that had tightened under his touch last night tightened once more into aching longing. Heat rushed into her cheeks. "Ah, that's it."

He seemed to touch her for an eternity, although reason told her it was only a few seconds. What a ninnyhammer she was to feel regret when he stepped back to survey her in the mirror.

"Lovely. Nobody tonight will question why I married you, my lady. You're incandescent."

Hamish had complimented her before, had even called her pretty a couple of times. But the blatant admiration in his eyes as he studied her set her lunatic heart leaping around like a frog in a jar.

"Th-thank you," she stammered.

Hamish smiled, which only encouraged her heart's ridiculous antics. He held out his hand. "Shall we go?"

"Yes," she said, so eager to escape this bedroom that even the prospect of meeting a tribe of unknown Scots seemed a reprieve.

CHAPTER THIRTEEN

Hamish told himself that so far things at his mother's house progressed pretty damn well. As he'd expected, Emily had made a good impression. She had a knack for making friends. In fact, the only person she seemed to have a prickly relationship with was that fine fellow Hamish Douglas.

They'd made it through dinner, and now everyone gathered in the elegant drawing room. Lord Liverpool had once said more legislation was formulated in this room than in the Houses of Parliament.

He and Emily stood in one corner, talking to his youngest sister Elspeth and her husband Brody. Fergus and Marina were nearer to the fire, bantering with each other. Their passion had always held a quicksilver, volatile quality. Diarmid was laughing at the sparkling repartee, his arm loose around Fiona's waist. They shared a secret smile, as Fergus swept Marina up for a quick kiss.

Hamish hated to admit it, but right now he was so jealous of his friends, he could spit. All the couples in this room enjoyed happy marriages. All the couples except one. He and his wife were as poorly matched as crab soup and chocolate sauce.

"Hamish?" Emily asked tentatively.

She stood at his side, with her hand tucked into his elbow. All night, they'd done their best to give an impression of ease in each other's company. One glimpse of his friends and how natural they were with one another told him he and his new bride failed to convince.

"Yes, my dear?" he said, his lips having trouble framing the endearment.

Not because she wasn't dear – while they had their difficulties, he'd never mistake Emily's quality – but because he knew she hated to hear it. Just as she must hate the falsehood of this evening. After the wedding, she'd looked ready to snap into pieces with the strain of pretending she was happy. Tonight was even worse, because the gathering was smaller and everyone knew Hamish too well.

Despite everything, pride blossomed in his chest as he looked at Emily. She was a wife to do any man credit. The moment he saw her, elegant and alluring in that deep green dress, he'd been dazzled. So dazzled in fact that he'd had trouble controlling his usually deft fingers when he fastened the diamond necklace around her graceful neck.

"You look like you're in another world," she said.

"I'm sorry. I was thinking what a lucky man I am."

Emily's smile froze. Brody and Elspeth missed the remark's shoddy ring and beamed with unfettered approval.

"Now, that's braw," Brody said. "I just hope you're half as happy as Elspeth and I are. Will we see ye in Scotland soon? Och, ye will want to show Glen Lyon to your bonny wife, I'm sure."

The glance that Elspeth sent Brody expressed fond impatience. "Darling, you know Emily's father is unwell. That's why there was no wedding trip."

"We're staying in London for the moment," Hamish said. "Perhaps we'll visit Glen Lyon next year."

"Have you ever been to Scotland, Emily?" Elspeth asked.

"Not yet. Papa gave a lecture in Newcastle a few years ago, and I went with him. That's as far north as I've managed to get."

"You have a treat ahead of you. Glen Lyon is glorious. Make Hamish take you in the spring. No, the summer, when the days are clear and warm."

Hamish snorted with amusement. "This is Glen Lyon that you're talking about, sis? Where it rains two days out of three, and on the third day, the wind is blustery enough to blow a man to Ireland?"

Brody laughed. "Och, ye know Elspeth likes to look on the bright side, Hamish. She's the eternal optimist. Why else would she have married me?"

Actually there was more truth in that than Brody might like to acknowledge. The young Laird of Invermackie had cultivated quite the reputation as a hell-raiser and ladies' man before he wed Elspeth. As a result, the family hadn't welcomed his pursuit of the youngest Douglas girl. Elspeth however had been convinced since girlhood that Brody was the one for her.

To the astonishment of everyone but Elspeth, she'd been right.

Now her eyes shone with love as she surveyed her tall, dark-haired husband. "She married you because she loved you, you silly man."

Acrid regret soured Hamish's stomach. Emily would never look at him like that.

"Och, *mo chridhe*..." Brody whispered, drawing Elspeth close for a tender kiss.

This time it was Emily and Hamish's turn to share a secret look. Not a look of mutual devotion. One expressing their horror at the cloying atmosphere. The air was thick as treacle with the joys of love fulfilled.

Emily started to laugh. So did Hamish.

"So lovely to see you in tune with each other," Hamish's mother said from behind them. "In my experience, if a couple can laugh together, they're well on their way to a good marriage."

All desire to laugh deserted Hamish. His mother's prediction was so far south of the truth, it might make a joke of its own.

This evening started to seem interminable. He felt a desperate need to be alone with his bride. Not for the usual reasons that newlyweds wanted to be alone. If only that were the case. But at least when they were in private, he needn't pretend that all was well.

Although tonight when he looked at Emily, beautiful, brave and just as desperate to bolster her pride, he admitted that if they were different people, if he was less temperamental and she was less opinionated, she'd make a fine wife.

If she wanted him, most of all.

But they weren't different people and their fundamental incompatibility should be apparent to anyone close to him.

Which made it strange that all his nearest and dearest seemed to accept his choice of bride as perfectly natural. The congratulations he'd received sounded sincere – and he should be able to tell, as he'd known everyone here for years, most of them since childhood.

So why couldn't they see that his marriage to Emily Baylor was a travesty? Devil take it, he and Emily could barely share the same room without bickering.

Still, he'd set out to convince his family that he was content. It was unreasonable to grumble when nobody spared him a hint of sympathy. The only explanation he could find was that because all these people loved their spouses, they couldn't imagine Hamish not loving his.

If only they knew the unpalatable truth.

"Happy marriages are a Douglas tradition." He heard the edge in his tone.

"They are indeed. I loved your papa dearly." Mamma had never ceased to mourn his father, and she showed no interest in remarrying. This was despite offers from some of the most eligible men in the kingdom, including at least one duke he knew of. "I hope you and Emily discover the same joy."

Hamish's gut twisted in shame. His mother's genuine pleasure in his ill-assorted match made him feel like an abominable liar.

"Thank you, Mamma." He hoped that she'd blame the rasp in his response on the strength of his emotions.

"Thank you, Lady Glen Lyon," Emily said in a small voice that he'd never heard from her before. She must feel as awkward as he did.

His mother's laugh held a fond note. "My dear, you're Lady Glen Lyon now."

"I...I don't feel like I am," Emily admitted. Hamish imagined that was true, not least because despite the wedding, she remained as virginal as the day she was born.

"You will. Give yourself time." His mother smiled at her new daughter-in-law. "It will all seem much more real once you visit Glen Lyon. The estate is so beautiful, anyone would be proud to be its mistress."

"My father's health—"

"I understand." Compassion softened his mother's expression. "But don't wait too long before you go to Scotland. Being chatelaine of Glen Lyon will go a long way toward making up for marrying my rapscallion son."

Ouch. That cut a little too close to the bone, although Hamish knew his mother was teasing.

"I hope we get the chance to travel there soon," Emily said in the same subdued voice.

His mother sent Hamish a look that told him she was about to issue a command. He was a foot taller than his mamma, but that look still had the power to send trepidation slithering down his backbone. "Go and talk to your friends, Hamish. There's no need to cling to Emily's side like a limpet. I'd like a word with my new daughter-in-law."

Hamish caught the flare of sheer terror in Emily's eyes. "I like having Hamish with me, my lady," she said in an even reedier tone.

His mother smiled at both of them with unconcealed approval. "That's lovely, my dear. But five minutes without him won't hurt. Hamish, I'm sure Diarmid and Fergus would love to have you to themselves, while I find out a little more about this delightful young lady you've brought into the family."

"Be gentle with her." Although he spoke lightly, he meant it. Mamma had ways of winkling out the truth. It was one of the talents that made her so brilliant in politics.

"Stop hovering over the girl like a mother hen, my son."

A limpet, and now a hen? He wanted to protest at the unflattering descriptions, however much truth they might contain.

Emily mustered a tremulous smile. "I'm looking forward to chatting with your mamma, Hamish. Go."

His heart heavy with foreboding, Hamish went.

"Shall we sit by the fire? It's probably the coziest spot in the room."

"As you wish," Emily said close to inaudibly, although nothing she'd seen in this huge house counted as cozy. She'd attended a dinner here to celebrate her engagement, and of course this was where her wedding breakfast had been held. On both occasions, she'd been so nervous and heartsick that she hadn't paid attention to anything beyond resisting the urge to run away.

Tonight it was too late to run away – it had been too late to run away the minute Hamish dragged her into the garden at Pascoe Place – and she finally took in the details of Douglas House. And felt sick with nerves all over again. Its grandeur could offer no greater proof that she'd wed outside her class.

She hadn't wanted to marry Hamish, but looking around this elaborate room, she saw why Hamish wouldn't want to marry her. Lady Glen Lyon – she might charmingly claim she was now the dowager and Emily held the title, but Emily didn't feel like she did – moved in the highest circles. His mother must have hoped her only son would make a better match than this one, with an impecunious scientist's daughter.

As she perched on the couch by the blazing hearth, Emily glanced across to where Hamish stood with Fergus and Diarmid. He was watching her, probably waiting for her to make some faux pas, she guessed. Although to be fair, he'd been true to his word tonight, staying nearby and helping her to navigate her way through all these people.

She mustered another shaky smile. When he crossed his eyes at her and made a scary face, a smothered giggle escaped, more hysteria than amusement.

Her mother-in-law took the place beside her. Hamish bore a strong resemblance to his mother. Both were tall and golden and resplendent. It had already struck Emily as wholly appropriate that these magnificent creatures should come from a place called Glen Lyon. There was something leonine and regal about both of them.

"I must say I'm so relieved to see such genuine affection between you and my son."

"Such genuine..." Emily cut off her horrified response before she said something unforgivable. While she and Hamish did nothing but argue, his mother didn't need to hear that. "I've known Hamish a long time, my lady."

"Yes, you have. But the gossip made me fear that this marriage came about purely to head off a scandal."

Emily blushed. Nobody at the previous family gatherings had dared to mention that night at Pascoe Place. Her heart sank as she braced for a scolding. "I hope all the talk didn't trouble you."

"I'm old enough to weather a bit of gossip." Hamish's mother sent Emily a searching regard from eyes the same bright blue as her son's. "Don't look so bilious, child. I'm not going to eat you."

Only because they'd just had a good dinner, Emily was sure. "It wasn't what people said it was," she said in a thin voice. "We didn't—"

"I know how tales grow as they spread. My son is a man of honor."

That at least Emily could agree with. "Yes, he is."

"And you've known him since you were a girl."

"Yes. He was always my father's favorite student."

"I met Sir John at the wedding."

"He's not what he was."

"I'm sorry to hear that. Hamish told me of your devoted care for your father. My son admires you most sincerely, you know."

No, she didn't, but she could imagine that he'd done his best to put their sudden marriage in the best light.

His mother was still speaking. "Hamish told me that you were discussing mathematics and lost track of how long you were alone."

"It's true. We were." After a hesitation, Emily dared to share at least a little of the truth. She'd approached this conversation sick with dread, but so far Lady Glen Lyon had been very understanding. "I told him the calculations in his paper were wrong, and he didn't want to quarrel with me in full view of the crowd."

To her surprise, Lady Glen Lyon laughed. "That sounds like my boy. Once his temper gets the better of him, there's no talking sense."

Encouraged, Emily went on. "He dragged me out into the garden to tell me I was mistaken. No harm would have come of it, except my dress snagged in a bush and it started to rain. He was trying to get me back to my carriage, when someone noticed us and we had to come back inside, looking like—"

"Drowned rats was the story I heard."

Emily felt her cheeks heat. The memory of that night still made her queasy. "I thought we could weather the talk, but Hamish was sure we couldn't."

"Hamish was right. The scandal was too delicious."

"Yes, his calculations about the comet might have been wrong, but his assessment of London's appetite for gossip was spot on," she said with a trace of grimness.

"And now you're wed." Hamish's mother smiled. "It's clear that you two are the perfect match, however the match was made."

Emily only just stopped herself from setting her mother-in-law straight. Hamish really must have told her some dreadful lies. "He's a good man."

"Yes, he is. And a kind and generous one."

"I'm not a conventional choice."

"No, but he's not a conventional man, and it gladdens my heart that he's found someone to share his life who can also share his interests. All of my children are clever, but Hamish outstripped the others from the first. His mind moves in a world where very few can follow him."

Emily regarded Hamish's mother in astonishment. "You really don't mind that he married me?"

Another of those fond laughs. "Good Lord, I don't mind at all. Why on earth would you think I did?"

Because we wed under a cloud of scandal.

Because he doesn't love me.

Because I don't love him.

"Because I have no fortune."

Lady Glen Lyon took her hand and squeezed it. "Nor did I – or nothing to compare anyway – when I married Hamish's father. He said he had plenty of money for both of us."

"That's what Hamish said."

"He's very like his father – although he looks more like me. No, my dear, you have it quite wrong, if you imagine the family disapproves. It was time for my son to marry, and I couldn't be more delighted that he chose a woman of brains and common sense."

"But the tattle..."

"The best revenge is living happily, and I can already see you've made an excellent start on that. I'm especially pleased to see that you don't put up with any of his nonsense. Never apologize, my dear, or fear you're not good enough. In my opinion, my son was lucky to find you. He's inclined to walk all over most people. It's that combination of charm and good looks and daunting intelligence."

Hamish wasn't the only Douglas who possessed those particular qualities. "You're very kind."

The lovely face brightened in another smile. "I can be a dreadful harridan, as I'm sure you'll discover over the coming years." She paused. "I can remember being a new bride. It was such a mad whirl of surprise and uncertainty and happiness. Nor is it easy to find your feet when you set up home with a husband. But you're clever and determined – and pretty enough to put a spark in my son's eyes. You'll find your way."

"Thank you. I hope so."

"If you'll take my advice—"

"Gladly," Emily said fervently, which prompted another laugh.

"See? I said you'd make an ideal daughter-in-law." Her voice lowered to seriousness. "Go to Glen

Lyon as soon as you can. Hamish may sound as English as the Duke of Devonshire, but he's Scots through and through. His intellectual life is here in London, but his heart and soul are in the Highlands. You have no chance of truly understanding him until you see him on his estates."

Emily's gaze shifted to the other side of the room, where Hamish seemed to be involved in an equally intense conversation with Fergus and Diarmid. "He always seems to fit in here."

"Yes, he does. He grew up in London, much as he hated it. But the war effort needed his father, and my Graham had a powerful sense of duty. As you'll discover does Hamish."

She already knew he did. If he didn't, he wouldn't have married her to save her good name. "Yet he stays in London."

"He has a career to make. Although I hope you'll encourage him to spend more time at Glen Lyon. It's good for him."

Emily wanted to say she had no influence over what her husband did, but stopped herself. Better by far that his mother continued in her happy fancies. She didn't need to know that her hopes for her son's marriage were fated to fail. "I'll try."

"Once you have children, Hamish won't need much persuading. He'll want the bairns brought up as good little Scots. He always claimed he'd marry a Scots girl, so nobody questioned whether his children belonged in the Highlands."

With that, Emily's pleasure at her mother-in-law's welcome corroded into guilt. Because there would be no bairns to roam Glen Lyon. There would only be two people yoked together for life, in what was sure to become worsening estrangement. Lady Glen Lyon would never dandle Hamish's babies on

her knee or watch a grandson groomed to become
the next laird.

Right now, Emily felt like the greatest imposter
in Christendom.

CHAPTER FOURTEEN

*H*amish tried to keep an eye on Emily, so he could dive in and rescue her from his mother if need be. But it was difficult when he had his own troubles, battling to convince the two people who knew him best that he was reconciled to his marriage. Not to mention hiding the humiliating truth that he'd never share his wife's bed.

Fergus and Diarmid might laugh. Even worse, they might feel sorry for him. That he couldn't bear.

"She's gey bonny, laddie. Did ye spark the scandal just so you could win her?" Fergus asked.

"It's not a bad idea, but no." He struggled to keep his voice even. As he bore their teasing, his smile had become more and more fixed. "I lost my temper with her when she told me I'd made a mistake in calculating my comet's velocity."

"She understands that guff ye scribble down?" Diarmid said. "I admire her even more."

"I told you this, Diarmid," Hamish said through his teeth.

His cousin's grin was mocking. "Aye, ye did. But I still like to see you squirm."

Fergus was watching Emily. "Well, who would have thought?"

Hamish shifted on his feet and smothered a growl. "That I could persuade a pretty girl to wed me?"

The flashing green glance Fergus shot him reminded Hamish that he hadn't liked the Laird of Achnasheen when he'd first met him. At fourteen, Fergus Mackinnon had been an arrogant bugger. He was even worse at thirty-four.

"There's that. But I'm actually talking about the miracle that your volatile temper has finally had a positive result. Most of the time, it lays waste to everything within a ten-mile radius."

To Hamish's regret, Fergus's description of the devastation he caused was accurate, even if he was wrong about the positive result this time round.

"Which doesnae mean ye should exercise it more often," Diarmid said. "A happy marriage requires patience and understanding, no' ye blowing up like a volcano every time things dinnae go your way."

Right now, Hamish would dearly love to tell his two dearest friends to stick their opinions up their arses. But he had a horrid feeling that would only confirm their smug assessment of his poor self-control. His tone was strained as he replied. "I don't need your advice, Diarmid. Or yours either, Fergus."

Diarmid clapped him on the shoulder. "Your marriage hasnae started under the most auspicious circumstances. Ye might want to listen to your more experienced friends."

"More experienced? Have you forgotten I always had more luck with the lassies than you did, chum?"

Which wasn't entirely true. Diarmid had that poetical, brooding air that made women weak at the knees. He suspected that he and his cousin shared equal honors when it came to catching a comely wench's interest. Not that Diarmid had eyes for anyone but his beloved Fiona these days.

Fergus studied Hamish with an expression that looked like pity, God rot him. "That's lassies, my friend. A wife is something very different."

"I don't see why," Hamish said mutinously, even though he might in private admit that his dealings with Emily had nothing in common with his bachelor conquests. For a start, she wasn't going to end up in his bed. At last, the world gave him permission to swive a female as often as he wanted – and his honor consigned him to sleeping alone. Somewhere the fates were rolling about laughing.

"Ye will." Diarmid's expression turned pitying, too. Damn it, did both his dearest friends want him to give them a bloody nose? "If ye dinnae, you'll never have a happy life."

"She'll come to heel." Hamish hoped they didn't hear the false note underlying his bravado.

"A wife doesnae come to heel. She walks at your side as a partner." Diarmid sent another glance toward Emily, who hadn't yet fled the room in tears. That was a good sign. Perhaps for once, his mother was behaving. "You'll never cow that lassie in a month of Sundays, anyway."

"She's a wonderful girl," Hamish said with some heat, although his cousin's remark hadn't sounded like criticism.

Fergus nodded. "That's the first smart thing you've said tonight. Aye, she is. Look at how she's managing your mother. So dinnae mess this up."

"Mess this up?" Hamish asked on a rising note. "You're treating me like the village idiot."

"I'm just saying that for a braw clever man, ye can do the stupidest things."

"You're all looking very serious over here, *tesoro*. I thought this evening was meant to be a celebration for Hamish and the *bella* new Lady Glen Lyon."

The arrival of Fergus's half-Italian wife Marina saved Hamish from having to respond to her husband's patronizing comment. Which was probably a lucky thing.

His best friends were mistaken to think he was blind to the changes in his life, now he was married. If nothing else, he was uncomfortably aware that his actions reflected on his wife, for good or ill. Which meant that he must forgo giving Diarmid a black eye and knocking that smirk off Fergus's face.

More was the pity.

"Thank you for saving me from these two blockheads." Hamish liked Marina, he always had. Although if anyone had told him before the marriage that Fergus would choose an independent, self-confident woman like this, he'd have scoffed. Fergus had always said he'd marry a meek little miss who would put up with his dictatorial ways.

But Marina was perfect for Fergus. She'd brought him down to earth and taught him that he wasn't the King of the Highlands.

Nor had Diarmid married the sort of woman Hamish imagined he would. After enduring a chaotic childhood with his vain, flighty mother, Diarmid had sworn he'd never wed a beauty. Yet Fiona was one of the loveliest women Hamish had ever seen.

So what lesson could Hamish draw from his friends' marriages? That an unexpected bride might end up the ideal choice? Emily was certainly unexpected. Even aside from their quarrels, she was English, when he'd always vowed that he'd wed a good Scots lass.

If only his wife's Englishness was the biggest problem facing them.

"They're both laying down the law, I'm guessing." Marina slid her hand around Hamish's elbow. "The gospel for a happy marriage, according to St. Fergus and St. Diarmid."

"Aye, and why no', *mo chridhe*?" Fergus asked. "We manage pretty well, would ye no' say?"

"*Si, caro*, I would. But it took us time to learn how to live together, and what works for us won't necessarily work for other people. It wouldn't be right for Diarmid and Fiona, for example."

"Aye. Dinnae take this the wrong way, but there's a wee bit too much push and pull between the two of ye for me," Diarmid said fervently. "I like a quiet life."

"Hamish and Emily will find their own way, too. You don't need to march in with your big heavy boots, my love. *Per l'amor di Dio*, sometimes discretion is the better part of valor."

Hamish took unworthy enjoyment in seeing his autocratic friend scolded by his spectacular wife. "Discretion isn't Fergus's style."

"I'm just giving him the benefit of my experience in taming a termagant," Fergus responded in a haughty tone, then looked offended when everyone around him burst out laughing.

"That wasn't nearly the ordeal we expected," Hamish said in relief, as they sat in the dark carriage on their way back to Bloomsbury.

"Speak for yourself," Emily retorted from the opposite seat.

If they had a real marriage, he'd be sitting next to her with his arm around her. If they had a real marriage, he'd take advantage of the privacy to steal a kiss or two and a few cuddles.

If they had a real marriage, those kisses and cuddles would lead to a night of bliss in Emily's bed. He'd long suspected that Emily would be a lover a man would never forget. Under her cool exterior, she was all fire. Even when she was annoyed with him, she was an exciting woman. The thought of how she'd flare up in the throes of passion made the blood thunder in his ears.

And all for nothing. They'd return home, say good night, and go their separate ways. What a waste.

He'd spent weeks telling himself there was no point getting het up about sleeping with Emily. It wasn't going to happen. But the company of all those happy couples tonight made his marriage seem more barren than ever.

"You didn't enjoy it? I thought you did. Everyone liked you, at least."

"They're putting a good face on things for your sake."

"I know them all well enough to see when they're just going through the motions. You impressed them."

How could she not? She was pretty and funny and clever, and interested in other people. The perfect wife, in fact. Hamish wondered why he'd never thought of marrying her before.

No, he didn't. They didn't like each other.

Except he did like her. He always had, despite her eternal quest to puncture his vanity.

"They're a remarkably handsome group. Are all Scots so picturesque?"

Hamish adopted his best brogue. "Och, lassie, we're a braw race of Adonises north of the border, ye ken."

It was too dark for him to see her roll her eyes, but he knew she did. That was another odd symptom of marriage. He'd always been aware of Emily – partly because he was waiting for her to pounce on his latest theory. Since they'd wed, he seemed to count her every breath.

Perhaps he was so attuned to her because he wanted her so badly. Most times when he took a fancy to a girl, consummation followed soon afterward. Perhaps he was so keyed up about his wife because there would be no consummation.

Or perhaps Fergus was right, despite speaking a lot of other rubbish, and a wife belonged in a special category of her own.

"Not just the men," she said, and it took him a moment to remember what they'd been talking about.

"So I don't need to be jealous?"

Her laugh was dismissive. "Given the trouble one particular Scotsman has caused me, I'm not lining up to take on another."

Hamish felt the old urge to say he was sorry. He was disappointed to see Emily so flat. He'd hoped she'd relish the welcome she'd received, but this wasn't a woman glorying in her social success.

"The women are splendid, too," she said before he could muster that apology. A good thing. She'd told him she didn't want him apologizing until the end of time. Even if he felt he owed that to her.

"You have nothing to envy them for. You look marvelous."

"Fine feathers."

"No, you just needed to be set like the jewel you are."

He heard her breath catch. "Hamish, that was almost poetic."

"I have hidden talents, you know." He shifted uncomfortably, bracing for a sarcastic response. Her last comment might have been sarcastic at that. Nobody made him feel like a blundering fool the way Emily did. It was a wonder he wanted her as much as he did.

Wanting her turned this carriage ride into torment. In the intimate darkness, he was too aware of her warmth and scent. He was too aware that if he leaned forward, he could take her hand. Once he held her hand, who knew where he'd end up?

Probably sulking in the corner after she boxed his ears.

Marriage was hell.

He leaned back and folded his arms across his chest, partly to stop himself reaching across the well between the seats and grabbing her. When he glanced out the window, they were only on Gower Street. A way to go yet before he could retreat to his lonely bed. It was late, and only a light or two glowed from the tall buildings on either side of the road. Although it wouldn't be long until the streets teemed with people bringing produce into the city.

"I nearly died when you left me alone with your mother," Emily said after a long silence.

Hamish stretched his legs out. "You seemed to cope."

"You checked?"

"Of course I did. Was it so bad?"

"I was waiting for her to denounce me as a wanton unfit to bear the Douglas name."

"She'd never do that. She likes you. Anyway, when I called on her to say we were engaged, I explained that the scandal was all my fault."

"You were just being gallant."

"No, I was telling the truth." Then he paused, shocked, as he digested what she'd said. By gum, that was almost a compliment. "And she knows me well enough to believe me. Besides, she wanted me to get married. It was becoming something of a cause with her. My mother on a crusade is a terrifying sight."

"I can imagine."

"I suppose she told you all sorts of ways to handle me."

To his relief, he heard a faint huff of amusement. "There might have been a bit of that."

Or a lot.

Emily didn't sound like she much cared. Why should she? After all, she and Hamish would lead separate lives, once they finished making this show designed to contradict what all London knew – that the Laird of Glen Lyon and his lady were together only to stifle a scandal.

When Hamish proposed, a separate life was the outcome he'd expected. Why now did that future seem so bleak?

Damn Fergus and Marina. Damn Diarmid and Fiona. Damn his sisters and their husbands. Damn every other blissfully happy couple at that dinner tonight.

The problem was that Hamish knew exactly what a successful union looked like. Which meant he was also wretchedly aware of how far his own fell short.

Was it worth trying to renegotiate his arrangement with Emily? He wasn't naïve enough to imagine she'd allow him into her bed just for the asking. But if she let him woo her, it would be something. It would give him a tiny thread of hope to cling to.

Only a few days into becoming a husband, and already he verged close to despair. Despair that worsened after tonight's reminder of what he missed out on.

As they turned into their street, for once he wasn't thinking with his prick. He was thinking about every aspect of the life extending ahead of him. He didn't want to be a stranger in his own house. He wanted friendship – love was too much to ask for – and companionship and trust. He wanted a home. He wanted...

"Something is wrong," Emily said sharply, leaning forward and staring out the window.

Her tone wrenched Hamish out of his fog of self-pity. In the Bloomsbury house, all the lights were on and people milled about on the doorstep.

"Don't expect the worst," he said, even as he cursed the remark's inanity. What else would she expect but the worst?

"It must be Papa," she said, opening the door and jumping from the carriage as it pulled up. "What is it, Roberts?"

"My lady, thank goodness you and Mr. Douglas are home. We just sent a groom to fetch you. Sir John has taken a very bad turn."

Hamish stepped down to the street and stood behind Emily. "What do you mean by a bad turn?"

"Miss McCorquodale knows more. She's been with him."

"What happened?" Emily asked in a voice Hamish had never heard from her.

"It seems he got up from his bed, determined to go out, then collapsed. We've sent for Dr. Allard."

In a silent attempt to share his strength with her, Hamish settled a hand on Emily's shoulder. She jerked away as if his touch offended her.

"I must go to him." She picked up her emerald skirts and dashed into the house without a backward glance.

Hamish, knowing he had no right to be hurt, but hurt anyway, followed her inside more slowly.

CHAPTER FIFTEEN

Sir John Baylor's funeral took place a week later. After the service, people called at the Bloomsbury house to pay their respects.

Hamish stood with Diarmid and Fiona beside the drawing room fire. He was grateful that Fergus and Diarmid and their wives had stayed in the south long enough to attend. The day was wet and freezing, typical December in London. With bleak surprise, he realized that it was only a couple of weeks until Christmas.

"How is Emily?" Fiona asked, as she sipped the sherry that Roberts had decreed was proper for this solemn occasion. What Hamish would give for a dram or ten of Bruce Mackenzie's finest whisky.

"She's in shock." Worried, he observed his wife where she sat wearing deepest black beside his mother, who had proven a rock during these difficult days. He supposed if anyone understood grief, it was Mamma. "I've hardly got a peep out of her."

A large number of mourners – the wake spread into the library and the dining room – lined up to express their sympathies to Sir John's daughter. Emily greeted everyone with the same frozen politeness. Not even Sir Humphry Davy managed to coax more than a few words from her.

"She told me she was very close to her father." During the last days of Sir John's life, Fiona had helped in the sickroom, and she and Emily showed signs of becoming friends. Marina had offered to help, too, but it soon became apparent that however good her intentions, she wasn't cut out for nursing.

"She wasn't just his daughter. She was his assistant and his sounding board and his inspiration. They were inseparable."

"Even when the end is expected, it's difficult to accept," Diarmid said. "You'll need to be patient with her."

"I don't think she even knows I'm in the house," he said grimly. When he tried to talk to her, she looked at him as if his words made no sense.

"The sharpest sorrow will pass with time," Diarmid said.

"Yes." But even after it did, Hamish couldn't imagine his presence would be any more welcome. Since her father's death, Emily spent most of her time in her room. The first night when he'd heard her crying, he'd knocked on her door and asked if she wanted company. She told him to go away. She'd been silently telling him to go away ever since.

He'd cooperated because what else could he do?

He had his own grief to cope with. It mightn't be on the scale of Emily's, but he'd loved Sir John. One of the few joys of this hurried marriage was how much it had pleased Emily's father.

"We're heading home tomorrow, laddie," Diarmid said. "The bairns have been out of their routine for too long, and they're getting fractious. We'd love to have ye and Emily to stay, if you can bring yourselves to leave London. Perhaps a change of scene will do ye both good."

"Thank you, cuz," Hamish said. "I appreciate you remaining for the funeral. I hoped we'd see more of each other during your visit."

"Cannae be helped." Diarmid clapped him on the shoulder and gave him an understanding smile. "Think seriously about the visit. Ye both need family right now, and things between you and Emily mightn't seem so strange and discordant when you're with friends."

Hamish would like to think so, but he doubted it. Right now, Emily seemed to hate him. She was locked away in a private world of grief, and his vitality and vigor offended her.

But how could he abandon her when she had nobody else? He'd noted at the wedding that she had no close family. The school friend who had been her bridesmaid had called once, but the visit had only lasted twenty minutes. She hadn't called again, although she was among those paying their respects today.

"We should go and say goodbye to Emily," Fiona said, her delicate features expressing concern. "Hamish, if you think it would help, we'll stay. Children or no children."

Hamish summoned a smile and stifled the urge to say that nothing would help. "Thank you, Fiona. You're a treasure."

She was. Diarmid was a lucky man.

"Not really. I care about Emily. I hate to see her suffer."

Fiona knew more than enough about suffering. Her happiness now had been hard-won, and Hamish knew she never took it for granted.

"It's very nice of you, but you should both go home. Emily needs quiet and time to find herself again. These last few years, caring for her father has been her whole life." Only as he said it did he realize how odd that sounded from a new husband.

"Be kind to her, laddie," Diarmid said. "You'll find your way back to each other in time."

Hamish was too heartsick to argue with his cousin's unjustified optimism. "I'll write."

"So will I – or at least Fiona will." They embraced, parting with a couple of hearty slaps on the back that did nothing to hide their deep affection.

"Goodbye, Hamish," Fiona said. "Come and see us for Christmas."

Hamish couldn't stifle a wince at the prospect of a big, boisterous celebration, brimming with jollity and love and laughter. "I'll let you know," he said, although they both knew that he'd be spending Christmas far from the Highlands.

He kissed her cheek, avoiding the pity he knew he'd find in her lovely blue eyes. "Goodbye, Fiona."

He watched as Diarmid and Fiona crossed to Emily. His cousin bent over her hand with the courtly elegance that came so naturally to him. Fiona leaned in to kiss her cheek.

As Emily raised her face to farewell Diarmid and Fiona, the window behind her cast stark gray light over her face. She was still beautiful. How could she be otherwise? But it was a beauty refined by sorrow. Hamish had suspected she wasn't eating much. Now he was sure of it. Her pale, perfect skin stretched tight across her delicate bones, and her great hazel eyes were dull.

He desperately wanted to make everything right for her. Just how desperately he wanted it surprised him, although he'd never wished her ill fortune, however much he might itch to give her a good shaking now and then.

But that was the old Emily, the smart-tongued, quarrelsome adversary who gave as good as she got. One rough word to this frail, exquisite creature sitting across the room would shatter her to dust.

By God, he loathed feeling so helpless.

Hamish was relieved when the reception drew to a close, although he saw that Emily had found comfort in the tributes that Britain's greatest scientific minds paid to her father. The last to leave the house was his mother. She looked magnificent in black silk. But then she looked magnificent in anything.

"Hamish, such a sad event to follow so close on your wedding."

Which for Emily had been a sad event, too. "I wish I could help Emily, Mamma. She looks so broken. Her father was her whole world."

His mother sent him a sharp glance, and he shifted in discomfort as he realized he came close to betraying the truth behind his marriage. "You need to help her through this."

Irritation with himself more than his mother had him answering with a touch of heat. "Of course I'll help her. What sort of heartless brute do you take me for?"

His mother was used to his mercurial temperament, and her voice stayed calm. "That's not what I meant."

He sucked in a breath and spoke in a more measured tone. "I'm sorry. It's been a difficult few days for everyone."

It had been a difficult few weeks. He and Emily had been wed less than a fortnight. Since then, Hamish felt like he'd lived through a lifetime.

"I'm trying in my ham-fisted way to say you'll need to use patience and care with Emily. And while you're kind enough, patience has never been easy."

His lips flattened. His mother did mean to chide him after all. "I'm not ten years old anymore."

"No, but you're still inclined to let your emotions rule you, especially when it comes to people you love."

He bit back a protest at her use of the word love. He and Emily didn't love each other. Right now, he'd lay good money she couldn't stand him, given her pained expression whenever she set eyes on him.

"It's not altogether a criticism," his mother said, when he didn't give an immediate response. "You're incapable of dissembling, and that's an attractive quality. But grief is a strange world to live in. Often people don't act the way they would in happier times. I'm asking you to be understanding and forgiving, and willing to take the long view. Emily isn't herself at present."

"That's true. She usually crackles with energy. She's like a ghost in the house."

"Under the pall of sorrow, she's still the woman you married."

"I wish I knew how to reach her."

"You'll find a way. Just let her set the limits for now."

He shot his mother a questioning look. "You really like her."

She looked startled. "Of course I do."

"I thought with the way the wedding came about..."

"I must admit I dreaded meeting a scheming hussy who had your fortune and your title in her sights. You're not the first young man caught in a sly girl's machinations."

"I told you the scandal was entirely my fault."

"Which I put down to natural gallantry. But the moment I met Emily, I saw she was perfect. Society misses bore you silly – not their fault, they're educated to be nothing but pretty little dolls. Emily has such substance, and she doesn't let you get away with being king of the beasts either."

Hamish struggled to hide his astonishment. As his mother said, he wasn't good at concealing his emotions. One emotion however he didn't have to conceal. "I'm so glad you welcome her into the family. I've only recently realized how alone she is in the world. You've been very kind to her since Sir John passed away."

His mother tilted her head with an effortlessly regal air. If he acted like the king of the beasts, he knew where he got it from. "It's easy to be kind to her. She'll find her place, Hamish. She has you and God willing, the children that will come. Life will offer consolations for her bereavement. It's what happens."

Guilt settled like a lump of melted iron in his gut. There would be no children, and he was no consolation to Emily at all. Guilt along with sorrow, because he knew his mother spoke from her own experience after his father's death eleven years ago.

The lost expression Emily wore was familiar. He'd often seen it on his mother's face.

He took his mother's hand and leaned in to kiss her cheek. The familiar childhood scents of vanilla and roses filled his head and made him feel better, despite the fact that he was a child no longer. "You found your way, Mamma. I'm sure Emily will, too."

His mother cupped his jaw in one hand. "You're a good lad, Hamish. You'll come through with flying colors. Just listen to your old mother."

He mustered a smile, although that blasted heaviness in his gut wasn't going anywhere soon. "You're not old, Mamma. Your beauty is immortal."

She responded with the famous husky chuckle that Lord Melbourne said was worth fifty votes in the House of Commons. "Oh, you're such a flatterer, my son." She glanced over at Emily who still sat on the sofa, staring into the distance. "I'll say goodbye to your wife and leave you alone. The two of you must be desperate for some quiet and privacy."

Emily was, he knew. All day, she'd looked strained. Now she appeared brittle enough to snap into a hundred pieces. The problem was that Hamish suspected her idea of quiet and privacy included the absence of her unloved husband.

Over the last few days, Hamish had taken his dinner in the library. While the dining room wasn't overly large, it felt overly large when he sat alone at the head of the shiny mahogany table. Since her father's death, Emily had retired to her room in the evenings. Avoiding him, he guessed.

He was staring with little enthusiasm at his congealing fish soup when the door opened. He looked up, expecting one of the servants, but it was his wife, still wearing the elegant black dress. Propriety frowned on women attending funerals, but he admired that she'd insisted on being there.

He smiled with surprised pleasure and waved toward a chair opposite the desk that served as his dining table. "Have you come to join me?"

She didn't accept his invitation, just stared at him out of her wan face as if she expected him to accuse her of some crime. "I thought you'd be in the dining room."

"It's too lonely. I prefer taking my meals in here." His pleasure ebbed. It was clear she'd come down at this time, specifically because she believed the room would be empty. He waited for her to make some excuse and disappear upstairs again.

She didn't go. Perhaps she took pity on him when he said he'd been lonely. "This has always been my favorite room in the house."

"Mine, too." He paused and hoped he wasn't overstepping the mark. "I can still sense your father in the air here. It's as if he might walk through the door, excited about his latest discovery."

To his surprise, a faint smile curved her lips. He was glad to see her step into the room and close the door behind her. This was the first time she'd sought his company since the night they'd returned from dinner at his mother's house.

"If his spirit lingers, this will be the place." She glanced around the walls lined with shelves crammed with books, mostly scientific texts. "He spent the majority of his life in here."

"I know. It was also where he brought his students when he wanted a private word."

"Because you were in trouble – as you often were."

When he'd lived in this house, he'd been dedicated to his studies, but he'd also been a high-spirited and willful young man. A young man who occasionally kicked over the traces when the capital's temptations proved too alluring.

"Your father wasn't one for ranting and raving."

The smile settled for a moment, so full of love that Hamish felt like weeping himself. He wanted to hug her, take her in his arms and tell her that everything would be all right.

"No, he wasn't. But he had a way of looking so disappointed in you that—"

"That you almost wished he'd shout. I know. I'm sure I'd have been even more trouble, if I didn't feel that every transgression broke his heart."

Emily ventured forward to sit in front of the desk, exactly where Hamish had sat as a youth, when he'd received a gentle rebuke for disrupting the house. "He always loved you, you know."

"I loved him. He was a great man."

"Yes, he was." For one fleeting moment, he met Emily's glance, and they shared an unspoken understanding. It was as if they drew together under the benevolent regard of her father's ghost. "He always believed you would surpass him. He never doubted your brilliance."

A jagged lump of emotion blocked Hamish's throat. "I didn't know."

"Well, it's true."

"I'll miss him. He was the wisest man I ever met. In that, I'll never surpass him."

"I'll miss him, too. I'm missing him now." Tears glazed her eyes, and her voice thickened. She fisted her hands in her lap and set her elegant jaw against losing control.

It hurt to watch her. "Why don't you cry, Emily? You've been so brave."

At the funeral, she hadn't shed a tear. He'd wished to God that she would. Her constrained sorrow seemed almost unnatural, and he feared the toll her proud suffering would exact on her.

"I've cried enough."

"You've cried enough when you no longer need to cry."

"Your soup is getting cold," she said.

He cast the bowl a dismissive glance. "I don't want it. Have you eaten?"

"I'll have a tray sent up to my room later."

Food she wouldn't eat, he knew, even if she brought herself to request a meal. "I could ring for something now."

Irritation shadowed her expression. "I'm not hungry. Don't fuss."

Their fleeting rapport evaporated. "I wish I could do something to help, Emily," he said, surveying her heavy eyes and pallid complexion.

He had a sudden poignant memory of how she'd looked that night at Greenwich in her blue dress. She'd been so alive and vibrant. It wasn't just her father's illness and death that oppressed her bright spirit. Her marriage provided no joy.

She watched him with an unreadable stare. "Yes, there is something you can do."

That was a surprise. He stood up, desperate to be of use.

"Anything." He meant it.

Emily twined her hands together in her lap. "You can leave me alone."

A silence crashed down like an avalanche. Hamish told himself he shouldn't feel hurt. After all, he already knew his presence grated on her.

"I...see."

"I want...I want a bit of privacy. I want to feel that nobody is watching me and judging me. I want quiet and space to grieve for my father."

It was the longest speech she'd directed at Hamish since her father's death.

Having promised to abide by her wishes, he had no choice but to obey. He bowed to her. "Then it shall be as you wish, Emily."

His voice was gentle, but his heart was heavy as he left the library to silence, a bowl of cold soup, and a lonely mourner.

The next morning, Emily slept late. Since her father's death, she slept more than half of every day away and woke wondering when she could seek oblivion again. She'd spent so long with one ear open for her father's call, that now he was gone, long-term exhaustion caught up with her. But all this sleep never left her refreshed.

A soft knock at the bedroom door. Upon her greeting, Polly entered bearing a tray. "Good morning, my lady. Do you feel like some breakfast today?"

Emily didn't, but she was sick to death of drifting around the house like a wraith. She sat up against the pillows. Everybody had been very tolerant – including Hamish to whom tolerance didn't come easily – but it was time she stiffened her backbone and took charge of her life. She'd never cease to miss her father, but he'd be horrified to think his passing had left her a complete wreck.

"Yes, I do," she said with an attempt at brightness. The unmasked relief in Polly's smile was indication enough that Emily needed to stop worrying everyone.

"That's grand," the maid said, carefully placing the tray over Emily's knees.

While Polly crossed to open the curtains, Emily began to butter a roll. There was a plate of eggs and bacon as well, but the sight of cooked food made her empty stomach heave.

"The master left you a note before he went, my lady."

Emily put down her roll and stared curiously at Polly. "Went?"

"Yes, he was off before first light. I'm surprised you didn't hear him."

She'd been sleeping like the dead, but now she had a vague memory of activity in the house in the early hours. And it wasn't like Hamish to leave her a note. He always assumed she had no interest in his comings and goings.

He was right. It was unfair to resent his presence, especially as he'd been marvelous in her father's last few days, quick, competent, considerate, indefatigable. But when she looked at her handsome, virile, lordly husband, all she could think was that her father, the only person in the world who had loved her, was gone.

Hamish came to represent a world that didn't care a fig about her. That world would trundle on its merry way, with or without Sir John Baylor and his daughter Emily.

She'd felt awful last night, telling Hamish to go away, especially when he was trying so hard to help. But for the present, his absence was all she wanted from him.

She stretched out her hand. "Where is his letter?"

Polly fished in her pocket and pulled out a piece of paper, folded and sealed. "Here it is, my lady. Shall I pour your tea?"

"Yes, please." Emily broke the seal, telling herself there was no reason for the dread that settled like lead in the pit of her stomach.

She hardly noticed Polly fussing around her. All her attention was on Hamish's letter.

Dear Emily,

I hate to see you so sunk in grief, and I apologize that I haven't been any comfort in this sad time. I should have guessed immediately that you found no solace in my presence. I had hoped that you'd gain some respite in knowing that I loved Sir John, too.

I appreciate your honesty in telling me that you'd rather be alone to mourn in private. I swore myself to your service when we wed. If the only service I can give you is to leave when you ask, that is what I will do.

I'm overdue to visit Glen Lyon, so if you need me, that's where you can reach me. I've written to Mr. Pond and told him that I'm unable to take up my post as his assistant at the Royal Observatory because of family commitments. In the meantime, I have instructed Henry Parnell, my man of business, to advance any funds you need. I've left details of how to reach him on the desk in the library, as well as the direction of Glen Lyon if you wish to contact me.

I can imagine my departure so close to our wedding will cause more talk. That's a pity, but can't be helped. Your wellbeing is more important than any amount of gossip. If you tell people my presence was urgently required north of the border, with luck they should accept my absence as nothing out of the ordinary.

I know that you have banned me from apologizing, my dear wife. But as this is a parting that is likely to endure for the foreseeable future, I humbly beg your pardon for all my sins against you, large and small. I hope you can forgive me for making these difficult days since your father's passing even more difficult than they needed to be.

With my sincerest respect and friendship – because despite your doubts, you have always had both,

Your husband, Hamish.

For a long while, Emily stared blank-eyed at the letter. Then she read it again to make sure she hadn't misunderstood its meaning.

Dear God, Hamish had left her. After a mere matter of days as a bride, she was a deserted wife.

Hamish, I didn't mean for you to leave me forever. I meant for you to go somewhere and grant me a few hours' peace. You could have tried harder.

"He tried as much as anyone could," said a sniping little voice inside her head.

The truth was that he had. He'd reached a point where he saw no purpose in trying anymore.

"The master has gone to Scotland," Polly said cheerily.

"Yes." Emily wondered at the weight of sorrow swelling her heart. Especially when she thought that her heart already brimmed with as much sorrow as it could hold.

"I'm sure he'll be back soon, my lady. Since Sir John died, he's been fair worried sick about you."

"Yes," Emily said, although she hadn't noticed. Not really.

Grief was such a selfish emotion. As she struggled to come to terms with her loss, she'd hardly spared a thought for Hamish. Now she suffered a second loss, and one which cut much more deeply than she'd ever imagined it would.

Hamish had gone to Scotland, her father was dead, and Emily felt more alone than she ever had in her entire life.

PART TWO

CHAPTER SIXTEEN

Glen Lyon, Highlands of Scotland, September 1823

A deafening pounding in his head smashed through Hamish's slumber. Bleary eyes cracked open to cruel sunshine. What the hell had he had to drink last night?

Oh, that's right. He'd been feeling sorry for himself and missing Emily like the very devil, so he'd taken a little too much whisky before he stumbled into bed. He should bloody well know better. During his long separation from his bride, he'd learned to place a tight lid on his loneliness. But he'd made the mistake of thinking how much his wife would love the immense northern skies, especially at night when the stars burned like fire.

He'd been so befuddled, with yearning more than with liquor, that he hadn't even closed the bedroom curtains. Now daylight cut like a knife. Hell, sunlight like this didn't belong in the Highlands. This part of the British Isles should be gray and cool and wet, but September had brought two weeks of warm weather.

The thunderous pounding continued, and he realized it wasn't inside his head, but came from downstairs. It seemed someone required his presence.

There must be some crisis down at Lyon House, he supposed, or perhaps a traveler had become lost in the maze of hills surrounding the estate. Except nobody ever came to this isolated peel tower. It wasn't on the way to anything, and the nearest neighbors were more than five miles away.

That was just how Hamish liked it.

He'd discovered this tower as a ruin when he was a boy. It was unusual to see one of these defensive structures from the Dark Ages so far north, but he'd known immediately that once restored, it would make the perfect observatory. It did. It also made the perfect refuge for a man with an aching heart who wanted to lick his wounds in private.

With a heartfelt groan, he rolled out of bed and staggered across the floor. He'd reached the top of the stairs before he recalled he was naked.

Stumbling back to the bed, he wrenched a linen sheet off the mattress and wrapped it around his waist. For a moment, a memory assailed him, of a frustrating wedding night when he'd confronted his uncaring bride wearing only a bedcover.

This time he was wise enough to push away all thought of his wife. Remembering Emily only paved the way to misery.

On unsteady legs, he made his way down the uneven stone stairs to the ground floor. The knocking continued. Damn it, whoever was outside must have a bloody tired arm by now.

"All right. All right. There's no need to try and wake the dead. I'm here."

After a few seconds' fumbling with the heavy iron latch, he flung the door open and squinted into dazzling brightness. The light was even more piercing outside than it was in his bedroom.

"What in sodding hell do you want?" he growled, hitching at the sheet which was inclined to droop.

"Well, that's a charming greeting after all these months apart," a dulcet voice said.

Hamish's headache evaporated in a flash, and he looked down his long nose at the two people on his doorstep. "Bugger me, if it's not dear little wifey."

Emily stared at the disheveled blond giant standing in the rough doorway and battled the urge to punch that firm stomach. An urge once too familiar, but absent from her life since last December.

She hadn't been sure what she'd feel when she tracked down her truant husband. Trepidation? Pleasure? Relief? A bitter regret that they'd turned into strangers? She hadn't expected to feel the way her fourteen-year-old self had, that Hamish Douglas was an arrogant ass who needed taking down a few pegs.

"Good morning, Hamish." Her tone was sweet as sugar, sharp as a needle. "No, pardon me, it's not good morning. It's gone four, so it's good afternoon."

"Good afternoon, Emily." The devil didn't display an ounce of embarrassment, despite sleeping the day away and appearing in front of her in nothing but a sheet. "What the deuce are you doing here?"

Beside her, Big Billy Mackay tugged his plaid bonnet from his rumpled orange hair and twisted it fit to rip it in two. "Och, did I do wrong, Glen Lyon? The lassie arrived at Lyon House around noon and said she was your wife and she needed to see ye. She is your lady fair and square?"

As if the reminder of her role in his life was enough to oppress his spirits, Hamish released a disconsolate sigh. "Aye, she's that, all right."

Emily's gloved hands clenched in the skirts of her stylish scarlet riding habit, but hitting Hamish would hurt her more than it hurt him. That outlandish garb he sported wasn't just a reminder of her wedding night, it revealed far too many impressive muscles.

However debauched Hamish's life might have been since he left London, he still looked fit enough to take on Gentleman Jackson and win. She told herself that the throbbing weight settling in her stomach had no connection to the superb, if scruffy, sample of masculinity before her.

Through the long journey, she'd worried about the reception her husband would give her. She'd hoped that at least they'd start out with politeness, wherever they ended up once she told him why she was here. Instead, it was as if she'd seen him only yesterday, and when she'd seen him yesterday, they'd squabbled.

"You look dreadful, Hamish." She wished to heaven that was true, but it wasn't.

Her eyes traveled over him, assessing the changes nearly a year had made. In London, he'd passed for a civilized man. Here in these isolated reaches of the kingdom, he'd set aside keeping up appearances. His bright gold hair tumbled around his massive shoulders, and he hadn't shaved in weeks. A shaggy beard hid the clean lines of his jaw and square chin.

How she'd like to say Hamish looked brutish and barbaric. He certainly looked like the Viking she'd always compared him to. But to her chagrin, the unkempt look suited him. It made her too aware of what a potently male creature she'd wed. Unwelcome heat made her pulses jump, battled with the urge to give him a good shake.

The blond colossus blocking the doorway arched a supercilious eyebrow. That was one London habit he hadn't abandoned, along with shaving and a regular barbering.

"If you turn up out of the blue, my dear, you must take me as you find me." Hamish glanced past her to Big Billy. "What the devil are you doing, bringing Lady Glen Lyon up here, over all this rough country? Anyone with a brain in his head would leave her in comfort at the house and come to fetch me."

"I offered to come and get ye..." the huge Scotsman stammered.

Emily stepped in front of Billy, although her slight figure did little to shield him from the laird's displeasure. Big Billy was even larger than Hamish. Something in this spectacular valley's water must turn men into giants. "I insisted on coming."

"Did you fear I wouldn't jump to your bidding?" More of that haughty drawl.

Her lips tightened. She remembered Hamish as annoying, but she'd forgotten quite how that acid tone could make her squirm. "Would you have come?"

He shrugged. "It depends why you're here."

"I told you – I want to see you."

"Is there some disaster in London? Last week's report from Henry Parnell didn't mention any trouble."

She supposed she should be outraged that he'd kept an eye on her activities, but something silly and female in her softened to know that he hadn't forgotten her altogether. In her darker days, she couldn't help remembering that out of sight was out of mind. "Your man of business spies on me?"

Again, not a shred of shame. "I like to know what's happening."

"You—"

Hamish looked over her head. "Billy, I see that my wife and I are overdue a long and frank discussion. Perhaps you could take her back to Lyon House. I'll follow, once I've packed up here."

"Aye, Glen Lyon."

Emily planted her feet on the ground, although she was woefully aware that if it came to a contest of strength, either of these brawny Highlanders could best her in a trice. "I'm not a parcel to be marked returned to sender. I'm your wife, and I insist upon staying. Billy can go back to the house, and you can escort me there once we've finished our business."

If she didn't strangle him first.

"Och, I'll just go and check the horses, Glen Lyon." Big Billy sounded eager to escape being caught in the middle of a marital quarrel. "Ye just tell me what to do when you ken what your plans are."

With ill-concealed relief, the large Highlander headed back to where the ponies nosed at the lush grass beside the stream.

"This dwelling is unfit for you, my lady," Hamish said, once they had a modicum of privacy.

"If it's fit for my lord, it's fit for me," Emily snapped.

Then she forgot Big Billy and Glen Lyon as a horrid thought struck her. If she wasn't so tired after miles of traveling, it would have struck her the moment that her husband opened the door.

It was clear that Hamish didn't want her setting foot inside. Was that because he kept his mistresses in this rough tower?

It explained why the staff at Lyon House had been so chary about bringing her here. It explained why her husband greeted her wearing only a bedsheet and why his face was slack with sleep at this advanced hour of the day. Not to mention that she'd never demanded his fidelity, once she'd barred him from her bed.

So the hot red mist that descended to blind her made no sense at all.

"Where is she, Hamish?" she asked in a voice that sliced like a razor.

"Where is who?" Hamish asked, sounding as innocent as a babe in arms. She'd wager all the money in her purse that he hadn't laid any real claim to innocence since he was that infant.

Emily growled deep in her throat and marched forward, wondering what she'd do if he didn't shift to let her by.

She might be smaller than him, but she was ablaze with fury. On this occasion, her temper trumped his size. After a hesitation, he fell back and let her shove past him.

The tower wasn't large. Her gaze swept the gloomy, windowless ground floor and confirmed even through the darkness that the uninviting space was empty. The shadows concealed no round-heeled Highland lassies.

Breathing audibly through her nose, she mounted the stone stairs to the next level. Another circular chamber with a few narrow arrow-slit windows and an unlit fireplace. A table and chairs, a couch, an untidy bookcase. No comely wench waiting here either.

"Emily, you're being foolish," Hamish said behind her, in the tone he'd used when he told her she was wrong about his calculations for his comet.

"Am I indeed?" she muttered, more to herself than to him.

She rushed up the next flight of stairs to the bedroom Hamish had just left, if the sheet missing from the bed was any indication.

The light was better here. This room boasted a ring of windows, offering a breathtaking view over the rugged hills. Not that Emily was in any frame of mind to appreciate scenery.

A round house offered no corners for the devil to hide in. The devil – or a brazen hussy. One comprehensive glance proved this room was empty, too.

Hamish stood at the top of the stairs leading up from below and spread his hands with more of that spurious injured innocence. "You see? I'm alone."

"There's another floor," she retorted. She was so furious that she felt like an iron band tightened around her chest.

Breathless by now, she climbed the last set of stairs to another round room. The tower was built like a spice jar, circular chamber set above circular chamber, tapering to the top.

No corners. No devil. No woman.

She glanced around the untidy space, encircled by windows like the one immediately below. This must be where Hamish worked – when he wasn't tupping the local talent. Papers littered every flat surface. Notebooks. Loose sheets. A quick scan took in drawings and calculations and reams of writing in a familiar scrawl.

Over the years, she'd transcribed enough of Hamish's work into a fair hand to recognize it. She certainly didn't recognize it from his letters to her in London because there hadn't been any.

She heard Hamish following her. He had no need to rush, she started to suspect, just as she suspected she was making the most frightful fool of herself.

Another stairway sloped up to what she guessed was the roof. More slowly, she made her way upward, already sure of what she'd find. Humiliation churned in her stomach and left a sour taste in her mouth.

Emily paused when she got to the top, not just because she was winded from climbing all those stairs, but because at last she took in the view. A view that didn't include any females rousted from her husband's bed, although it did include a large telescope on an elaborate stand and a couple of tables heaped with scientific instruments. Around her stretched a vista of treeless hills offering no signs of human habitation, apart from the faint dirt track that she and Billy had followed to get here and Billy himself. Billy was leading the ponies toward a grove of Scots pines that grew beside the tower.

Mortification crawled along Emily's backbone. It felt like a host of spiders. Another crowd of spiders waged a battle inside her stomach.

"You've been working," she said flatly, turning to where Hamish stood near the parapet.

He watched her with steady blue eyes. "Yes."

"I thought—"

"I know what you thought." Of course, he did. What made her cringe was that he'd understand that her outburst proved she was far from indifferent to him. She cursed herself for showing her hand so early in the game.

"That's why you were still in bed at four o'clock in the afternoon."

His gesture encompassed the empty wilderness surrounding them. "It's the perfect place for an observatory. No light to interfere with the stars."

She regarded him without pleasure. "You can't try and tell me there have been no women, Hamish. I won't believe it. It's been nearly eleven months since our wedding."

He looked annoyed, although whether at her accusation or at being caught out, she wasn't sure. "Why should you care?"

She shouldn't. After all, she'd faced the possibility – certainty – of him straying since she'd agreed to marry him. If he lost his temper, for once Emily couldn't blame him. She'd acted like a madwoman. But the idea of Hamish finding physical pleasure in this isolated love nest made her want to smash something.

Something like his handsome face.

"Nobody likes having their nose rubbed in the sins of an unfaithful spouse."

"I'm miles from the nearest dwelling. I have no visitors, apart from the people who bring my supplies up from Lyon House." The way he hitched at the slipping sheet reeked of offended virtue. "If I brought twenty women here, I wouldn't be rubbing your nose in it."

Every muscle in her body tensed. "Have you?"

"Have I what?" he asked huffily, folding his arms over his bare chest.

"Have you brought twenty women here?"

"It's none of your business," he said snidely. "You gave me permission to pursue my entertainment elsewhere, remember?"

Damn it, she had. Even then, she hadn't liked the idea, but she'd been trying to play fair. Right now, playing fair could go to the dickens. "Discreetly."

He made an exasperated sound deep in his throat and spread his hands to indicate the beautiful if rather desolate view. "I'm stuck in a blasted tower in the middle of nowhere. How much more discreet can a man be?"

His theatrical gesture threatened to dislodge the sheet. Her attention dipped to his waist where crumpled linen drooped to reveal a nest of golden curls at the base of his stomach.

She didn't want to blush, but she did. She didn't want to keep looking, but she did.

Her gloved hands closed into fists at her sides, as she couldn't help remembering what he looked like naked. Their long separation had done nothing to diminish the vividness of that particular memory.

"Emily, for God's sake..." he said in a strangled voice, as shaking hands hauled the sheet back to his waist.

Her cheeks might feel ready to catch fire, but that didn't stop her from subjecting his body to a slow inspection before she raised her eyes to his face. She'd remembered him as handsome, almost offensively so, but after all these months apart, his leonine magnificence struck her like a blow.

Hamish was thinner than he'd been in London, and he must have gone shirtless in the summer, because the skin of his chest and arms was tanned deep gold, heightening the leonine impression. When she'd seen him naked, the dim candlelight or her own innocence must have prevented her from taking in a lot of details. Like the way gilt hair curled across his chest and arrowed down his flat stomach to disappear beneath that dratted concealing sheet.

Every drop of moisture evaporated from her mouth, and her blood set up a deep slow pulse. Whatever he might say, her husband hadn't spent all these months locked away in scholarly pursuits. Unless her recollection betrayed her, the muscles of his arms and torso were more defined than they'd been after the wedding.

"If you keep looking at me like that, you'll discover just what the local lassies have been lining up to enjoy," he sniped.

"You have the nerve to taunt me?"

"You have the nerve to hiss at me like a scalded cat, when you sent me away in the first place?"

Emily hardly heard what he said. She'd always acknowledged the beauty of that bass drawl, but had it always made her very bones vibrate?

She licked parched lips, as she studied the man she'd married. How on earth had she missed what a splendid creature he was? After their long separation, it was as if she saw him for the first time. And what she saw was more compelling than she'd ever imagined.

"Emily?"

She came back to herself enough to note the bewilderment underlying the irritation.

"How many lassies?" Where did that husky tone come from?

Hamish glared at her as if she'd lost her mind. She supposed she should be grateful that he wasn't crowing over the lack of incriminating evidence uncovered in her frantic search. But she wasn't quite at that point yet.

"You may as well tell me. I'll find out anyway," she said coldly. Once he did, she'd hunt down every one of those Scottish trollops and scratch out their eyes.

He sighed and ran his fingers through the tumbled mane of golden hair. "You're not going to let this go, are you?"

"No."

Hamish turned and stared across the hills. Emily appreciated the back view of her husband almost as much as the front one. Especially since when he looked away, she could feast on the sight unobserved.

Broad shoulders tapered to a narrow waist, and the sheet outlined firm buttocks and long, strong legs. Those acres of smooth golden skin across his back were taut. He must be having trouble finding the words to confess his sins.

"Have you lost count?" she asked with a hint of acid.

He turned to her again. In his tanned face, the blue eyes were bright as cornflowers, and his thinness made his cheekbones as sharp and pure as those on a medieval sculpture. "No."

"Then?" Her stomach tightened in squirming anticipation. She didn't want to know. She couldn't live another moment without finding out.

A wry smile creased his cheeks. She really couldn't get used to that beard. "It doesn't take long to count to zero."

Every ounce of breath left her in a whoosh, and she sagged. Such powerful relief rushed through her that it turned her legs into wet string. "None?"

He shrugged as if he hadn't changed her world with a single sentence. "I told you, I've been working."

Incredible as it was, she believed him. Hamish didn't lie. Her head was swimming. She still had trouble getting enough air into her lungs. "All these months."

"Pretty much."

She slumped into a plain wooden chair and shook her head in self-disgust. "I've made a complete spectacle of myself." She shot him a resentful glance. "And you let me."

Amusement lit his features. "There was no stopping you."

"At first." He dragged another chair across the roof and sat opposite her.

"But afterward…"

He spread his hands to indicate his blamelessness. "Your tantrum was too intriguing. Never in my wildest dreams had I pictured you as jealous."

"I'm not jealous," she said in outrage, sitting up as straight as a ruler and scowling at him. Jealousy implied she cared about this great galoot. When she didn't.

Hamish let the silence extend. After a few seconds, the odious truth stuck its claws into Emily and her eyes flickered away from his knowing sapphire stare.

How utterly devastating. How utterly disagreeable. Plague take him, she had been jealous. In fact, she'd been so jealous, she'd gone quite demented.

Who knew she harbored such possessive feelings about her husband? She'd come to Scotland for a rational discussion about their future. Yet she'd launched her campaign with a fit of fireworks that revealed far too much and put her at a distinct disadvantage.

"Why?" she managed to ask.

"Why was I working?"

He was playing games. She knew he understood her question. It was her turn to subject him to an uncomfortable silence.

After a while, his lips flattened. "Nobody took my fancy."

Her arched eyebrows told him that she found that explanation inadequate.

He shifted on the chair, making it creak. "Damn it, Emily. This is my home. I'm the laird. I'm a married man." He sounded nettled. "I owe it to my clan to set an example."

"Didn't you get lonely?"

She'd seen Hamish lose himself in his work until nothing else existed, but for heaven's sake, he'd been away since last December. That was a long time for a lusty male to go without female company. She'd spent their time apart battling not to dwell on what Hamish might do to amuse himself in her absence. The subject was too painful, even at that distance. Now she knew there had been no other women, she was curious.

His grunt was self-derisory. "Of course I bloody did."

"So…"

"So nothing." He went on with such reluctance that she couldn't doubt his sincerity. "The shameful truth is that I missed you like the devil. There. You came up here determined to hear a dreadful confession, and now you have."

"You missed me?" That seemed even more unlikely than the fact that her red-blooded husband hadn't tumbled every strumpet between here and Inverness.

"Yes, laugh if you like." He sounded so grim and miserable, she had to believe he'd missed her. "It's dashed funny, after all."

She spread her hands in bafflement, even as insidious warmth squeezed her heart. "If you missed me, why on earth didn't you come back to London and blooming well see me?"

"You told me to leave you alone." The deep voice was flat.

A dismissive snort escaped her. "That didn't mean you had to forsake me forever."

"It sounded like it. I said in my letter that I wouldn't bother you again, unless you asked me to come back."

"So you decided I didn't want to hear a single word from you in the meantime?"

He frowned. "You haven't inundated me with mail either."

Hamish had a point. "I assumed once you'd returned to your real life, you wouldn't want to hear from me."

"We seem to have made a lot of assumptions."

"We do." She paused, then went on in a more measured tone. "Perhaps a few of them were wrong."

For a long moment, they stared at each other. Emily wondered how different things might have been if Hamish had stayed in London. She had an inkling that he was thinking exactly the same thing.

Eventually he straightened in his chair and sent her a direct look. "Just what are you doing here, Emily?"

She swallowed. The moment had arrived to explain why she'd come in pursuit of a neglectful husband. She was sick with nerves. Which made no sense at all. She'd traveled for days to reach this tower. The whole way, she'd practiced what she had to say, and for a good few weeks before she left London.

Now she knew that Hamish had missed her and that he'd stayed faithful, her task should be easier. But those revelations remained too astonishing for her to feel like she could rely on them.

She swallowed again and cursed the way her voice emerged reedy and unsteady. "I decided my place was with my husband."

If she expected him to greet that announcement with any gratification, she was to be disappointed.

The chiseled features remained unreadable as he said slowly, "Did you indeed?"

She rose on legs that still felt wobbly. Perhaps standing might make her feel less at a disadvantage.

"I did." When Hamish didn't respond straightaway, she forced out the hardest bit. "I hoped...I thought if you were willing, we might try to find some common ground in this marriage."

Hamish stood, too. He hitched the sheet higher and wheeled toward the steps.

Speechless, Emily watched him go. What on earth was he doing? She felt as though she'd sliced out her heart and laid it at his feet, and all he did was run away. Again.

"Hamish?" Her voice shook. "Did you hear me?"

"Yes," he said without turning back.

"So what do you say?"

At least she no longer sounded like a squeaky ninnyhammer. Shock receded under the more familiar urge to biff him with the nearest hard object.

Hamish didn't glance back as he started to descend the stairs. "I say that if this is what you've come all this way to talk about, I need to be wearing more than just a bedsheet."

CHAPTER SEVENTEEN

Fuming, Emily stayed behind on the tower roof. Since the moment she first contemplated this expedition, she'd questioned the wisdom of coming north. Never more than now, when she felt so vulnerable. And her husband, instead of reacting with joy or even, curse him, meeting her halfway when she suggested a normal marriage, turned his back on her.

She heard voices below and crossed to look over the stone parapet. From here, it was a long way to the ground.

Hamish, still in his bedsheet, was talking to Big Billy. Probably arranging for the removal of his inconvenient wife back to Lyon House. Or London, more like.

Emily was too far up to hear what they said, especially with the wind rising. She'd never been to Scotland before, but the weather on this first visit proved mercurial. Once she crossed the border, her carriage spent a lot of time bogged, or making little headway through driving rain. Although the sun had shone as she journeyed further north. What a pity that it didn't turn out to be an omen for a brighter future.

Hamish wasn't sending her away, it seemed. Billy bowed and went off to catch his piebald pony. He left her stocky gray grazing near the trees. Wondering whether she should be pleased or alarmed at being marooned here with Hamish, she watched the brawny Highlander trot down the narrow track.

Hamish glanced up to where she stood and gave her a brief wave before he went inside.

It seemed he was willing to keep her here to discuss their situation. Although she wasn't sure what he might say. Whatever it was, he'd ensured their privacy.

She waited for him to seek her out, but there was no sign of him. The breeze strengthened, and she was getting cold. More of that mercurial weather.

With a long-suffering sigh, she went down to the floor below and surveyed the chaos. All this proof of industry, however messy, confirmed her husband's story that he'd spent their time apart working.

When Hamish still didn't appear, she began to tidy. It turned out he'd been dabbling in all sorts of things. The moons of Jupiter. Pages of observations of Saturn. Further work on his comet. Notes on a host of stars. Paintings of the northern lights. Detailed descriptions of the Perseid meteor showers, which she imagined were spectacular in this isolated corner of the kingdom.

She became so interested in tracing his observations and placing each scrap of paper with its companion pieces that she forgot the time.

"Emily?" Hamish said from the top of the stairs. "Come down to the parlor. I'll make you breakfast."

Startled she glanced up from a beautifully drawn chart of Orion. "Breakfast?"

"Well, it's breakfast for me. For you, I suppose it's getting on for dinner." As if to confirm that remark, the clock on the mantel chimed five o'clock. Through the windows, the light softened toward evening, lending the endless lines of hills a golden glow. "I'm guessing you're hungry. I certainly am."

"Yes, I'm hungry." She paused. "But I'd like a chance to freshen up first. I've been traveling all day."

He raised a hand to his bare chin. The beard had gone, which partly explained why he'd taken so long to come back to her. He'd tied that wealth of hair back in a neat queue.

He might no longer look like a pillaging barbarian, but wearing a clean shirt and a kilt, he didn't look like the Hamish she'd known in London either. There was something fiercely stirring about this new guise. He seemed more untamed, more primitive, more...magnetic than any other man she'd ever seen.

"I straightened my room and changed the sheets. While you're here, please consider the bedroom yours."

She narrowed her eyes on him, wondering if he'd taken her reasons for coming here at face value. Before she shared her body with him, she wanted to straighten out a few things. "Where will you sleep?"

His lips twisted in a sardonic smile. "That rather depends on how our discussion goes."

Elephants started performing a quadrille in her stomach. "Hamish..."

He laughed with a trace of chagrin. "Don't worry. I'm not about to demand my conjugal rights. There's a chaise longue in here." He waved toward a corner. "In fact, your sterling efforts have uncovered it."

They had. She hadn't even realized it was there, until she shifted the books piled around it. The dust had set her sneezing.

She regarded it doubtfully. "It doesn't look big enough."

He shrugged. "I'll manage. I've become such a strange, nocturnal creature since I've been here, I'll probably be awake all night anyway."

She made a sweeping gesture around the room. "You've been busy."

"Now do you believe me when I say the women of Glen Lyon have slept unmolested in their beds?"

She'd believed him upstairs. He'd never been a liar. "Yes."

"Good."

He turned and went downstairs again, his voice rising to where she stood. "Come to the parlor when you're ready."

By the time Emily joined him, she'd had a wash and tidied her hair. She'd needed to use Hamish's comb because she'd left her luggage at Lyon House. At least now she felt more prepared to deal with her troublesome spouse.

In the middle of the afternoon, this room had been cold and forbidding. Now as twilight drew in, it seemed cozy and welcoming, with a fragrant peat fire burning in the huge medieval hearth.

"Please sit down. I'll scramble some eggs. There's bacon and fresh bread and cheese and dried apples. I'm sorry for the humble fare."

She straightened her shoulders and told herself to be brave. "Hamish, I've come up here to—"

He waved her to silence. "You're tired and hungry. Take a little while to eat something and catch your breath. Then we'll talk."

She released a relieved breath. Hamish was right. Far better not to rush into negotiations. She wanted his full attention when she addressed the issues that had brought her all this way north.

Emily noticed the trivet over the flames and the makings of their meal on a wooden stool near the fire. "You cater for yourself?"

"I'm not one of your soft English gentlemen, needing a servant to button up his trousers and wash his hands for him."

He kneeled to pour the egg mixture into a skillet. As she sat at the table, she couldn't tear her eyes away from her big, powerful husband cooking with noteworthy competence. The reference to English gentlemen had been a joke, she knew, but she wondered how many of her father's aristocratic pupils had the first idea how to prepare a meal. There was something deeply satisfying about having an attractive man working for her comfort.

"You sound like an English gentleman," she said, so hungry that she tore a roll in two and slathered it with rich golden butter.

"I do," he said, still watching the eggs. "I've always hated that."

"I imagine it made life in London easier."

"Yes, it did. But not life in Scotland." His tone was neutral, but she had a feeling that his calm response hid deep emotion. "To many people up here, an English accent remains the sound of the enemy. It's not that long since Culloden, after all, and there are folk on the estate who lived through the suppression of the Highlands after the Jacobite uprising."

Surprised and concerned, she set her roll back on its plate. "But I'm English."

He forked rashers of bacon onto the plates he had ready. "You are indeed."

"Does that mean the people of Glen Lyon will hate me?" Everyone had been kind to her on the way north, and while she'd only spent an hour at Lyon House, the welcome had seemed warm.

Hamish gave the eggs another stir, sprinkled a few herbs over the top and glanced at her over his shoulder. "My choice of an English wife wasn't cause for celebration, but they'll give you a chance. If you decide to stay, you'll win them over."

"Will I?" she asked doubtfully.

Disquiet churned in her belly. She could think of a host of reasons for his kinsmen not to like her, not least that she'd lingered in London while her husband lived alone up here.

He divided the golden eggs between the warmed plates and rose to carry them across to the table. "Of course you will."

She wasn't so sure. As she looked down at her meal, her appetite shrank to nothing. It had been hard enough coming to Glen Lyon to win over a reluctant spouse. Now it seemed she had to make headway against the prejudice of the entire Douglas clan.

But Hamish seemed to be in an unusually confiding mood. She wasn't going to waste it. His mother had already told her why such a proud Scot sounded like an upper-crust Londoner, but Emily would love to hear Hamish's views on where he belonged. "You say you hated sounding like an Englishman."

"Loathed it. This is my home, yet I always felt like an outsider when I was a boy. Too many people doubted my claim to be a Highlander, when I'm a Highlander through and through. The Douglases belong here. The land's been ours for centuries." The ringing pride in his voice lifted her heart in a way she couldn't quite explain.

He wasn't the same man she'd known in London. It wasn't just his clothes that were different. What made her nervous was that in this rugged Highland setting, he was even more attractive than he'd been in London. And in London, she'd feared that she might fall under his spell, when she had no guarantee that he cared for her at all.

She still didn't. Except that he'd remained faithful. And he'd said he missed her. Not a guarantee, but perhaps something to build on.

Hamish began to eat with gusto. She forked some eggs into her mouth. She feared they might stick in her throat, but hunger overcame her roiling uncertainty about her future.

"This is good." The bacon was just as flavorsome as the eggs.

"Thank you. We have venison steaks for tomorrow."

"Are we still going to be here tomorrow?" After he heard her out, he might decide to ship her back to Bloomsbury. Or Tierra del Fuego.

Half his plate was clear already. "We don't have to decide tonight." He used a linen napkin to wipe his mouth. "Would you like wine or ale or water?"

"Ale, please." Emily watched him fill two horn beakers and pass her one. "You were telling me about your childhood."

His beaker paused on its way to his lips. "Good God, was I? I'm sure we can talk about something more interesting."

The problem was that everything else was much more fraught than his life story – and anyway she wanted to know. The simmering hostility that had always marred her dealings with Hamish left her woefully ignorant of so much about this clever, complicated man. "No, tell me."

He shrugged, took a long drink, and set the beaker down. "While both my parents are as Scottish as haggis and I was born at Glen Lyon, Papa placed his considerable abilities at the nation's service during the war. Throughout the troubles with France, he was one of the most powerful figures in the War Office. Mamma and Papa loved each other too much to live apart, so when I was a wean, the whole family relocated to London."

"Your mamma still misses her husband."

"She does. They were wonderful together."

Her lips turned down in a rueful smile. "I suspect they were terrifying."

"Mamma has changed over the years. She was more approachable when I was a boy. That steely edge only appeared after she lost my father. I think she had to become harder, or grief would have destroyed her. Papa left us far too early. He was only in his fifties when an apoplexy took him. Overwork, I always thought."

She set down her cutlery. This was the closest she'd ever come to sharing confidences with Hamish. And for once, their interactions held no edge. She was surprised that she almost felt at ease, despite the difficult conversation ahead of her.

"My parents were in love, too." Strange to think that they had this in common.

"I know they were." Hamish's response was gentle. "Your father talked about your mother with such affection. It was clear that he never ceased to miss her. He often said you were very like her."

"I'd like to think that was true. She was wonderful." Emily swallowed the knot of sorrow that blocked her throat. Her mother's loss still hurt. Her voice was husky as she changed the subject. "Did you see much of Glen Lyon as a child?"

"We had summer holidays in Scotland. Mostly that meant a visit home and a few fistfights when someone called me a cursed Sassenach." He spat the word out, as if it had a rotten taste.

"Did you win?"

Hamish gave a huff of self-derisive amusement. "Once I started to grow into my size, I did."

"One would think that your tenants would treat you with deference because you're the heir to the estate. They would in England."

He refilled his beaker. She'd hardly touched hers. "The Highlands are more democratic. The shepherd's son is perfectly happy to knock the block off the laird's son, if he feels the laird's son deserves it."

"I see," when in fact, she didn't.

A reminiscent smile curved Hamish's lips. "I met Fergus during one of those holidays north. When Diarmid and I had got lost in the hills, he rescued us. By the way, you and he have something in common."

"Oh?" She couldn't imagine what. She'd found the Laird of Achnasheen almost as daunting as she found Hamish's mother.

Laughter danced in Hamish's brilliant blue eyes, made him breathtakingly appealing. "It took Fergus a while to recognize me for what an all-round excellent fellow I am. He didn't like me much when he met me. In fact, he might have dared to use the S word."

Emily smiled, although she didn't feel much like laughing. Hamish told this tale as if it was a high old adventure, but she knew enough now to see the unhappy, displaced child at the heart of it. "So did you like growing up in London?"

"Not much. I missed Scotland like the very devil, although I'd have missed my family more if I stayed here. And life was no easier south of the border than it was in the north. When I went to Eton, I had to defend my honor even more often than I had to up here. I was too English for my clansmen and too Scottish for the stuck-up swine who went to school with me."

So in the end, Hamish had belonged nowhere. When he swaggered into her father's house, Emily had immediately resented his cocky self-assurance. Now she wondered if his pride had led him to overcompensate, to hide his fears of being the eternal outsider.

"You make school sound lonely."

"It wasn't too bad, especially once I started winning the fights."

More pride. At last, she learned to recognize it and the fierce defenses he placed around it.

"And of course you were clever."

"That doesn't translate to universal popularity."

He spoke with uncharacteristic hesitation, as if afraid he betrayed himself. But it was too late. She'd caught a glimpse of the boy beneath the glamor. She couldn't view him through the prejudiced eyes of her childhood ever again.

"Cambridge, however, was a lark." His expression brightened. "Lots of high jinks, plenty to drink, clever chaps to hang about with, and people who taught me all they knew about the stars. I was happy as a pig in mud there. And afterward, I came to your father. That was best of all."

"You were happy with us."

"When my professor's daughter wasn't glaring at me, I was."

After what she'd learned tonight, she had the grace to feel a stab of guilt for how she'd treated him. When it came to placing blame for their prickly relationship, she deserved her share. "I was a snotty little madam."

"You were, but I suspect I was insufferable." He shrugged. "I suspect I still am."

Blindly she stared down at her empty plate. "You're not so bad," she mumbled.

"What did you say?"

She raised an unwilling gaze to his face. "I said you improve upon acquaintance."

He cupped one hand around his ear and did a fair impersonation of a deaf old man. "No, I still can't be sure I heard you aright."

Emily struggled not to laugh. What a revelation. She felt like she shared a sweet moment with someone who understood her better than anyone else in the whole wide world. How strange, when she'd braced for an encounter bristling with antagonism and recrimination. "Hamish, don't tease."

He lowered his hand, and the laughter drained from his face. The expression in his eyes made the eggs she'd eaten coagulate into a cold lump in her stomach. The preliminaries, gentler than she'd ever predicted, reached their end. It was time for the main bout.

She wasn't surprised when Hamish came around to pull out her chair, with a courtesy she remembered as innate.

"I should wash up." She cursed the quiver in her voice. Now the moment arrived, she was desperate to put it off for a little longer.

"Later." Hamish took her hand and seated her in a leather chair in front of the fire.

Emily watched him settle in the chair beside hers. With his long hair and traditional Highland costume, he could be a man from another age. The ancient tower rising about them deepened the impression of the past crowding in upon the present.

He stretched his long bare legs toward the hearth and turned to her. Flames flickered across his chiseled features and made him look like a stranger. Her heart fluttered with fear – and with something that she now recognized as sensual awareness. Ten empty months had given her plenty of time to examine her own confused reactions to the man she'd married.

"You've come a long way to see me, Emily. After nearly a year without a word." His voice was deep and persuasive, with no hint of belligerence. "Will you tell me what you want?"

Ah, that was a question indeed.

She curled shaking hands over the worn lions' heads carved into the arms of her chair and made herself answer. To her surprise, the words emerged smoothly. Those unexpected revelations about Hamish's lonely childhood gave her a shred of hope that he might understand.

"I don't want to be alone anymore."

CHAPTER EIGHTEEN

*H*amish frowned unseeing into the fire, as those astonishing words ricocheted through his mind. The whole day had been astonishing. He'd never expected to see Emily here at his bolt-hole. The sight of her had awoken his desire to almost painful life.

Now his wife was here, asking for...

Just what was she asking for?

"Hamish, are you trying to work out some tactful way of telling me to go back to London?" She sounded touchingly young, like the adolescent girl he'd met all those years ago at her father's house.

He raised his eyes and studied her. She looked nervous. She also looked like she struggled to conceal her nerves under a show of bravado. How very like her.

"Even after all these months apart, you must recall that tact isn't my forte."

His attempt to lighten the atmosphere didn't succeed. Her expression remained austere. "So what do you think?"

He thought that he needed a lot more information before he took on what could be just more heartache and frustration. "Tell me why you want this."

The spread of her hands indicated an inability to explain. "It's a long story."

He rested his shoulders on the back of the chair. "I'm not going anywhere."

The question was – was Emily?

She twined her hands in her lap, a sign of disquiet he'd become familiar with in London. "I...I missed you, too."

Startled, he sat up straight. "The devil you did."

"The devil I did." At last, those lush lips twisted in a wry smile. "It caught me unawares, too."

"After your father died, I couldn't do anything right." The memory of those difficult days was still painful. "It was obvious I was driving you utterly mad. When you told me to go away, it seemed the only thing I could do to save your sanity."

Regret turned her hazel eyes deep green. "I was so sad, I wasn't in my right mind. It wasn't you in particular."

"I'm sure you were relieved when I went," he said somberly.

"Perhaps I was." The stark honesty in her gaze made his heart clench. "Although believe me, I didn't mean to exile you all the way to Scotland. And the relief didn't last."

"I'm sorry. I hoped my absence would help."

She bit her lip. He could see that she found this confession difficult. She didn't like to leave herself vulnerable. Nor did he. Mutual defensiveness had contributed to their thorny relationship.

"Without Papa to care for, without you to fight with, the house seemed appallingly empty." Her lips turned down, and he saw that revisiting that time made her wretched, too. "The hours hung so heavy on my hands. I had too much leisure to stare into space and miss Papa."

"And regret your decisions," he said with a hint of grimness.

"I regretted some of them."

"Marrying me being the principal target, I'll wager."

To his surprise, she shook her head. "You might think that's true, but it isn't."

Another shock. More powerful than the one that he'd felt when she admitted missing him. And perhaps just a tiny glimmer of hope. "It isn't?"

Her gesture expressed her confusion. "Oh, I regretted the way we married. Coming to terms with that was never going to be easy. But once you left, I found myself thinking that you weren't nearly the nightmare to live with that I imagined."

"Thanks very much," he said with an edge.

Another reluctant smile. "Tact has never been my specialty either. So you know I'm being sincere when I say I looked back on our short time together and found myself remembering how kind you'd been, both to me and to Papa. I remembered how you tried to make my new life as smooth as you could. I remembered how you took so much strain off my shoulders, and in a way that I hardly noticed until you'd gone and it was too late to thank you." She paused. "I remembered how you kept your word about not sharing my bed."

Damn it, that wasn't a subject he was ready to broach. He was trying not to get too excited about the thought of possessing his bride. She said she wanted a real marriage, but she hadn't said that meant taking him as her lover. If he let himself hope too hard and then she insisted he kept his promise, the disappointment would be too much to endure.

Surely she must want him to keep his promise.

"No decent man would behave differently," he said.

Approval tinged her smile. The expression was so unfamiliar, it took him a few seconds to identify it. "That's the crux of it – it turned out that I married a decent man, when I feared I was taking on a selfish, temperamental child in a man's body."

He shifted uncomfortably under all this praise. "I can be a difficult sod when the mood takes me."

"Yes, you can, but at heart, you're a good man. And I treated you so shabbily."

He was unaccustomed to Emily saying nice things about him. Most of the time, she looked like she wanted to pitch a vase at his head, the bigger, the better. "You were worried sick about your father."

"He'd always been the center of my world. More so, after he became ill."

"So you found yourself at a loss, once he was gone."

"That's true." She paused. "I was also a wife without a husband. Even during my mourning period, that made life difficult. There were nasty remarks and a string of questions about your whereabouts. Things got much worse, once I was out and about again. I couldn't appear in public without meeting prurient curiosity. I almost think I'd rather be scorned as a scarlet woman than derided as an object of pity. But everyone knew that I hadn't managed to keep my husband with me for more than a few weeks."

"It isn't unusual for me to visit Scotland."

"It is when you left so soon after our wedding and my father's funeral." She sounded sad rather than angry. "It is when you didn't come back."

Guilt pricked at him. Perhaps he should have stayed. "I'm sorry, Emily. I guessed there would be talk, but I came to the conclusion that you'd prefer the gossip to my company."

"You were wrong."

If that was the case, the gossip must have been horrendous. "So is that what this is about? Have you come to ask me to join you in London? You could have done that in a letter."

A wave of her hand dismissed the suggestion. "You could ignore a letter. And I didn't know how you felt about coming back. In the letter you left me, you sounded piqued."

He gave a bleak huff of laughter. "I was hurt, not piqued."

When distress darkened her remarkable eyes, he repented his honesty. "Oh, Hamish, I'm sorry. I didn't think you cared about me at all."

"You're wrong. I do care," he said gruffly.

"I didn't know," she said on a breath. His confession left her looking troubled, not pleased. What else did he expect? A declaration of undying love?

"Well, now you do."

After a resonant pause, she asked, "So will you come back to London?"

"To save you from the gossip?" Bitterness sharpened the question.

Emily rose to her feet, her chin angled with familiar defiance. "I don't like all the nasty cats pointing at me and smirking. I didn't like it after Greenwich. I don't like it now."

"Surely you're not excluded from society." He stood, too. "What the hell has my mother been doing? If anyone can give you countenance in the beau monde, she can. Nobody dares cross her."

"Your mother has been good to me, but even she can't stop the spiteful whispers about how you and I made our bed and now must lie on it."

Hamish still didn't want to think about beds. Not when he had this night to get through. He closed his eyes to avoid looking at her, so lovely here where he never thought she'd be.

She'd taken off that spectacular, figure-hugging scarlet jacket and now wore only a blouse and the red skirt. Fabric covered her from collarbone to instep. Only a ravening beast would take that plain, practical outfit as an invitation to strip her naked.

Clearly he was a ravening beast.

In fact, this room was altogether too dark and intimate. He began to prowl around, lighting every lamp in the room. "You weren't a regular at society events anyway. I doubt the scientific community still cares about our private life."

"However great their minds, most of your colleagues are old women when it comes to gossip. Their wives and daughters are certainly avid to spread any tattle."

Hamish lit the last lamp and turned to face her. Only to strangle a groan.

Why the dickens had he decided that it was a good idea to make the room brighter? Emily was as alluring as she'd ever been in the gloaming. More. Now he could see the intelligence in her eyes and the shine on the rich sable of her hair. He still dreamed of those magical moments in the library, when he'd taken down her hair.

"The talk will die down in time."

"It hasn't so far."

"So you want me back to salve your pride?"

"That's part of it. But not the most important part." The tilt of her chin became even more pronounced. "I told you – I'm tired of being alone."

He made a frustrated sound deep in his throat. "You say that, but what do you mean?"

Her defiance faded, and she eyed him warily. "I don't want us to live apart. When we wed, I assumed we'd be under one roof. You certainly spoke as if we would be. I want to set up home with my husband. It's about time I did."

He drew a shuddering breath. In her innocence, she didn't know what she asked. "Emily, forgive me if I speak bluntly."

She stood her ground. "I wish you would."

After he finished, she wouldn't say that. "When you told me to leave, I was heartsore and worried sick about leaving you grief-stricken and alone."

"It was awful."

"I'm sure it was." He paused. "But leaving you was also a blessed relief."

When he saw her whiten, he was sorrier than ever that he'd lit the lamps. She reached out to hold the back of the chair, as if her legs threatened to give way beneath her. "You wanted to get away from me so much? You said you like me. You said you...cared."

He swallowed, wishing there was an easy way to make her understand the unacceptable truth. "I did. I do."

"It doesn't sound like it." Resentment cracked in her voice.

He sliced the air with one hand. "Damn it, the problem is I like you too much. I like you to the point where sleeping alone became the purest torture. I made you a promise before we married. But each day we spent as man and wife, that promise became shakier and shakier. With every mile that I traveled north, you were a mile safer from my need."

She was still ashen. "So you're saying if we live together, our arrangements must change?"

Arrangements? What a namby-pamby term to describe the storm of desire that swept through him at the merest thought of her. He stood as straight as if he faced a firing squad. He had to make this clear, if they were to have any chance of rescuing anything positive from the disaster of their marriage.

"Yes, I am. I know it's not fair. I know I told you I can keep my word. But, Emily, if you and I are going to reconcile, I can't live as your chaste partner for the rest of my days. If we live together, we live together as man and wife. With all that phrase encompasses."

CHAPTER NINETEEN

*H*amish waited for Emily to storm out of the room in disgust. But although the wariness in her expression deepened, she didn't move. She didn't even look particularly shocked. Which shocked him.

Then a horrible thought occurred to him. "You do know what I'm talking about, don't you?"

A wry smile twisted her lips. "Do you mean am I aware of the mechanics of conjugal relations? Yes, I am. A girl at school told me. I didn't believe her, but I've since had the opportunity to read some animal husbandry manuals. If we mate as animals do, I understand the basics."

Despite the tension vibrating in the air, Hamish laughed. "That is such an Emily answer."

She blushed. "I had nobody to ask. I couldn't talk to Papa about this."

No, he supposed she couldn't. She'd been lonely growing up, too.

"I can imagine those books were all practicality and no poetry," he said bleakly.

She still eyed him as though she expected him to ravish her if she blinked. "I've read enough poetry to guess that with people, it's not so matter-of-fact. I imagine when passion carries one away, it feels different from the ram tupping the ewe."

If he wasn't so close to the edge, he might laugh at that. "So it's just me you don't want to sleep with."

There was a spiky pause. "I'm not as opposed to the idea as I was."

He shook his head. Surely he'd misheard. "What?"

She leveled wide hazel eyes on him. "Don't make me say it again."

He took a step forward but stopped bewildered when she raised one hand. "Don't come any closer."

"But you just said..." Hamish struggled to master his primitive impulses.

It suddenly seemed a very bad idea that he hadn't rushed her straight back to Lyon House the moment she arrived. They had far too much privacy here at the peel tower, and he wasn't sure she could trust him in private any longer.

"We've been apart for months. I'm not jumping into bed the minute I see you again."

He slumped so heavily into a dining chair that it gave a loud creak. With a groan, he buried his face in his hands. "Damn it, Emily, this is torture."

When he raised his head, she hadn't shifted an inch. He strove to sound like a reasonable man. "What's changed? You were adamant that you'd never allow me to put my filthy paws on you."

With considerably more grace than he'd demonstrated, Emily sank into the chair beside his. "When you proposed, it was—"

"Unwelcome?"

"I'd never thought of you as a potential husband."

"I'd never thought of you as a wife. But once I came to terms with the idea, I thought we had as good a chance as anyone else."

"Except I placed an impossible condition on the match."

"You were afraid."

"Yes." She must have read his horrified expression, because she went on quickly. "Not of you. Or only a little. I was afraid of losing my grip on everything I was. You are rather overwhelming, you know."

"You're up to my weight."

She raised her chin. "I think I just might be."

"So you're no longer afraid that my wicked wiles will turn you into a cipher?"

His exaggerated description of her fears didn't spark a smile. "I am still afraid of that. You're a force of nature, Hamish. But I'm more afraid of going the rest of my life without the consolations of family life. I'm afraid I'll never know my husband's tenderness or a child's love. I've had ten long miserable months to admit that I'd painted myself into a corner. I might be safe there, but it's a barren safety. I've had time to wonder how it would feel if you touch me. I must admit I'm...curious."

"In a purely academic sense?"

A soft snort of amusement escaped her. "I doubt purity has much to do with it."

Hamish straightened from his slouch and stared at her. "Do you want me to play the suitor?"

Her lips twitched. "I've led a sheltered and scholarly life. I like the idea of a big, handsome Scot wooing me."

He relished that Emily called him a big, handsome Scot. He liked how she looked. It was encouraging to hear that she liked how he looked, too.

"I could do that," he said slowly, hoping to hell that he could control his urges until she said yes.

If she said yes.

Relief flooded her face. "Would you?"

"The prize is worth the winning."

Emily was right about one thing. The future was bleak unless they turned this hastily constructed union into a real marriage.

She frowned. He'd forgotten how expressive her face was. Or perhaps over their long separation, he'd learned how to read her. "If you take another woman into your bed, I won't remain complacent. I can't accept a husband who strays, if he's also the man who uses my body."

He burst out laughing as he stood up. "I believe you made that clear after you arrived – and at that point, I still had leave to take a mistress."

When she blushed, the pink in her cheeks was adorable. "I jumped to conclusions."

"I did answer the door in the middle of the afternoon wearing only a sheet. And you had no particular reason to trust me."

"That's still no excuse for turning into a lunatic."

"I love that I can make you jealous. It means that I can make you want me." He paused and spoke from the depths of his heart. "Emily, you're the woman I want. I wouldn't invite some substitute into my bed, just because I had an itch to scratch."

Wondering eyes fixed on him. "I like that you want me."

"You didn't in London."

"I did." She sighed. "And I didn't. How was I to accept your desire when we fought all the time?"

"I suspect we fought because we were attracted to each other but resisted acknowledging it. At least I was always attracted to you."

He waited for her to deny her interest, for pride's sake, but she looked thoughtful. "The moment you opened your mouth, I'd bristle up. None of my father's other students had that effect. In fact, I have trouble remembering most of their names. From the beginning, you took up more than your fair share of my attention."

"I spent a lot of time thinking about you, too." In ways that would shock her if she knew.

She subjected him to a comprehensive survey from the top of his head to his toes. Heat sizzled wherever her eyes focused. "Partly because you're so spectacular to look at. When you arrived at the house, I thought you looked like a handsome prince in a fairy story."

As hot color flooded his face, he shifted uncomfortably. Odd how Emily's compliments overset him." Oh, go on with you."

"Hamish, you're blushing," she said in delight.

"Yes, well..."

"I still think you're handsome. None of my father's other students would look nearly as good in a sheet." She paused. "Or out of it."

Ridiculous to feel his cheeks get even hotter. It wasn't as if she was the only girl to see him naked. "That night, I feared you'd run screaming from the room."

To his astonishment, sensual nostalgia tinged her smile. His blood churned with excitement, although she'd made it clear that there would be no consummation tonight. However, now he dared to hope. If he played his cards right, there was a good chance a consummation loomed in his future.

Her sideways glance sent his pulses rocketing. "Actually I was curious."

"Were you indeed, you shameless hussy?"

"My father trained me in scientific method."

"So I was a specimen."

Her lips quirked. "An impressive one. You're magnificent with your clothes on, but that's nothing compared to how you look undressed."

He was blushing again. "You're playing a dangerous game, sweetheart."

She looked startled. "You've never called me that before."

"Do you mind?"

Another thoughtful frown. "You know, I rather like it."

He took a risk, although to an outsider it would seem the most natural of actions. He extended one hand. When she hesitated, his fragile hopes dimmed.

Then she leaned forward in her chair and curled her fingers around his. His heart lurched into a drunken dance. Fergus and Diarmid had told him a wife was different from every other woman in a man's life. They were right. Emily was holding his hand, for God's sake, and he couldn't be more stirred up if London's most expensive courtesan gave him the wink.

He wondered just when Emily had stopped being the thorn in his side and become the one woman in the world he could imagine sharing his life. The change had happened before he left for Scotland. She'd already made her mark on his soul before he traveled north, stricken with grief after Sir John's death and the failure of his marriage.

She squeezed his hand and smiled, although uncertainty still shadowed her eyes. "In the meantime, I'm not against a few experiments."

Hamish told his idiot heart to settle down. He didn't yet know what she was offering. "Oh?"

"I've never been kissed." She bit her lip, then spoke in a rush. "I'd like it very much if you kissed me, Hamish."

CHAPTER TWENTY

*E*mily stared into Hamish's face, desperate to read his reaction to her confession – and her request. She pulled her hand free, then was sorry that she did. She liked the warm strength of his grasp. After months of feeling abominably alone, his touch soothed her loneliness.

"Have I shocked you?" The question was unsteady.

"You've made me lose what little respect I ever had for the Sassenach male. How does a pretty girl like you reach the advanced age of twenty-five without men fighting to kiss her?"

Heat flooded her cheeks. And other parts of her. She shifted on her chair. "You're flirting with me."

"I am indeed. But that doesn't stop me from being appalled."

She spread her hands. "You know what Papa's house was like. Everything was dedicated to science."

"I was dedicated to science. They didn't stop me from thinking about the naughty things I wanted to do to you."

"You never tried to kiss me."

"No, but I wish I had now. I certainly wanted to."

He had, hadn't he? Looking into his intent face, she could tell that he still did. How intriguing. "We were too busy fighting to kiss."

"Nobody is that busy. I suppose you terrified all those other clodpolls, because you're so clever and pretty. Even I found myself daunted – and very little daunts a gallant Scotsman."

Emily regarded him doubtfully. "You never seemed daunted."

"Inside I was shaking with dread."

She struggled not to smile. "You're such a fibber."

"And I suppose your father's colleagues are all past it – although I noticed that a couple of those old goats had an eye for you."

"A few of them chased me around the library."

He looked startled. And displeased. "Did they, by God?"

"I only worked for Lord Pascoe once. It turned out he wanted more from me than verification of his arithmetic."

"Frightful old duffer. He never caught you?"

"No, only you did that."

"I did, didn't I?" Hamish looked thoughtful. "It's my duty as a man of honor to give you a first kiss to remember."

"Are you going to kiss me now?" Despite her best efforts, her voice shook as she rose. He suddenly seemed awfully tall and...male.

"Yes, I am," he said with a solemn expression, although the glint in his eye told her that even now, he teased her.

Emily snatched at his hand. She needed something to keep her upright. Her knees felt like blancmange.

She'd known that kissing would be involved when she approached Hamish about making their marriage work. Good heavens, more than kissing. This craven reaction to the prospect of a kiss hinted that she'd be catatonic with nerves when it came to the marital act.

On the way north, she'd looked forward to learning what made people go silly when two pairs of lips met. But when she imagined kissing Hamish, she'd forgotten how big and powerful he was. While she wasn't a tiny woman, compared to him she felt like a mere speck.

"The setting leaves something to be desired." He glanced around the parlor. "You're lucky you married an astronomer, my girl."

"I am?" she said faintly. "Because you'll make me see stars?"

He responded with a soft laugh. She liked his laugh. She liked the way the low rumble of amusement resonated in her bones. "I do hope so. Although I meant something else. An astronomer keeps a close watch on the phases of the moon. As luck would have it, there's a moon out tonight and the evening has set fair. That's not always the case in this beautiful country of mine."

"You're taking me outside." She wasn't sure whether she was relieved or disappointed at her reprieve. Once she mentioned kissing, she'd expected him to jump on her.

"Doesn't every maiden dream of a kiss in the moonlight?"

She swallowed to ease a dry throat. "I dream of discovering a new planet like Herschel did."

The burgeoning delight in his smile puzzled her. "Emily, you're the most marvelous girl in creation, and I'm so happy we got caught *in flagrante* in Greenwich."

"Hardly *in flagrante*—" She stopped and regarded him in amazement. "What did you say?"

Hamish lifted her hand and placed a fervent kiss on her palm. Heat rippled along her arm and set her heart beating even faster. Since Hamish said he meant to kiss her, it had been galloping fit to win the Derby.

"I'm deuced glad that you didn't marry one of those milksops who hung on your father's every word. I'm even gladder that you didn't settle for a doddering old codger like Pascoe. I'm so happy you decided to marry me instead."

"I am..."

Good heavens, she didn't know what she was. She'd never imagined Hamish saying such things. When he'd proposed, his manner had conveyed a grim determination to do the right thing, no matter what it cost him. Or her.

His smile filled with the sweetness that she so rarely saw. Which was a good thing for her health. That smile did wicked things to her heart, made it bounce and bound about.

His other hand rose to touch her lips. "You are lovely."

The sensation of his lips on her hand had made her feel most unlike herself. The touch of his fingers on her lips turned out to be equally devastating. And when all that was combined with what sounded like a heartfelt compliment, her head reeled.

Goodness, he hadn't even kissed her on the mouth yet. Already she was completely doolally.

Emily's reading about copulation had described a purely physical process. It hadn't prepared her for this hazy, shivery, restless reaction. That time Hamish had mistaken his room, she'd thrilled to his touch on her breast. That was the limit of the physical pleasure they'd shared, although she often dreamed of those charged moments when he'd taken down her hair.

"Do you still want me to kiss you?" His thumb rubbed the back of her hand. The caress's erratic rhythm made her blood simmer in a way that was both disturbing and enjoyable.

Did she want him to kiss her? From the first, she'd feared that if she married Hamish, his larger-than-life personality would swamp her. On the brink of sharing her body with him, she recognized that she was about to change forever. In ways her innocence prevented her from imagining.

But her answer emerged before she stopped to consider it. She'd come too far toward him, physically, intellectually, emotionally, to retreat now.

Nor did she want to retreat. She just had to recall the desert of her life in London to admit that.

"More than ever."

Another breathtaking smile rewarded her. "Then come out into the moonlight, fair maiden." He tucked her hand through his arm and paused to collect one of the lamps. "It's as dark as Satan's coalmine downstairs. My plans for you don't include a broken leg."

She shivered in anticipation, as she wondered what his plans might include instead. For the first time, she pressed close to Hamish's side. She didn't want anything to separate them, which was a frightening admission from someone who had always prided herself on her independence.

The closeness worked well until they reached the stairway. It was so narrow that she let him go ahead. "I must ask you about the history of this tower," she said, as the weight of expectation between them grew oppressive.

He squeezed her hand as they navigated the stairs. "Not now."

"No, not now."

They crossed the stone floor to the door. Hamish set down the lantern and raised the latch. He pushed the door open and stood back to let Emily precede him. She stepped across the threshold into a world of enchantment.

The moon turned the dramatic landscape to silver. The brook chuckled its way across the field. The breeze created its own music through the grove of Scots pines growing beside the tower.

"You approve?"

"I approve," she murmured.

He kept hold of her hand and turned to face her. In the moonlight, his sculpted features were all mystery.

"You're so beautiful," he said, after a long while.

Emily trembled and swayed forward to catch his scent. She'd missed that scent since the day he left. The deep breath she drew was rich with his spicy male tang and the pure clear air of the Highlands. "Shut up, Hamish."

Even in the dark, she saw him jerk in surprise. "Shut up?"

"Yes, shut up and kiss me before I die of longing."

"Well, damn me for a porridge-brained fool..."

He caught her around the waist and hauled her against his body. She had a moment to gasp in surprise before he bent his head, blocking out the moonlight. His lips found hers, and she instinctively opened. He tasted hot and delicious, and when his tongue flicked her lower lip, her stomach turned over in immediate pleasure. It was all so unfamiliar and fascinating, she wasn't even frightened when his tongue slid deep inside her mouth.

He did it again, and her knees gave up the fight. On a sigh of surrender, she sagged and her arms found their way around his neck.

She'd expected something tentative and gentle, if only out of respect for her innocence, but the instant his lips met hers, he swept her up into a whirlwind. This time when his tongue moved against hers, she responded.

He gave a growl of appreciation and gathered her closer. Her blood ignited to flame. The whole world turned from dark to light. The onslaught of physical pleasure made her head swim. A demanding pulse set up in her belly.

When he raised his head, he was breathing roughly, while Emily felt as if he'd waltzed her through every constellation in the Milky Way. After that swirling voyage through the galaxy, it was difficult coming back to earth.

"Good Lord, Hamish, if I'd known you could do that, I'd never have left off pestering you."

His low laugh made her skin tingle with pleasure. "I've had plenty of time to think about how I'd like to kiss you, sweetheart."

"Do it again," she whispered, leaning closer. This greedy wanton couldn't possibly be self-sufficient, self-contained Emily Baylor.

Except she wasn't Emily Baylor anymore. She'd been Emily Douglas since November, even if it was only now that the name felt like hers.

"With pleasure," Hamish murmured. They kept their voices low, although there was nobody to hear. The occasion seemed to demand reverence, even as her body awakened to a carnal delight she'd never known. "And I mean that most sincerely."

She thought she'd learned passion from his first kiss, but this one was even more voracious. Caught up in tumultuous response, she forgot that she was a novice, she forgot to fret over whether she was making a mess of this because of her inexperience. She just sank into the warm ocean of Hamish's passion.

Emily greeted the entry of his tongue into her mouth with a flutter of her own. Through the blood thundering in her ears, she heard another of those rumbles of approval. He sucked her tongue into his mouth and she, eager for more of this dazzling new experience, copied him.

When his lips left hers, she couldn't suppress a moan of disappointment, until he began to kiss her face and her ears, dizzying little contacts that made her burn for more.

This time his groan expressed frustration. She pulled away to see his face. Or as much of his face as the moonlight allowed. Her earlier uncertainty came flooding back. "Have I done something wrong?"

"Hell, no." His hair hung loose, ruffled from her roving hands. The cord that had confined it must be lying on the grass somewhere. "You're a dream come true."

She blinked. "I wish you'd said these things to me years ago. We wouldn't have spent so much time at odds."

He gave a grunt of amusement and kissed her quickly on the lips. Another thrill raced through her. It had been an altogether thrilling night. "You'd have laughed in my face."

She smiled, although she couldn't help thinking how much time they'd wasted. Time when they could have been in each other's arms. "Not if you'd been kissing me at the time."

"So whenever you disagree with me, I should kiss you?"

"If it means more kisses, I approve."

Hamish laughed and kissed her again, and she dived deep into the pleasure and heat. He stroked her back and when his hands lowered to clasp her bottom through her skirts, another of those giddy thrills rushed through her. He hoisted her up and clamped her into his body. Her hands curled around those brawny shoulders, and she growled when her skirt hindered her from getting as close as she wanted.

Hardness pressed into her stomach. Thanks to her wedding night, she knew what that meant.

An hour ago, this excitement would have perturbed her, made her retreat. Now she rubbed luxuriantly against him and basked in his groan of frustration. Desire rushed through her, and the place between her legs turned hot and liquid.

In her naivety, she'd imagined a kiss would be a simple thing. She'd been mistaken. This passion between them was profound and earthy and urgent. Somewhere at the back of her whirling mind, she knew Hamish would need little encouragement to lay her down on the soft grass at their feet.

Under her hands, he was shaking and his scent had turned humid and musky. Their kisses had flared into a conflagration so quickly that she'd lost her grip on reality.

She pulled back and sucked in a huge breath to feed starved lungs. When he stared down at her, the moon was bright on his face. "You're wearing too many clothes."

"Oh," she said, disturbed and excited at the same time.

To her regret, he set her down. "Let me."

"Yes," she whispered, although even in her heightened state, she knew the risks of letting Hamish remove her garments. "You're shaking."

She found it disarming that his fingers fumbled as he undid the tiny pearl buttons fastening her shirt's high collar.

"You strike straight to the heart of me, Emily, and that's the truth."

More poetry. Here in Scotland, he unleashed a strain of Celtic romanticism that he kept under wraps in London. His mother had told her that she'd never understand the man she'd married until she saw him at Glen Lyon.

He brushed away the material covering her neck and began to kiss her there. Volleys of breathtaking thrills sizzled through her, and she released a helpless gasp as her knees buckled.

She grabbed the front of his linen shirt. "Hamish…"

Until now, her neck had seemed a prosaic part of her body, a mere apparatus for holding up her head. Under the depredations of Hamish's lips, it turned out to be a location ripe for delight.

As he kissed along her shoulder, Emily was vaguely aware of his fingers tugging more buttons loose. When his hand insinuated itself under the shirt to cup her breast through her stays, she cried out in surprise.

Gently he squeezed, and the breath caught in her throat. The pulse between her legs hammered so frantically that it shook her whole body. Her nipples tightened, and her undergarments turned into instruments of torture. She wanted his hands on her bare skin. She wanted her hands on his bare skin.

Emily realized that she needed to decide here and now whether she meant him to continue. The wild woman he'd conjured to life was more than ready to lose her maidenhead on a rugged Scottish hillside. Anything, so long as he didn't stop touching her. The more cautious creature who had held sway all her life reminded her that this was an experiment. Now she'd satisfied her original question, it was time to stop.

She'd wanted to know what a kiss was like. More, she'd wanted to know if she enjoyed Hamish's kisses. It turned out that kissing was a splendid pastime, especially when her husband did it. This was the best experiment she'd ever conducted.

"Hamish," she said in a breathy voice that bore no resemblance to her throaty murmur only moments ago.

"Hmm?" He kissed her behind the ear. For a second, she was tempted to consign prudence to perdition. His thumb idly brushed her nipple and even through her shift, the effect was shattering.

"Hamish..." She heard failing will in the quivering sound.

"Yes?" He nipped at her ear lobe. "May I take down your hair? I love your hair."

She knew he did. She knew now how close he'd come to kissing her during those charged moments in the library at Bloomsbury. "That's not sensible."

"Sensible can go to blazes," he muttered against her neck.

She really shouldn't, but she tilted her head to give him greater access. "You don't mean that," she said with no conviction whatsoever.

"By God, I do."

It seemed that if she intended to bring this seduction to a halt, the first move was up to her. But, oh, what regret burdened her heart as she strove to bolster legs that had turned to jelly.

"You're going to let sensible win." He raised his head and stared down at her.

His unconcealed disappointment made her exult. She hadn't only learned how it felt to kiss a man. She'd discovered how it felt when a man wanted her to the edge of desperation.

Emily had never thought of herself as a girl who could make a man shake with need. Yet Hamish, handsome, clever, worldly Hamish, was completely at her mercy.

How astonishing. *How...delicious.*

"I am." Regret didn't only weigh down her heart. It weighed down her answer, too. "This was meant to be a kiss, and only a kiss."

In the moonlight, she caught the flash of his straight white teeth when he smiled. As the tension eased, she breathed a sigh of relief. He meant to abide by his word and let her set the pace.

At that moment, Emily realized with harrowing clarity that somewhere in all their topsy-turvy dealings, somewhere since that chaotic night at Pascoe Place, she'd fallen in love with her husband.

Oh, no, this promised to be a disaster. She had absolutely no idea what to do with this irresistible, uninvited, all-encompassing love. Because even if she became Hamish's wife in every sense – and it was inevitable that she'd end up sharing his bed – love was a step too far. They'd spent most of their time together squabbling. This new concord might not last. In fact, it was likely that it wouldn't.

"What is it, Emily?" He didn't sound like the man who'd been lost to pleasure such a short while ago.

Oh, dear, she forgot how perceptive he was. Was she capable of hiding her love from him? Could she bear for him to feel sorry for her? When he said he cared, did that mean he could come to love her?

One thing she did know – tonight's revelations were so fresh, so powerful, she needed time to consider them before she took any action.

"Nothing." She winced at the faint sharpness. She'd like to think that their old combative relationship was gone forever, but so many years of quarreling couldn't disappear without a trace.

He frowned, but she couldn't read his expression. Curse this moonlight. It hid as much as it revealed.

"I didn't frighten you, did I? You won't believe me, but I came out here with good intentions. Once we started, I lost my head. You're..."

He spread his hands, and she realized that even with his unexpected poetic bent, he couldn't find the words for what they'd experienced. The magic they'd summoned was beyond description.

"No, I wasn't frightened. That was a wonderful first kiss, Hamish. Thank you."

He smiled, and her poor aching heart cramped in longing. For renewed physical pleasure, but even more, for him to love her as she loved him.

What would it take to earn the love of a man like Hamish Douglas? Did she have a chance? His mother had thought so. From the first, she'd been convinced that this was a love match. That was back in the days when Emily could barely speak a civil word to her new husband.

Emily straightened her shoulders and told herself she'd do her best to win his heart. She had his desire. It was a good start.

CHAPTER TWENTY-ONE

*H*amish regarded the chaise longue in his study with contempt. The "longue" part of its name was a foul lie. If he lay down, his legs would wave off the end.

He wasn't sleepy anyway. During his time at the tower, he'd become used to staying awake most of the night, so he could stargaze. This morning, he'd tumbled into bed after dawn and slept like a log until Emily turned up on his doorstep.

Emily...

His surfeit of sleep wasn't at the root of his restlessness. Unsatisfied desire was.

He'd imagined he couldn't want his wife more than he did. He'd been wrong. When he'd kissed her, she'd been a wonder, sweet and passionate and more responsive than any woman he'd known. The instant he took her into his arms, good intentions went up in smoke. One taste of those lush lips, and he drowned in carnal hunger. When she called a halt to an encounter that rapidly spiraled out of control, he'd been an inch from tossing her down on the ground and seeking his pleasure.

Once his brain returned to working order, he was grateful that she'd stopped him. For her first time, she deserved better than a quick tumble in the open air. And his pride insisted that she came to him, fully aware of what she did. His turbulent past with Emily had beaten down his arrogance. He'd give half his fortune to hear her admit she wanted him. If she placed no more conditions on their union, he'd hand over the other half without a qualm.

He was too conscious that he was a mere floor above her. If he lay down in this room, he'd only stew in his frustration. So he did what he'd done every fine night since he'd holed up in this tower, hoping to heal the scars that his failed marriage had scored into his soul. He took off his shoes, picked up a lantern, collected a notebook, and climbed to the roof. While all the time, his animal self shrieked that he was heading in the wrong direction.

For once, the beauties of the night sky failed to hold Hamish's attention. He couldn't shift his mind from the softness of Emily's lips, her salty honey taste, the beguiling little sounds she made as he kissed her. His hand didn't want to grip a pen and record his observations. It wanted to cup Emily's luscious breast and shape the perfect curve of her rump. He didn't want to focus his mind on planetary orbits. He wanted to lose it in the delights of seducing his wife.

After an unproductive hour, he released a weighty sigh and turned away from his telescope. The only stars he could see tonight were the ones he'd found in Emily's eyes. He'd kissed her with lingering enjoyment before he abandoned her to her solitary bed, and she'd looked at him as if he set the sun in the heavens.

Only as he stood did he notice that he wasn't alone under this glorious clear sky. "Emily…"

She perched on the parapet near the steps, wearing something dark. As she rose and ventured toward him, he realized that she'd put on one of his jackets. She must have one of his shirts on under that. A line of pale material showed beneath the black.

He bit back a groan. The shirt covered her to her knees and revealed the sweetest calves and ankles he'd ever seen. Her luxuriant dark hair was loose and tumbled around her shoulders. The lantern's frail light turned her into a creature of mystery and enchantment.

"I couldn't sleep," she said softly.

"Neither could I."

She might trust him, but when she came to him half-naked in the middle of the night, she tested his willpower to breaking. If the angels had a scrap of mercy, she'd stay where she was, well out of reach.

The angels weren't feeling in a generous mood. Emily approached, to stop an arm's length away. Hamish braced as if for a blow and told himself that he'd lived for eleven long months without claiming her. What was one more night of longing? Or even a hundred?

Except her presence made abstinence bite so much deeper. When she was a whole country away, he'd endured his futile desire because he had no choice. With only a pace separating them, it became impossible to keep his hands off her.

But Hamish was horribly aware that so close to achieving his goal, he was at the greatest risk of losing everything. If he broke her trust, if he pushed her beyond what she was willing to give, if he frightened her with the magnitude of his craving, she could just as easily hie back to London and consign him to a lifetime of loneliness. So while every cell in his body urged him to seize her and carry her downstairs to the empty bed, he kept his hands by his sides.

"What are you working on?"

How to woo a skittish wife. "I might have found a new moon for Saturn."

He sounded brusque. Hamish didn't want to discuss heavenly bodies, when the only heavenly body he gave a rat's arse about was Emily's.

"Hamish, that's wonderful."

He sucked in a breath and forced the curtness from his tone. "I'm still confirming my observations. It's an odd bugger – a strange shape and the orbit is unlike anything I've ever seen."

Interest sharpened her expression. "Show me."

"Emily..."

"What?"

"You're not...dressed."

She couldn't be that ingenuous. Surely she knew that it was cruel to flaunt herself like this. Girls were always wrapped up in layers of undergarments. Even unworldly creatures like Emily Baylor learned in the nursery that the sight of too much feminine flesh turned men into beasts.

He couldn't read her expression. Blame it on the lamplight. Blame it on the fact that he was going insane.

"I'm not cold."

Nor, God damn it, was he. He ground his teeth until they hurt and pulled out a stool. "Then help yourself."

He struggled to ignore how the jacket parted down the front and the hem of his shirt rode up as she settled in the place where he'd devoted so many lonely nights to staring at the skies. He also failed to ignore the jiggle of her breasts as she wriggled around to find a comfortable angle for the telescope. To facilitate his observations, he had the lamp turned down low, but it still revealed far too much of his beautiful wife.

She was going to kill him stone dead. And just as he was on the verge of a major scientific breakthrough, too. He was surprised steam didn't come out of his ears, he was so hot for her.

"I can't..." she murmured.

For pity's sake, she really would kill him. He set his jaw until it threatened to crack and leaned in to help with the focusing. He caught a drift of her jasmine scent, always alluring, doubly alluring since he'd kissed her and tasted her skin and glimpsed the passion locked inside her luscious body.

"Ah," she said in satisfaction.

"Can you see Virgo?"

Most girls – most people – would have no idea where to look, but Emily was Sir John Baylor's daughter. She'd known how to find the constellations before she could read. "Yes."

"Look west. It's small. Tiny really. Just a pinprick of light. It could be a distant star, but it acts like a moon."

While she scanned the sky, he kept silent.

"I don't..." Then she gave a glad cry. "I see it."

"I need to do a lot more work before I'm ready to present my findings."

"But how marvelous." She turned her head. "Congratulations."

He was so close, her breath was warm on his cheek when she spoke. If he shifted an inch, he could kiss her. Every muscle went taut as he imagined taking her in his arms again.

Blast it, he didn't dare kiss her. After their kisses, it had nearly broken him to relinquish her to a chaste bed. He jerked away and only came to a panting standstill halfway across the roof.

Even that wasn't enough. His shoulders slumped, and his hands fisted so tight that his nails dug into his palms. He was bloody grateful when Emily went back to observing the sky.

Don't balls this up, Hamish. You're close to getting what you want. But you can still lose it all.

It had been bad enough thinking he'd lost it all, when he'd been convinced he never had a chance of gaining it. The prospect of losing it all when he teetered on the brink of winning was too agonizing to contemplate.

He stared up. From the moment he was old enough to understand that there were worlds upon worlds above him, he'd found peace pondering the skies. Tonight his earthly troubles were too overwhelming for those twinkling lights in the heavens to offer any solace.

"This is a wonderful telescope."

He told himself to act like a civilized man. "It's based on Herschel's forty-foot reflecting telescope."

"But only a quarter of the length. Yet it gives such a clear image."

"I reconfigured the mirrors. I didn't have room up here for either a forty-foot telescope or that huge ungainly stand he had to build for it in Slough." William Herschel, who had discovered the planet Uranus late last century, had always been his hero.

"It's brilliant. No wonder you're doing such good work here."

"I'll take you through what I've done, if you like." Few people in the world would be able to follow the course of his investigations. He was fortunate that his wife was among those few. He hadn't only missed Emily's physical presence. He'd missed sharing his work with her.

"I'd like that." She stood up. "Now?"

Now? When she was only half-covered and he could still taste her kisses? Not bloody likely.

"Aren't you tired after all that travel?" he asked with a hint of desperation.

"Yes."

"Then wouldn't you like to go to bed?" He closed his eyes in dismay at his lamentable phrasing. He rushed on. "I spent most of the day asleep. You didn't."

"I'm...keyed up."

Hell, Hamish could write a thesis on feeling keyed up. "Let's go downstairs. Some of Bruce Mackenzie's finest might help you to settle."

She smoothed down the coat. He restrained a groan. The material pulled too tight against the body beneath it for his comfort. "What on earth is Bruce Mackenzie's finest?"

He made himself continue and hoped she'd put the hoarseness of his voice down to tiredness. "Whisky. Not entirely legal. The best distiller north of the border lives on the Achnasheen estate, devil take Fergus's good luck. If Fergus feels in charity with me, he sometimes lets me have a bottle or two."

"I'm not sure spirits will—"

"A little bit won't hurt you. And if you're planning on becoming a good Scotswoman, you need to learn to love the water of life."

"The water of life?"

"*Uisge beatha.* It's Gaelic. That's where the word whisky comes from."

A faint smile curved her lips, made her breathtakingly lovely. And breathtakingly approachable, which was the last thing he needed when they were alone together in the middle of nowhere.

"It really is a new world up here. How fascinating." She cast him a searching look. "You're different, too."

Hamish paused in the act of picking up the lantern. His notebook could stay where it was. Tonight, it contained no new observations. "Oh?"

Emily watched him with that steady, perceptive gaze that always made him feel like she cut to his soul. As usual, it made him uncomfortable. It was worse tonight when his soul was crammed with a thousand depraved intentions.

"Yes. You seem more...yourself, more true to Hamish Douglas than the man I knew in London."

He shifted under her assessing stare. "Go on with you, lass. It's just the romance of the hills and the stars, and sleeping in a tower that the Vikings built."

"The Vikings? So you're part Norse."

"Aye, a lot of the people in the glen are. There were longboats up and down this coast."

A pleased smile curved her lips. "That's how I've always thought of you, you know. As a fearless Viking. No wonder you never fitted in with those pale, skinny Londoners. I thought it was my imagination, but it wasn't. You come from a long line of marauding warriors."

Hamish bit back an offer to show her just how marauding he could be. "You really have fallen for the romantic Highlands."

He waited for her to deny it, to remind him she was a cool-headed scientist just as much as he was. If William Herschel was his hero, Herschel's brilliant sister Caroline, with a string of scientific achievements in her own right, had always inspired Emily. Caroline Herschel offered Emily a model for a female who made her mark in the world of the intellect.

That mysterious smile still flickered across Emily's face. "You know, you might be right."

Heaven save him. He needed to get off this rooftop. He needed to cover up his wife – preferably in a suit of armor. He needed to jump into the burn and cool off before he did something he was sure to regret.

With a sigh, he trudged toward the steps. "Let's get you a wee dram then put you to bed."

He stamped downstairs, once he checked that she followed. Sending Big Billy back to Lyon House had been a mad, reckless act. The peel tower was too small, when it came to Emily trusting him with her chastity.

Hamish began to wonder whether the whole wide damned world was too small, when it came to keeping his hands off his delectable wife.

CHAPTER TWENTY-TWO

*E*mily picked her way down to the study and paused in the doorway to watch Hamish dig two small glasses and a squat flask from a corner cupboard.

"Are you sure you're not cold?" Hamish asked without looking at her.

"No, I'm fine, thank you." Scotland in early autumn was warm, much more so than she'd expected.

However, she was most definitely suffering an agony of self-consciousness. When she'd prepared for bed, she'd considered sleeping in her crumpled shift. But much more appealing was one of Hamish's clean white shirts, smelling of herbal soap and mown grass and sea salt – and the tiniest, most intriguing hint of him.

After those incendiary kisses in the moonlight, she hadn't been able to sleep. Her blood fizzed like champagne shaken inside the bottle, and a needy restlessness made her feel like ants crawled over her skin.

It wasn't just her body that was in a ferment. Her heart brimmed with the overwhelming love she'd only just acknowledged.

Was falling in love with her fascinating husband a blessing or the worst calamity that could befall her? For ten years, she and Hamish had fought each other to a standstill. If anyone had suggested she was likely to fall in love with her father's swaggering protégé, she'd have laughed her head off. Yet now she ached for him to take her in his arms and tell her that he loved her, too.

Emily was accounted a clever woman, but she found herself conflicted and confused. This dilemma was beyond the powers of science or mathematics to solve. Unless the equation really was as simple as one and one made two.

Troubled and unhappy – yet, strangely happy too, because love was a gift, whether returned or not – she'd stretched out on a bed that smelled like Hamish's shirt. Trying to quiet the turmoil in her heart, she told herself that tomorrow, she'd make some decisions.

Then all she did was lie there, tired, mentally alert, *physically*...

Physically, every fiber of her body insisted that it was wrong to be alone.

Hamish had touched her with desire. But at least as important, they'd spoken like intimates. Joy had flowered in her soul when he'd trusted her enough to confide in her. There had been occasions tonight when he'd felt like her dearest friend. Could she rely on this surprising, erratic harmony that sprang up between them here in this magical place?

She wished to heaven she'd taken the trouble years ago to talk to him properly. Tonight's revelations had shown her that her husband was a million miles away from the impervious rock of arrogance she'd once believed him.

At last Emily came to know him as someone other than a rival. Because she was ashamed to admit that he had been a rival, both intellectually and for her father's affection. She'd now grown up enough to see that jealousy rather than pique had inspired a large part of her hostility toward her father's favorite pupil.

She loved Hamish's mind. His intelligence left her in awe. But she began to wonder if perhaps his heart was even bigger than his extraordinary brain. If that was the case, it was time to clear away the obstacles standing between them and seek a genuine closeness.

She burned to tell him that she wanted him, too, that she was tired of being a virgin bride. If he kissed her the way he had tonight, he could do whatever he liked to her.

But when she sought him out, her courage failed. The words inviting him to take her refused to emerge from her lips. Some cowardly element hoped that when she showed up half-naked, he'd take the decision away from her.

He hadn't, curse him. She should have known that he wouldn't. He had too much honor. At last, she acknowledged what a fundamentally good man Hamish was.

Sometimes, like now, she wished he wasn't quite so good.

"Here." He passed her a glass half-full of golden liquor. "This should help you sleep. *Slainte mhath.*"

"What?"

"It means 'your health.'"

"Slong chee..."

He laughed softly. "Speak the English, lassie. Gaelic takes a bit of wrapping the tongue around."

Inevitably that made her remember how his tongue had danced inside her mouth. That had seemed such a bizarre thing for him to do, yet in practice it had been wonderful. That disturbing yearning surged again, and she shifted from one bare foot to the other.

"Cheers," she mumbled and took a gulp of the whisky.

Aromatic fumes filled her head and made her cough. She was barely aware of Hamish taking her glass and pushing her into a seat.

"Emily, are you all right?"

Sucking in a broken breath only made her cough again. She stared up at him out of watery eyes and forced a response past her burning throat. "You drink that for pleasure?"

He went down on his haunches in front of her, resting one hand on her shoulder. "It's probably an acquired taste."

"Probably?"

"Have a drink of water. It might help."

She hadn't realized he held a glass of water in his other hand. When he lifted it to her lips, she gulped down a mouthful. "Bruce Mackenzie is a poisoner," she said, her voice still raw after her coughing fit.

"Never tell him that," Hamish said with theatrical horror. "He's an artist and deuced sensitive."

She gave a cracked laugh. "I'll remember that."

To her regret, Hamish stood and stepped away. "More water?"

"No, thank you."

"More whisky?"

"You're so funny."

He stared down at her with that special smile that always made her heart perform somersaults. At least now she knew why. A dizzying wave of longing flooded her. "Hamish…" she began, but he spoke over her.

"You really should go to bed. You'll be tired in the morning."

"What about you?"

"I'll sleep now, too."

Her burgeoning hopes suffered a setback. If he could sleep, her presence mustn't disturb him anywhere near as much as his disturbed her. She watched him pick up his glass and empty it in one swallow. Although why anyone would want to drink that vile brew, she had no idea.

"The chaise longue is too short." She spoke before cowardice silenced her again. "Why not sleep downstairs with me?"

He turned to her with a stern expression. "Emily, that's not a good idea."

Yes, it was. It was the best idea she'd had in years. "We're married."

He sighed. Which wasn't exactly the response that she'd expected when she offered him a place in her bed. "Very well."

Feeling sick with nerves, she preceded him down to the bedroom. She took off his coat and crossed to the big bed to slide between crisp white sheets. Hamish set down the lamp he carried and blew it out.

"You sleep naked, don't you?" she asked through the darkness.

"Usually." There was a thorny pause. "Not tonight."

The bed sagged as he lay down and Emily braced for him to reach for her. After their kisses, she'd hoped that lying beside him might feel more natural. After their kisses, she'd hoped that he'd be on fire to possess her.

"Good night, Emily," he said gruffly, staying as far away from her as he could.

"Good night, Hamish," she whispered. Had she come so far only to make an utter fool of herself at the end?

Hamish lay as still as a block of wood. He feared if he moved, he'd move in Emily's direction. If he moved in her direction, all would be lost.

He felt like he was stretched on the rack. Why the hell had he agreed to sleep beside her? Although precious little sleeping would take place, he already knew.

He'd understood it was a terrible idea the moment he agreed, but he loathed the idea of leaving her, even for the few hours left of this endless night. After all these months of missing her like the very devil, he'd been so bloody desperate for her company. But he hadn't factored in how her closeness would torment him.

Now he knew how it felt to kiss her.

Now he knew that she responded to him.

Now he only needed to move his hand a few inches to touch her.

He should have stayed on the damned roof.

Her scent enveloped him, set his blood clamoring. He didn't need to see her. The image of Emily a mere shirt away from naked was etched on his aching eyeballs.

Closing his eyes, he fisted his hands in the sheets and prayed for control.

He didn't know how long he lay unmoving and burning with desire before she spoke. It was a surprise he could hear anything at all over the pounding pulse in his ears.

"Hamish?"

"Yes?" he whispered.

The mattress dipped as she rolled in his direction. "Will you...touch me?"

Hell's bells. His heart crashed against his ribs so hard, he feared they might crack.

He didn't trust himself next to her any longer. He rolled out of bed and fiddled with the lamp. "What in Hades did you say?"

The answer emerged in jerky fits and starts. "I want you to touch me. I want you to kiss me."

"Emily, if I touch you, you know what's going to happen," he said wearily. He broke off to swear at the uncooperative bloody lamp. "Light, you blasted useless contraption."

Finally a glow filled the room, enough for him to see his wife. She was sitting up against the heaped pillows, the sheet pulled up to her waist. Her magnificent hair cascaded about her, and her eyes were dark with uncertainty and what just might be longing. His gut twisted into a knot of ravenous hunger.

"I know what I hope is going to happen."

He hardly heard her. Instead his attention focused on the way her breasts swelled against soft white linen. "You wear that dashed shirt better than I do."

"Hamish, did you hear me?" Impatience drew her brows together. "I'm saying yes."

His breath hitched, and he froze where he was as he struggled to make sense of what she said. Through his bewildered astonishment, a fragile seedling of hope unfurled at last.

Had his beautiful Emily consented to be his? After all the cross purposes and misunderstandings, did they finally see their way clear?

He swallowed and warned himself to be cautious. She wasn't his first lover, but he was painfully aware that she was the first lover to mean so much. He'd already made so many mistakes with her. He had to be sure this wasn't one more.

"You told me that you needed time to decide." He forced himself to look into that unforgettable face. Why had it taken him so long to understand that this was a face he'd happily look at for the rest of his days?

She was rosy with embarrassment. "Your kisses helped me to decide. It's time. It's past time. I want us to be a real couple. I want a true marriage, with both of us living together, not you in Scotland and me in London."

He still didn't move. "You won't change your mind?"

"I'm steadfast once I commit to something, Hamish. You know that."

"And you're sure now?"

A faint smile lifted her lips, and she indicated the space beside her. "Are you waiting for an engraved invitation to come through the mail?"

Dear God above, what the hell was wrong with him? And what the hell was he doing over here, when he could be lying beside her?

Elation swelled inside him, swept him out into a whirlpool of hot anticipation. In one huge stride, he landed back in the bed.

CHAPTER TWENTY-THREE

*E*mily was almost sorry Hamish lit the lamp. The determination in his face sent a jagged thrill through her, half-panic, half-excitement. Then he came back to bed, and there was no time for second thoughts or fear or, heaven help her, retreat. He was kissing her wildly, madly, rapaciously, as if he starved for her. She hadn't liked the taste of the whisky when she'd tried it. On Hamish's lips, it turned into smoky nectar.

She imagined she'd already learned about kissing, but this storm of passion proved she had no idea. As his big body crushed her into the mattress, she sank down and wrapped her arms around him. His arousal, hard and heavy against her belly, made all her secret places clench in wicked anticipation.

An eternity of heat and hunger later, he wrenched far enough away to speak. "You make me so happy, Emily."

He didn't sound like the domineering Scot who always set up her hackles. He sounded vulnerable and desperate. As she gazed into his face, she understood that he had indeed longed for her. He'd been as lonely without her as she'd been without him.

One trembling hand rose to his cheek, feeling new whiskers scrape under her palm. A tenderness so piercing it was painful filled her and briefly swamped her physical excitement.

"You make me happy, too, Hamish," she murmured. He was infuriating and stubborn, and often wrongheaded. But he was also clever and principled and stalwart in his affections.

And she loved him more than she loved anyone else in the world.

At this profound moment, it didn't even matter that he didn't love her. She'd been married for almost a year. It was past time that she knew her husband's body.

The feverish urgency drained from his blue eyes, replaced by a glow that only heightened her poignant emotion. He shifted until they lay facing each other. He took her hand in his strong, capable grip. "I swear I'll always do my best for you, Emily. You have all my loyalty."

His rich bass voice was even deeper than usual. He spoke as if he made a sacred vow. Tears pricked at her eyes, not just because of his words but because of his intense expression. This wasn't a mere meeting of bodies, powerful as that promised to be, but something much more significant. A matter of souls. For him as well as her.

"You have my loyalty, too, Hamish. Always." *You have my love.*

He dipped his head and kissed her with such reverence, her heart swelled and threatened to break free. She answered with all the unspoken love she'd only just recognized. For a space, sweetness reigned, before inevitably passion surged once more.

Hamish was panting when he drew away. So was she.

She lay silent, overcome by her tumultuous feelings, while he rose to his knees and tugged his shirt over his head. Twice before, she'd seen him without a shirt, but his male magnificence trapped the breath in her throat just like the first time.

With an unsteady hand, she smoothed a path across one firm pectoral. The whorls of hair beneath her palm were soft, and his skin radiated heat. He closed his eyes and made a deep sound in his throat like a purr.

Her lion of Glen Lyon. She smiled as she lifted her hand away.

He smiled back and waved toward the crumpled shirt she wore. "Your turn."

Trembling, she shifted up and drew the shirt over her head, casting it to the floor. She lowered her eyes, not sure she was ready to see his reaction. She'd never been naked in front of a man. Hamish's stare felt like a physical force.

She waited for him to catch her up in his arms, but he didn't touch her. After a few seconds, she dared to meet his gaze. The appreciation in his eyes warmed her skin, and she found the courage to straighten her spine and endure his wondering attention.

"You're lovelier than a clear night sky," he said softly.

With a sigh of purely feminine pleasure, she curled her toes into the sheet beneath her. For the first time in her life, Emily felt genuinely beautiful. She basked in the waves of desire radiating off him.

Hamish caught her around the waist and hauled her up for a deep kiss that felt like the promise of pleasure to come. He started to explore her body, kissing her nose and her chin and her cheeks while his hands discovered her curves. Sensation after sensation rioted through her. She shivered and twisted beneath his touch, encouraging more daring forays. His lips trailed delight down her neck, then ventured lower until he took one pearled nipple into his mouth.

She cried out in startled pleasure when his tongue flicked against the aching point, then again when he drew on her. Arousal rushed through her and settled as a simmering weight in the pit of her stomach. She arched up in shameless appeal for more and buried her hands in the heavy silk of his hair. When his fingers teased her other breast, she moaned and gripped his hair harder.

"I love your hair," she gasped, as it tumbled over her hands. *I love you.*

He gave an unsteady laugh against her breast.

"Ooh," she said, as that sent a new sensation to join the others shooting through her. The brush of his breath on her flesh gave her goosebumps.

He raised his head. "I look like a vagabond."

The glittering amusement in his eyes made her smile back. She smoothed the tumble of rich gold hair away from his face. "You do indeed. If the London girls saw you now, they'd swoon."

"Devil take the London girls. There's only one girl I'm interested in, and she's much closer than London."

That was true. Wasn't she lucky? Her smile widened. "I'm glad I came to find you."

"So am I," he said fervently.

"I'm sorry I made you wait so long."

His expression turned serious. "Emily, we weren't ready to come together when we married. I needed to know you. You needed to know me."

"There's still so much to discover."

His answer emerged on a husky note. "You're my constellations and my galaxies, darling. You're as lovely as any star in the heavens. You're as mysterious and spectacular as the stellar clouds. Of course there's more to discover. A mere lifetime won't be enough to reveal your secrets."

She'd called him a poet. She'd had no idea. His words turned her into a puddle of syrup. "Oh, Hamish..."

"What a voyage awaits us, my beautiful wife. We set out with joyful hearts."

"That's..." She swallowed to shift the giant boulder of emotion blocking her throat. "That's a good start."

He kissed her, one of those long, voracious kisses that made her quake with yearning. But beneath the passion, tenderness lingered. Hamish began to kiss her stomach then inched lower to the feathery, dark brown curls hiding her mound. When his mouth brushed her there, shock banished the daze of pleasure.

"Hamish!" She wriggled away.

For the first time since he'd started this exquisite torture, she tried to cover herself. Her legs had eased apart, and he must be able to see her...*there*.

"I promised you joy." He caught her fluttering hand and brought it to his lips for a kiss. "Let me show you."

She stared into intent blue eyes the color of a midnight sky, and shook her head as much in puzzlement as in denial. "Down there?"

A faint smile lifted his lips. "Down there."

"It seems...strange."

His hold tightened. "To a virginal maiden such as yourself, Lady Glen Lyon, much of what we do together will seem strange. At least at first."

His teasing didn't ease her uncertainty, although the warmth in his eyes made her feel all shimmery inside. "Perhaps we should wait."

"Is this Emily Baylor, the fearless seeker after scientific truth?"

"This isn't like plotting a planet's orbit."

"It's a chance to discover something new."

Without question. But she shook her head. "Would you mind if we don't do that tonight?"

"I want to give you pleasure. I want you to feel free to enjoy the magic we make together." His voice lowered into persuasion. "I want you to trust me."

Helplessly she stared at him. How could she say no to that? Gingerly she lay down and stared up at the plaster ceiling. "I trust you."

He kissed her again. "I can't tell you what that means, Emily."

She braced for his lips to touch her cleft, but he devoted his attention to her breasts. She'd feared all that lovely pleasure might be lost, but under his skilled hands, she was soon squirming again. When he tugged at her nipples, heat sizzled all the way to that place between her legs, a place that suddenly seemed so very empty.

He stroked her as if he created her anew with every caress. No more lonely, scholarly, prickly Emily Baylor. Instead she was queen of a new, sensual world.

So this time, when his hands moved to her thighs and gently parted them, she didn't protest. He traced tormenting circles over her stomach and legs. With every touch, that emptiness at her core became more acute. As she tilted her hips toward him, an incoherent grumble of frustration escaped her.

Finally, his hand traced the hot, wet folds of her sex, and she cried out in pleasure and surprise. When his attention focused on one place in particular, violent sensation crashed down over her. She shuddered and cried out and all her muscles clenched into flaring bliss. Her tumultuous reaction left her shaking and gasping.

When she came back to earth, her nails dug into his brawny forearms and her legs sprawled across the sheets. Modesty became so irrelevant that she had no idea why she'd ever asked him to stop.

"Hamish, what on earth was that?" she asked breathlessly, trying to straighten cramped fingers.

He smiled at her. "That, my darling, was the first of many climaxes. Or at least I hope so."

"Climax?"

"Didn't it feel like a climax?"

"It felt like... It felt like a mountainside of pleasure slid down to bury me. And you can stop looking so smug."

"But I feel smug. Would you like to do it again?"

She swallowed to shift a swirling mixture of trepidation and excitement. "Again?"

"And again and again."

"I'm not sure I'll survive."

The gentle mockery in his laugh made her want to snuggle closer. "I'll save you if you're in danger."

When she lifted her hands from his arms, she was horrified to see the crescent marks of her fingernails on his golden skin. "I think you're the one in danger."

He glanced at the scratches. "Wounds of honor."

His grandiloquence made her giggle. "Wounds of lust, more like."

The tremulous, otherworldly feeling receded, but the glow lingered. What an extraordinary experience. Emily felt like he'd combed out all her bones and laid them out in line under the sun.

Except if Hamish was right, it wasn't so extraordinary at all and he could make it happen again. How...*marvelous.*

Confusion stirred under her anticipation. "I don't understand what just happened to me."

He stretched out on his side and crooked one elbow so he could rest his head on his hand. Those bright blue eyes surveyed her with unmistakable approval. "You want me to explain what I did?"

"No." Except while she thought about it, his capacity for drawing such reactions from her body was interesting. She would like to know more. "Well, yes. But not now."

"Then what don't you understand, you absurd miracle of a woman?"

That melting feeling was back. "Oh, Hamish..." she whispered. "How am I meant to put two words together when you say such wonderful things to me?"

He reached out to play with her tangled brown hair. "Do you like it?"

"You know I do."

More than his astonishing words, the affection in his tone launched her heart on a dizzying swoop. She struggled to remind herself that only one person in this bed was in love, and it wasn't her husband. But clinging to that thought was impossible when Hamish stared at her as if she was another new comet for him to discover.

Another comet? An entirely new galaxy.

"Stop thinking so hard. I've never taken a scientific lady to bed before. I had no idea of the challenges she'd present."

"Too many challenges?"

"I'm up to them," he said, with another of those gravelly laughs that made her bones dissolve with yearning.

He caught a handful of her hair in his fist and leaned in to kiss her again. His lips soothed her uncertainty, but not her curiosity. In fact, it was his...*upness* that troubled her.

"You said you wanted me," she said against his lips.

He frowned as he lifted his head. "Good God, you can't doubt that."

"I'm beginning to."

He sat up and stared at her in consternation. "What the devil..."

Explaining this was difficult, not least because she still trembled after those extraordinary moments when she'd flown free of the world's bounds. Her explanation emerged in a breathless rush.

"I thought you'd be in a hurry. I thought there would only be...hurry." She scowled as she sat up, clutching the sheet to her bosom. "Now you're trying not to laugh at me."

"Actually I think we're both rather funny."

"Why? What am I meant to think? You haven't even taken off your kilt."

"I was trying not to frighten you." She saw he, too, struggled for words. "This is your first time with a man. I want it to be good for you, so I'm—"

"Preparing the ground?"

This time he did laugh, although with a bashful note that made her susceptible heart contract with adoration. "If you like. I'm...big all over, you see."

He certainly was. She remembered his rampant virility from their chaotic wedding night. When she felt bereft without him, she'd often let her mind dwell on the image as a naughty pleasure. Now when she thought about that hefty organ invading her body, she began to see the problem. "You're saying you won't fit?"

Hamish started to blush. "I'm saying things might be somewhat painful, at least the first time. So I'm trying to make you as...relaxed as possible first."

"When you touch me, it's not relaxing," she said emphatically.

"It's not?"

"No, it's exciting and stirring and—"

He groaned and closed his eyes. "Stop, Emily. Or you'll get your rushed coupling after all."

As she stared at him sitting beside her, she realized that caught up in her unprecedented responses, she'd missed the signs of how he was reacting. He wasn't nearly as at ease as she'd thought. Tension bunched in those broad shoulders, and the angle of his masterful jaw told her he fought to rein himself in. "You're being...kind again."

Another agonized groan and this time, she heard the strain behind the sound. "Don't you believe a word of it. It's all self-serving. I don't want you deciding once is enough."

She placed her hand flat on his chest, where his heart thundered. "Hamish, I hate to see you suffer. I'm sure I can cope with—"

His large, warm hand covered hers. "I don't want you merely coping. I want you transported with ecstasy."

A smile curved her lips. "That sounds lovely."

"It is." He stared into her eyes as if he plumbed every corner of her soul. "At least it can be."

"Show me." Then she spoke the words she'd never said before. "I want you, Hamish."

Brilliant excitement flared in his features, made his golden beauty blaze like lightning. Her wayward heart upended into a dizzying tumble of trepidation and desire as he swept away the sheet and came down over her. "Then let's be on our way, lassie."

CHAPTER TWENTY-FOUR

hrough a turbulent storm of kisses and caresses, Hamish managed to unwrap his kilt. It was a damn sight easier than stripping off his English clothes, thank God. Although he resented even those few seconds, because they stopped him from kissing Emily.

She wanted him. He'd known it when she responded so ardently to his seduction, but hearing her speak the words was a dream fulfilled.

He stroked the delicate petals of her sex, finding the center of her pleasure and teasing her until she was gasping and he felt the liquid rush of her arousal. How he loved the way her face changed, when she gave herself up to delight. She closed her eyes and parted her lips and released a long voluptuous sigh of surrender. That sound of female rapture made him feel like a king.

While she still trembled in the afterglow, he settled between her legs, poised to join his body to hers. With exquisite care, he edged forward, watching her face all the time. When a faint wince tightened her expression, he made himself stop.

"Are you all right, Emily?" he asked in a raw tone.

She opened her eyes and summoned a smile. Her hands clenched hard on his shoulders. "Don't wait, Hamish. We've waited too long already."

By heaven, that was true.

He kissed her with all the reverence he felt for her. Gradually the stiffness seeped from her body, and he shifted deeper. Then deeper again, until she cried out and dug her fingernails into his skin. Tomorrow, he'd bear her mark. Dear God, he'd bear her mark for the rest of his life, whether the world could see it or not.

To his dismay, he saw a tear trickle from the corner of her eye. He stopped moving, although every atom in his body insisted he push home and claim her. "Emily, I'm sorry. I've hurt you."

"No," she said in a husky voice.

"Liar."

To his surprise, she angled up and kissed him with clumsy but volcanic passion. "It's a little uncomfortable, but not too bad. I feel so...stretched."

Yes, she must. She closed so snug around him. The sensation was glorious – for him, at least.

Emily kissed him again, and he felt her desperate grip as he inched further. With a shaking hand, he reached down and tilted her upward. The change in position drew a guttural sound from her. This time, it wasn't a whimper of pain but a moan of pleasure.

Encouraged, he kept going. As the delicious pressure built, she released another of those beguiling little hums of enjoyment.

She wriggled, and he felt her body loosen in sudden welcome. With a naturalness he would never have expected, he seated himself fully inside her.

"Hamish..." In that soft contralto, his name was a caress.

"My wife." Profound emotion flooded his heart. It vied with this unrivaled physical pleasure for the most powerful experience in his life.

Fergus was right. A wife wasn't like other lassies. Or at least Hamish's wasn't. This connection he formed with Emily beggared previous encounters the way the sun outshone every other object in the solar system.

He rose on his elbows until he could see her face. She was flushed, and her eyes were heavy and dark with arousal, green as forest pools. After his ferocious kisses, her lips were swollen and red.

When he'd taken her, she dug her fingernails into him. Hamish was a barbarian to admit it, but the sting had added extra spice to this first extraordinary connection.

Now she released her frantic clutch on his shoulders and began to stroke him, touching his arms and neck and chest. It was like she discovered him through touch alone, while all the time, her body held him as if she never meant to let him go.

"I had no idea," she murmured. Her hands trembled as she explored his damp skin. "The...closeness is astonishing, isn't it?"

"Sublime." He dipped his head to kiss her. The urge to move became irresistible, but he was reluctant to shatter this radiance. "Does it still hurt?"

"A little. That's part of the pleasure."

"Yes," Hamish said, glad she started to understand.

"You've occupied every inch of me," she said in that same wondering tone. "I don't know where I end and where you begin."

His heart expanded to the point of bursting. "My darling..." he whispered and kissed her again.

Her roaming hands moved up and down his back, tracing his spine and the long muscles over his ribs. Her touch felt like a benediction. Wherever she stroked his skin, she made him whole in a way he'd never felt before.

He started to move and transcendent stillness changed to furious action. As he withdrew and thrust forward again, she made a raw sound of appreciation. Her grip on his back tightened. The next time, she lifted to greet him. He lost himself to the blazing dance of desire.

Emily crossed the barrier first. As her body clenched around him, she cried out on a high pure note that would echo in his ears forever. He held still while she shuddered and convulsed around him.

Not a moment too soon. Keeping himself back as she attained her peak tested his limits. He retreated, the wondrous friction threatening to blow his head off. Then with a mighty roar, he plunged forward and gave everything he was into her keeping.

Emily still soared in the dizzying heights, when she felt the hot spurt of Hamish's seed. Their joining had already spun an intimacy between them that left her reeling. But this moment, when she received his essence, was the most intimate act of all.

He exhaled audibly and rolled to the side. Overwhelmed by all that had happened tonight, she remained flat on her back staring up at the beams on the ceiling. Gradually her breathing eased, her heart steadied, and her mind wafted back to earth after wandering out among the stars. She became aware that she was still naked. So was Hamish. His arm lay along hers, a physical connection to remind her of the more profound physical connection they'd just shared.

The long night drew to an end. A bird started to sing outside. The dawn came early here in Scotland. Already sunlight edged the curtains to compete with the lamplight.

Lying here beside Hamish without a stitch to cover her, she started to feel awkward. She shifted to find the sheet.

"Not yet," Hamish said, his voice more subterranean than she'd ever heard it.

"I thought..." she began, then forgot what she meant to say when he caught her hand in his and brought it to his lips.

"Just lie with me."

She shifted until she could see his profile. The straight, commanding nose and determined chin gave little away. "If you wish."

Then her fleeting unease evaporated as he drew her into his arms, until she lay with her head on his chest and her legs tangled with his. Immediately the closeness returned. She'd feared it might belong purely to the marital act.

"Thank you, Emily." Drowsiness thickened the words, as he dropped a kiss on the crown of her head.

"Thank you, Hamish." *I love you, Hamish.*

She felt tired and stretched and on edge. She wanted to dance and jump and run. She wanted to stay just where she was, resting in her husband's arms in the sweet aftermath. Her body felt strange, as if it didn't belong to her anymore. There was a stickiness between her legs, and her neck and breasts stung where the beginnings of his beard had chafed her skin.

Her mind inevitably drifted back to that explosion of ecstasy. It had been like her earlier climax – thank goodness Hamish had given her a word to describe that flaring moment. But the experience had been longer and more powerful when he'd been inside her. At the end, her pleasure had risen so high, surely she must have rattled the gates of heaven.

She cuddled closer to Hamish and winced as strained muscles made themselves felt when she moved. A climax was a marvelous thing. She hoped Hamish meant to give her another before too long.

And if a climax was a wonderful thing, she began to think a skillful lover for a husband might be even better.

CHAPTER TWENTY-FIVE

They stayed in the peel tower for a week, enjoying a long-delayed honeymoon.

Emily became used to plundering Hamish's wardrobe, although the wicked truth was that she spent much more time naked in his bed than she spent dressed in his shirts.

"You've turned me into a lazy sensualist," she said to her husband now as they rode back to Lyon House.

They were making their way along a narrow defile. From her first trip to the tower, she remembered that this track led to a ridge overlooking Lyon House in its pretty valley. She'd ridden up to the tower only seven days ago, yet the Emily who retraced this route was a completely new person.

Hamish turned back in the saddle to give her the flashing smile that sweetened her blood to honey. "You're surely not blaming me."

"I surely am."

"Then I cry unfair. There I was, dedicating every waking hour to the cause of science, when a wild and wanton woman landed on my doorstep and demanded I abandon my studies and put myself at her service."

"That's not how I remember it."

"Damn this pass. It's too narrow."

"What?" She'd drifted into a reverie, reliving some of the decadent things Hamish had done in her service. "Are we in danger?"

He faced forward, his low chuckle carrying back to her. "The only danger is that I want to get off this horse and kiss you."

"That doesn't sound too dangerous."

"It is, if you want to reach Lyon House before nightfall."

Her smile faded, and she dared to voice what troubled her. "Hamish, will we be the same when we get back to civilization?"

He pulled his horse to a stop and turned to face her. "My darling, it won't be the same, but it will be just as good."

She reined her horse to a halt, too. "I know we can't live like castaways on a desert island forever. You're the laird, and you have responsibilities. But I fear in the real world, we'll go back to being hostile strangers." Her voice broke. "I'd hate that."

Her time with Hamish had sparked so many discoveries, not least that now they set aside their defenses, they got along surprisingly well, and not just in bed. So well, that Emily wondered why it had taken her so long to find out what excellent company he was.

He slid to the ground and walked back to her. "Are you really fretting about this, Emily?" Ahead, his mount ambled forward to nibble at some grass sprouting from a cranny.

She struggled to find the words to explain her disquiet. "This last week has been like something from a fairy story."

He grinned at her. "You must have read more exciting fairy stories than I did."

Emily didn't smile. "You know what I mean."

His expression sobered. "Yes, I do. It's felt like time out of mind."

He did understand. "Like we were whisked away to an enchanted kingdom."

To her surprise, he reached up and dragged her down into his arms for a long and passionate kiss that knocked her stylish hat to the ground. By the time he raised his head, she was trembling and breathless.

"Dear Lord above, what was that for?" she asked, unsure if her knees would hold her up.

He remained serious. "That was proof that we carry our enchanted kingdom with us. You and I create the magic. It's nothing to do with where we are."

"Oh," she said, dazzled. "What a lovely thing to say."

He kissed her again, and this time he was smiling when he drew away. "Have faith, Emily. We've started our journey together, and it's going to take us to marvelous places. There might be a few stumbles along the way, but that's all part of the joy of travel."

"When did you become so wise?" She stared up at him in wonder. "I'll swear in London the man I knew was a stubborn blockhead who needed a good thrashing."

"It must be something about Scotland, my love."

His love...

If only that was the case. But he'd already given her so much, it would be churlish to ask for more. "It must be," she said faintly.

Hamish smiled and kissed her again. "Anyway, you'll like Lyon House."

Emily did like Lyon House. The large gray mansion with its tall casement windows was set on a rise overlooking a spectacular sea loch. Hamish told her that he kept a yacht tied up at the quay, and he promised to take her sailing to Mull and Iona and Skye.

Now, the morning after their arrival, her husband showed her around her new home. She'd toured the kitchens and met the staff. She'd heard more stories about Douglas exploits through the centuries than she could keep straight. She'd visited the morning room, two drawing rooms, and an imposing dining room. There had been a pretty little room full of delicate china – Hamish's late grandmother had been an avid collector. They'd wandered through a large conservatory and a glittering ballroom.

But her favorite room downstairs was the well-stocked library with its walls of bookcases and views south across the loch and hills. Or at least she thought it was her favorite. She couldn't be sure, because Hamish had kissed her there and she'd lost all interest in architecture or furnishings.

Upstairs were twelve bedrooms, including a suite for the clan chieftain and his wife. She'd slept there last night, in the clan chieftain's huge four-poster bed, covered in carvings of the Douglas harp and sword emblem.

In truth, she'd done precious little actual sleeping. After the strenuous night, all this marching up and down stairs and along endless corridors made her feel like a nap.

"How are you holding up?" Hamish asked, as they followed yet another corridor.

They were holding hands like sweethearts. He'd touched her all morning, and each contact only made her heart yearn more desperately for his love.

"I had no idea you owned a house the size of Blenheim Palace."

He responded with an appreciative grunt of amusement. "It's not that big."

"Not far off. Please don't let go of my hand. Without you, I'll never find my way to dinner."

"The house is easy enough to navigate. The southern side faces the loch and so do most of the main rooms. The northern side looks across the hills. You'll find your feet."

"In a year or two."

"There's no rush." He released her hand and curled his arm around her waist. "And if you're afraid of getting lost, it gives me an excuse to stay by your side."

"Either that, or I'll have to carry a ball of string like Ariadne so I can retrace my steps."

"Go on with you, lassie. I'm much more fun than a ball of string."

Emily smiled with nostalgic pleasure. "You are at that."

What a fascinating man he was. She thought that she'd known him in London, yet she'd had no idea what he was really like. At the peel tower, she'd imagined that she ventured closer to his true self. And she had. But only now that he guided her around his clan seat with such pride did she start to understand the depths of his generous heart.

And that heart, despite his crisp English accent, was as Scottish as bagpipes.

He turned another corner and brought her into a long, light gallery lined with family portraits.

She paused in front of a large canvas. "It's your whole family."

"It is. Me with my four blasted sisters." His older sisters, Prudence, Charity, and Grace, wore floaty white dresses and posed as the three Graces, their lovely golden hair caught up in the classical style. Elspeth was a baby in her mother's arms. Emily could see how a vigorous young rascal like Hamish might feel smothered, surrounded by so much femininity.

"Sisters you love to death."

"Yes, I do. But when I was a lad, they drove me mad with their tears and tantrums and endless talk about dresses. By the way, that's a devilish becoming dress you're wearing today. Is it new?"

After running around in Hamish's shirts for most of last week, it had felt like an imposition to put on stays and petticoats. She'd compensated by choosing one of her favorite gowns, a pretty calico printed with flowers and peacocks.

"New since you were last in London. I'm afraid I was so annoyed with you for decamping to Scotland and leaving me to face the gossip, I spent every penny of the allowance you made me. Or at least I did, once my mourning period for Papa came to an end. Not to mention that the house in Bloomsbury is looking quite *à la mode*."

"Heaven forfend, my lady, must I sell the family silver?" He dropped his arm from her waist and staggered back, looking overcome. "My dear old father warned me against taking an extravagant bride. The bailiffs will be at the door any minute."

Emily sent him an unimpressed glance, trying not to smile at his nonsense. She'd always known Hamish was charming, but now that he turned that charm on her, she realized quite how devastating he could be to a girl. No wonder the London ladies had been in a flutter over the young Laird of Glen Lyon.

"You're not upset. I can tell."

He laughed and caught her hand up for a quick kiss. Her silly heart performed a somersault, although he'd done much saucier things last night than merely kiss her hand. These constant little caresses kept her in a ferment, both physical and emotional. She wondered if he'd join her for that nap after lunch. She had a yen for him now and didn't want to wait until they retired for the night.

"What's the point of having a pretty wife, if not to show her off?"

"Right answer." She examined the painting in front of her. "How old were you here?"

"About ten. Thomas Lawrence sketched all of us in London, then traveled up here to paint the background. Papa was too busy to leave the War Office and bring the family to Scotland for something as trivial as a portrait. That was the year my parents rented a hunting lodge near Achnasheen for the summer, and Diarmid's family joined us."

"That was the year you met Fergus."

"Yes, he saved my life and gave me a puppy called Blackie. Best damn dog that ever lived. I was twenty-five when he died, and I cried like a lost bairn."

"Oh, Hamish," she said softly, laying her head on his shoulder. When he put his arm around her, her wayward heart staggered like a drunken sailor. She loved the glorious things he did to her in bed — how could she not? But their growing emotional closeness made her soul ache with longing. "You didn't bring Blackie to London?"

"No, he wasn't a dog for the city, although we both pined when we were apart."

She returned her attention to the group portrait. "Your father and mother look happy. I've only seen that rather stern picture of him that your mamma keeps in the dining room in London."

"Yes, they were happy together. Unlike Diarmid's parents who were in continual strife. I remember that holiday at Achnasheen as a paradise of masculine company. Diarmid and Fergus, and nobody nagging me to look at hats in the *Belle Assemblée*. But the adults didn't have nearly so carefree a time of it. Diarmid at twelve was old enough to understand what was going on. I learned later that the holiday was a failed attempt to get my aunt and uncle to reconcile, but I remained oblivious. A ten-year-old boy is pretty blind to emotional undercurrents."

"Poor Diarmid." She'd liked Diarmid. She'd particularly liked Fiona, who had been such a support during her father's last illness.

"Yes. I'm so glad he's found happiness now. He deserves it."

The painting still captivated Emily. This glimpse into the childhood of the man she loved intrigued her. "I'm always astonished at how beautiful your mother was. No wonder she took the beau monde by storm."

"Yes, she was a stunner, wasn't she? Her sister was just as lovely."

"You're a good-looking family. I remember being overawed the first time I saw you all together. It was rather like a mortal daring to set foot on Olympus."

Hamish kissed the top of her head. She was in such a bad way. Whenever he did that, she felt like swooning. "You'll always be my goddess, Emily."

What on earth could she say to that? And the worst of it was that he sounded like he meant it.

She rested in his embrace, before she lifted her head to look down the long narrow room. "I suppose you should show me the rest of this rogues' gallery."

He smiled at her with a hint of devilry. "These musty old daubs can wait."

"They can?"

"Yes. I brought you up here to see Granny Phyllis's cabinet of curiosities."

"She really did have collecting mania, didn't she?" Granny Phyllis was responsible for the priceless porcelain downstairs.

"Mad old bat she was. But she had an eye for a treasure, and we keep the pick of her ferreting in a private room."

Too little sleep clearly affected Emily's intelligence. Only when she entered the small chamber at the end of the gallery and she watched Hamish lock the door behind him did she twig to the significance of the word "private." She subjected her husband to a narrow-eyed stare. "I'm guessing that I won't be doing much art appreciation."

His smile was roguish in the extreme. "I think you're going to be very appreciative."

"That you're set on despoiling me in the middle of the day?"

"I did at the tower." He frowned. "Don't tell me you're shocked. I won't believe it."

When she laughed, the sound was resonant with anticipation. "I was going to suggest we retire to our chambers this afternoon."

"We can do that as well – but it's too far off. I had a fancy to have you on one of the library tables, before I saw the damn gardeners scratching around in the parterre. It was easier to have my wicked way at the tower, by God."

She glanced around the confined space. High windows cast light across shelves of exquisite curios and a wall of miniatures. Her attention focused on the chaise longue in the middle of the floor. It seemed an odd inclusion.

"Did you have that carried in?"

"No. It's been here for years. I suspect my parents worked out that this was a fine place to escape their rambunctious offspring."

She stepped across and sat, her gaze unwavering on her handsome husband. "If it's a family tradition to dally in the cabinet of curiosities, who am I to object?"

"We'll make a Douglas of you yet." Laughing, Hamish came forward and fell to his knees before her. When next he spoke, his voice held no teasing. "Do you trust me yet?"

She frowned. "Given everything we've done together, I must."

"Good." He lifted the frothy skirts of her dress and gently pulled her knees apart. "You're wearing drawers."

Silly to blush. "We're back in civilization now."

Emily had an inkling what he intended to do. Since their first night at the tower, this had felt like unfinished business. In their encounters, he'd used his hand on her but not his mouth. The thought of him kissing her between the legs still struck her as perverse, but she'd progressed a long way beyond the nervous maiden of a week ago.

"Slide your bottom forward to the edge of the seat and keep your legs spread."

"You're going to do...*that*, aren't you?"

She waited for him to mock her mealymouthed phrasing, but his eyes were grave as they met hers. "If you really don't want me to, I won't."

She leaned back on her elbows and widened her legs to fit his imposing shoulders. "You're set upon this course."

"If you agree, yes."

"I can't see how it will give you any pleasure."

His lips quirked, and the sly knowledge in his expression had her shivering with anticipation, whatever her quibbles. "Giving you pleasure gives me pleasure."

"How very...unselfish."

"I told you that you married a prince."

Emily gave a disdainful huff of amusement then subsided into trembling silence as he untied the tapes holding her drawers up.

"Lift your hips for me," he murmured.

She cooperated. He'd seen her secret places before, but this time, something about his deliberately stated intentions awoke all her uncertainties.

Gently he straightened each leg and drew the sheer linen down, teasing her with every inch. Her drawers slipped over silk stockings and pretty pink slippers with their ribbons crossing over her instep and ankles.

He touched one of her pink embroidered garters, tied below her knee. She felt the contact like an earthquake. "Nice."

"Are you going to take off my stockings?" she asked in a shaky voice.

He leaned in to kiss the soft flesh behind her knee, flicking his tongue against her bare skin in a way that made her tremble. "I don't think so."

"What should I do?"

When he spread her legs again, he didn't glance up. Instead he stared at the apex of her thighs. Emily thought she'd overcome her old modesty, but she had difficulty resisting the urge to shield herself from his curiosity.

The strange thing was that while she remained deeply unsure about what was to happen, a whirlpool of arousal agitated her blood. And Hamish had barely touched her yet.

"Lie back and enjoy yourself. I'll do all the hard work."

He usually did all the hard work. When they came together, her inexperience meant she ceded control.

As she lay back at his command, a wicked thought struck her. If Hamish gained such satisfaction from placing his mouth on her sex, could she return the favor? A week ago, the idea of taking his rod into her mouth would have revolted her. At this moment, the notion offered tantalizing possibilities.

The brush of his lips on her inner thigh wrenched her out of her depraved musings. When he ventured a little higher, her womb clenched in longing. She braced for him to kiss her cleft, but he began to stroke her legs and place soft, almost innocent kisses across her thighs and stomach.

Every time his lips skimmed across her skin, a bolt of heat sizzled through her. Those touches weren't innocent at all.

Hamish started to linger on each kiss, varying the sensations until Emily whimpered with need. Sometimes he'd graze his teeth over a sensitive spot. Sometimes he'd give her a soft nip. Sometimes he'd use his tongue.

Her fingers curled into the velvet seat beneath her, as thrill after thrill rocketed through her. Her vision of the pink and white angels painted on the ceiling grew misty. While her body softened into liquid readiness, hunger churned in her belly.

"Hamish, I want you," she gasped, wriggling forward to get closer to that tormenting mouth.

His grip on her thighs tightened. "Soon."

"Now, you brute," she said in a hoarse voice.

He answered her with a nip to the top of her leg. Then he placed his mouth over her and every muscle tightened in immediate reaction.

"Hamish!"

The capacity for speech left her entirely, as he licked her with a luxuriant languor that threatened to hurl her heart from her chest.

"Oh," she shuddered, blindly reaching forward to bury her hands in his soft, long hair. "Oh, yes."

His low growl told her that he was lost in sensual delight. He licked her again, then pushed his tongue inside her. A surge of warmth welcomed him, and Emily gave another incoherent moan of encouragement.

For a long time, he toyed with her, using his mouth to take her to places she'd never been. When he sucked on the pearl of flesh, she raised her hips in astonished pleasure. He sucked again, harder, and she plunged into bliss. She cried out and quaked against his mouth for what felt like an eon.

She'd felt rapture so often before. He'd given her pleasure with his hands and his body. He'd even taught her to pleasure herself and watched with delight as she dissolved into forbidden joy.

Every time was different. Every time she thought that it couldn't get better. Then God help her, it did.

Breathless, she slumped back against the seat, while he lifted his head and smiled at her with unconcealed triumph.

"You smug devil," she said without heat.

CHAPTER TWENTY-SIX

"Can you blame me?"

Emily gave a weary laugh as she struggled up onto her elbows. "No." Her voice lowered to husky sincerity. "That was wonderful, Hamish. Thank you."

"You're welcome." He placed a kiss on her thigh, very near where he'd taken her to paradise. Shifting back, he pulled down her colorful skirt.

With a shock, Emily saw that he meant to leave it there. She sat up and stared at him in consternation. "Aren't you going to…"

"I wanted to show you pleasure." He rose to his feet, towering above her. In this small chamber, his great height was even more noticeable than usual.

"You did." She summoned all her courage and held out her hand. "Now let me give you pleasure."

"You do." His smile was sweet. "Surely you know that."

Those stray thoughts that had tiptoed through her mind returned with a vengeance. "I want to do more."

He went as still as a statue, an arrested look on his face.

She lowered her hand, uncertainty rising anew. After all, she was a novice when it came to dealings between men and women. Beyond the things that she and Hamish had already done, what did she know about pleasing a husband?

Still, she'd launched this ship. She'd sail on aboard it, until she either foundered against the rocks or reached safe harbor. "You always take the lead."

He looked a little disgruntled, and she reminded herself to be careful. She didn't want to hurt his feelings. To think that once she wouldn't have thought Hamish had feelings to hurt.

"That's because—"

"You've done this before. I know. And I appreciate your expertise. When I'm in your arms, you make me feel like the most desirable woman in the world."

His eyes sparked at her declaration. "It's not just technique. It's the two of us together. You make me feel more than I have with any other lover."

Speechless, she stared at him as she struggled to make sense of what he said.

He gave her a rueful smile. "Shocking, I know. But a clever girl like you must have noticed that I'm utterly mad for you."

Cautious happiness seeped through her. Could he be closer to falling in love with her than she'd ever dared to imagine?

Mad for her didn't equal love, but it was a damned sight better than being his inconvenient bride. "I know you've been eager to..."

"I have indeed. That's because I'm quite addicted to you, Emily Douglas. With every day that passes, I only want you more."

Well... Her heart turned into a ball of warm, sticky nectar. Who would have guessed that the bond between them was special for Hamish, too? Certainly not Emily Douglas, although even an innocent would notice his appetite for her. "This isn't what usually happens to you?"

He sighed and ran one hand through his untidy hair. "Devil take it, Emily, I can't think of anything but you. I spend every moment away from bed wanting to carry you back to bed. You've turned me into an utter wreck. I used to be a worthwhile member of society. Those days are gone." He frowned at her, although the glint in his blue eyes belied his intense expression. "Now who's looking smug?"

She stopped trying to contain her smile. "I suppose I must be." She hesitated before she spoke again, although surely there could be no risk in the admission, given what he'd just said. "I'm quite mad about you, too."

I love you, Hamish.

But she backed away from that ultimate confession. Because gratifying as it was to hear how she turned his life topsy-turvy, desire wasn't love.

Could it be the pathway to love?

She was too inexperienced to know. But if she had to formulate a theory, she'd speculate that at last her marriage headed in a positive direction. Which made her more determined than ever to become an equal partner when she and Hamish came together.

For a worldly man who had had far too much feminine attention in his life, he looked ridiculously pleased. "Well, I'll be a Dutchman. Mutual lunacy?"

She couldn't help laughing. "At least it's mutual."

"That's true." He looked thoughtful. "You'd like to make our encounters more mutual?"

Heat stung her cheeks at having to have this conversation, which given what he'd just done to her seemed insane. "I'd like to make you feel the way you make me feel."

He seemed to understand, despite her mixed-up sentence. "I should have known you'd start wanting to order me about."

Once resentment would have honed those words. Now they emerged with an affectionate tolerance that made her want to hug him. "Not always. Just now and again."

"You want to wreak havoc on my innocent body?"

Her lips quirked. "Not so innocent."

He didn't smile back. "You could be right."

She frowned. "I'm not saying I don't like what we've done so far. I love it."

"I never doubted it, darling." He still looked like he made some abstruse calculation in his head. It was a familiar expression. "But you feel like the recipient, not the giver."

"Exactly."

"That's not true by the way. I've never enjoyed a lover more than you."

Another of those excited little jumps of her heart. Another catch of emotion in her throat. "Thank you."

"You're welcome."

"So do you mind if we try something different?"

Hamish spread his hands in surrender while a broad smile covered his face. "Mind? I'll wager I'm the luckiest cove in Scotland."

Hamish watched relief flood Emily's features. She was such an intriguing mixture of confidence and shyness, much more interesting than the prickly, if attractive little termagant he'd once thought her.

Her laugh held a note of surprise. "Really?"

"I'm at your disposal, Lady Glen Lyon. What would you like to do first?"

A wicked smile curled her luscious mouth.

Heat blasted Hamish. Was she thinking of putting that mouth on his prick? That particular fantasy stretched all the way back to his youth, when he'd first noticed that Emily Baylor might be annoying, but she was also deuced pretty.

"Take off your shirt."

He cooperated. She licked her lips, as she conducted a leisurely survey of his body. He groaned. "If you keep looking at me like that, I won't be responsible for the consequences."

"Patience," she murmured, rising from the chaise longue and prowling toward him like a panther on the hunt.

At that moment, he realized how much she'd changed. This was a woman who claimed her right to sensual pleasure. So far he'd called the tune. Emily was right about that. He had a suspicion that after today, that would no longer be the case.

For a week, he'd basked in unrivaled physical satisfaction. He'd relished watching Emily's tentative responses transform to blazing ecstasy. She was perfect in his arms, the most wonderful lover he'd ever known. But this predatory version of his wife set him ablaze with an excitement he'd never felt before. She was dangerous and daring and full of unexpected surprises. He couldn't wait to see what she did next.

What she did next was run her hands over his bare chest with an appreciative languor that turned him as hard as an iron bar. He exhaled in an agony of delight. "You're going to spin this out, aren't you?"

A superior smile hovered around her lips. "You have somewhere you need to be?"

"I'm sure I can spare the time." The last words escaped as a gasp, because she kissed his chest. The heat of her lips on his skin shuddered through him like summer lightning.

She ran her hands up and down his arms. "You're a magnificent figure of a man, you know."

"Thank you." Another groan escaped him, as she flicked her tongue over one nipple then the other. Shaking hands reached for her. "Emily…"

"No." She dodged out of reach. "I want to find out what gives you pleasure. It's…it's a scientific investigation."

Despite his frustration, a laugh escaped. "Even if you kill your subject?"

She kept smiling. "It's in a good cause."

He raised one eyebrow. "You like having me at your mercy."

"Definitely."

"Then go ahead." He set his jaw and told himself he could endure. "Anything to further the sum of human knowledge."

Her smile widened. "I hoped you'd feel like that."

She went back to kissing his chest. He trembled as she dipped her head low and traced a sizzling path down his belly to the belt that cinched his kilt. She moved to his back, scraping her teeth across his skin. He sucked in a deep breath, then released it when she bit him. His cock twitched, and he nearly came there and then.

Her incoherent sounds of pleasure only heightened his arousal. He always relished Emily's unabashed enjoyment of what they did together.

He'd thought her an exciting lover when she followed his lead. Now with her dedicating that impressive brain to his titillation, he wanted to get down on his knees in thanks.

He might yet fall to his knees. Under this slow, thorough seduction, his legs didn't feel too steady.

The tendons of his neck tightened as she nibbled a line across his shoulder. He'd never had a lover take this amount of trouble over him. The close focus was as arousing as the touch of her lips.

Well, almost.

"You're so warm," she murmured into his skin.

Warm? Hell, she had no idea. One stray spark and he'd burst into flames.

"And so large and strong."

"Emily..." Her name was a drawn-out plea to stop tormenting him.

She shifted behind him again and fiddled with the tie in his hair. Her sigh when his hair slipped about his shoulders made his gut clench in longing.

She smoothed his hair, stroking him like a big cat. "I suppose you'll have to chop your hair off when we go back to London."

He closed his eyes, reveling in the sensation. He already knew she liked his long hair. That was one of the reasons he hadn't cut it. "They won't let me into Almack's if I look like a Norse raider."

"Then devil take Almack's. We'll just have to stay here forever."

Through the storm of arousal swirling through his veins, he registered that she seemed content to remain in Scotland with him. Then all coherent thought fled as she stood in front of him and began to undo his belt. The lingering seduction was taking its toll on her, too. Her usually deft hands were unsteady, and the time she spent loosening the buckle turned into an exercise in excruciating self-control for Hamish.

Finally... Finally she slid the belt free. His blue and gold Douglas plaid slid to the floor in a colorful heap.

"Goodness me..." she whispered. "No wonder you've been huffing and puffing like an overworked draft horse."

He gave a grunt of wry amusement. "Goodness has nothing to do with it."

"Oh, I hope not." She reached out and curled her fingers around his throbbing dick. Reaction jolted through him and turned the world red hot. He thrust his hips forward in encouragement.

Her hand formed a fist and began to move up and down, milking him. He closed his eyes, giving himself up to flaring delight. She'd touched him before, and he'd shown her what gave him pleasure. Now she turned those lessons upon him with a few variations of her own that had him shaking and panting like a man in a fever.

"If you...keep doing...that...this is going...to be...a quick encounter," he bit out as he braced against spilling into her hand.

Her thumb teased the sensitive head, already slick with moisture. "I love that I make you burn."

Her voice rang with new confidence. He opened hazy eyes to see her drop to her knees in front of him. Surely she wouldn't...

By God, it turned out she would.

A long guttural sound of surrender escaped him, as she fitted her lips around the head and her fingers encircled the base. He staggered and reached for her shoulders.

The slide of her tongue on his swollen flesh struck him like cannon fire, then the world turned scarlet as she tentatively sucked. When she increased the pressure, he tangled shaking hands in her thick hair.

For endless blazing seconds, Hamish submitted to her clumsy, arousing, glorious attentions. He was so close, yet he couldn't come in her mouth. She'd blasted through barriers that he'd imagined no lady would cross. But that would be a step too far. He couldn't bear to think that anything he did might repulse or frighten her.

"Emily…" His fingers tightened on her scalp. "Emily, sweetheart, you must stop."

With voluptuous slowness, she released him. He'd always thought her pretty. Now on her knees before him, her hair a tangled mess, her eyes heavy with desire, and her mouth damp and swollen after pleasuring him, she was the most beautiful sight he'd ever seen.

"Don't you like it?" Her husky question almost made him lose himself.

"I like it too much." He bent and kissed her with a succulent carnality that did nothing to promote control. Her lips tasted of salt and musk. The knowledge that she'd been willing to do that for him shuddered through him like a tidal wave.

"Lie on the chaise longue," he said roughly, too stirred up for politeness.

Dark eyebrows arched with a haughtiness that reminded him of the girl he'd known in London. She'd been exciting then, but he'd never have imagined quite how exciting she'd end up becoming. "No, you lie on the chaise longue."

Disbelief turned Hamish as still as a rock. "What the devil…"

"I want to sit on you."

"Sit?"

She looked disconcerted. "Won't the physics work?"

What an Emily question. He'd laugh, if he wasn't so close to the brink. "Yes, it will work."

"Then?"

He seized her in his arms and kissed her with all the astounded gratitude rushing through him. He'd called her exciting? He'd had no idea.

"Hamish..." she gasped, looking enchantingly rumpled.

He released her and arranged himself on the chaise. When he spread out before her, her sizzling survey made his cock even harder. He struggled to hold himself in. In return for her extraordinary generosity, he owed her pleasure. Anyway, he wanted to be inside her when he spilled his seed. A week of wedded bliss had convinced him that nothing compared to the feeling of his wife's muscles gripping him as he lost himself.

She crossed to straddle him, hitching her skirts to give him a glimpse of the sweet nest of curls below her stomach.

"Please don't delay," he said in a hoarse voice as she balanced over him. "I'm only human."

"You? Only human? Don't make me laugh." The anticipation in her smile made him shake. Clever hands gripped him, ready for her descent. "You're the heroic Laird of Glen Lyon."

When she slid down, it was even more perfect than he could have imagined. There was a delicious slippery moment when he realized that what they'd done had aroused her to madness, then he was deep inside her. With a gasp of female excitement, Emily clenched around him. Every time she moved, sensation crashed through him like hot gunfire.

Hamish fought for control, but he was too close. A ragged groan escaped him, as she leaned forward to press an openmouthed kiss to his lips. When her tongue thrust into his mouth, she squeezed him. He bit back a whimper and slipped one shaking hand between their bodies.

She bucked and cried out. Hamish's control shattered. On another broken groan, he lifted his hips and filled her. He dived headlong into a fiery inferno where the only reality was his wife's passion and the incendiary pleasure they created together.

When he came back to himself, an exhausted bundle of fragrant femininity sprawled across his chest. The air was thick with sexual satisfaction.

He firmed his grip on Emily and smiled up at the painted ceiling. The luckiest man in Scotland? He was the luckiest man in the entire world.

Eventually Emily stirred and raised her head. She looked happy. She looked tired. She looked beautiful. For a long time, they stared at each other before he reached forward and stroked the tumble of sable hair back from her forehead.

He drew her down for a kiss that spoke of tenderness rather than desire. "Thank you."

Hamish shifted, bringing her with him so they rested against the back of the chaise longue. She draped across his lap, boneless with exhaustion and the lingering remnants of her climax. Emily buried her face in his chest, and he felt her lips move in a kiss. Her sweetness in this aftermath touched him anew.

He was startled to hear a muffled giggle. "What is it?"

Sparkling hazel eyes more gold than green focused on him. "I can't believe I was so very wicked – yet somehow I'm still wearing my dress."

"I'll fix that next time."

"I can't wait."

It was his turn to laugh. "You may have to – at least until I've recovered. You drained me to the dregs." His voice lowered. "You're the lover a man dreams of, Emily."

She blushed, which he found touching, given what she'd just done to him. "I'm sorry I was so afraid when we married. If I had any idea—"

"Shh, sweetheart," he crooned, stroking her back. "What we have now is worth any amount of waiting."

"The things you make me feel..." Her gesture conveyed what words could not.

He smiled at her, enthralled anew. "Do you know what we should do now?"

Eyes shining with curiosity leveled on him. "What?"

His smile widened. "I think we should have a party."

CHAPTER TWENTY-SEVEN

These Scots certainly knew how to celebrate.

Emily clung to Hamish's arm and surveyed the crowd of jubilant people crammed into Lyon House's vast ballroom. Most of them were strangers to her, and the throng included all levels of society. Crofters. Villagers. Neighbors. The local grandees. All mixing with an ease that impressed someone from the much more class-ridden south.

Most of them were strangers, but not all. Big Billy towered over everyone. There were the people she'd come to know who worked at the house. And standing with her and Hamish were Diarmid and Fiona and Fergus and Marina.

The noise was terrific. Chatter. Laughter. A cohort of fiddlers doing their best to be heard above the cacophony.

"Not like a London party," Hamish said, smiling at her.

"No, not at all," Emily said faintly. In this riotous gathering, she felt awfully English and hidebound and out of place. Yet it was so important that these people liked her and welcomed her to the glen. For her sake and for Hamish's.

"You look wonderful, Emily," Fiona said. "The clan will take you to their hearts."

Emily wore a red silk gown trimmed with gold braid, and the diamond necklace and pearl pins Hamish had given her in London.

"I hope so," she said, still staring out at the chaos.

"How could you fail?" Marina said. "*Coraggio, ragazza*. These are your people now."

"Yes, you're my wife, and the Lady of Glen Lyon." Hamish stepped away and held out his hand. He looked every inch the laird in his blue and gold kilt and his black velvet formal jacket. Her susceptible heart skipped a beat at how handsome he was. "Let's show them the way to dance a reel, sweetheart."

When Emily looked into his eyes, she saw that he was proud to show her off to his friends and kinfolk. An uncertain smile curled her lips. "We haven't danced together since our engagement."

When they'd seethed with mutual resentment and dread for the future. Now the future was here, and she'd never been happier, if she ignored the tiny niggle that Hamish didn't love her. But compared to the joy these last three weeks had brought, that was a small niggle indeed. She and Hamish passed their days in harmony and their nights in passionate communion. The marriage which had started so badly promised a lifetime of joy ahead.

"Then it's time ye danced together again." Fergus looked magnificent in the red Mackinnon plaid.

Diarmid had chosen to dress in the English style. He and Fiona made a spectacular couple, with her silvery beauty set off in pale blue organza and him so dark and brooding at her side.

The night turned into a whirl of excitement. The dances were different up here, too, but fortunately most people tolerated Emily's mistakes. Once she'd danced with Hamish, she partnered his neighbors and even shared a jig with Big Billy, who swung her around so fast, she became dizzy. It was a relief to return to Hamish and feel his arms slide around her.

"Having fun?" he asked.

"Oh, yes," she said breathlessly. "If this is what you grew up with, you must have found London balls very staid."

"Those Sassenachs have no idea how to celebrate. May I have this dance? It's a waltz."

At Emily's request, the band had played some of the dances she knew, amongst all the unbridled Scottish measures. She smiled at her husband. "I'd love to, but I promised the first waltz to—"

"To me." Fergus spoke from behind her.

"Hamish, *caro*, perhaps you and I can show the world how it is done," Marina said. She held her tall, redheaded husband's arm, and her olive skin was flushed. She'd danced every set with a Continental élan that Emily admired.

Hamish released Emily and bowed to the gorgeous brunette. "It would be my pleasure, Marina."

Marina cast him a flashing glance from her bright black eyes. "By the way, I approve of this mane *d'oro*, Hamish. It makes you look like a Viking."

"That's what Emily says," he muttered with the hint of self-consciousness that never failed to melt Emily's heart. "She won't let me cut it, although I told her I only let it grow because I was holed up in my peel tower stargazing. And pining for her."

Emily bestowed a smile of fond approval upon him. She believed he'd been pining for her. Hadn't she been pining for him down in London? Although she'd been too proud to admit it, even to herself.

"It makes you look *molto bello*, like a hero from a Minerva Press novel." Marina surveyed Hamish with the strangely impersonal air that she sometimes adopted.

Emily had come to realize that it usually meant that she'd moved into artist mode and her mind flooded with abstract shapes and colors. Having grown up with one scientist and married another, Emily didn't find the change too disconcerting, but she'd noticed other people caught out.

"Before you cut it, let me paint you. *Madonna*, with all that hair, you look like the King of the Highlands."

"Pardon me, *mo chridhe*, but should I be jealous? Surely in my wife's eyes, I am the King of the Highlands," Fergus protested.

Marina's laugh was low and sensual. "*Tesoro*, you're king of my heart. Don't be greedy."

Emily had so much to be grateful for, especially when she thought back to her marriage's unpromising start. But the look of love and perfect understanding that passed between Marina and her husband stabbed a knife through her. How she envied the love the Mackinnons shared. How she wished Hamish was devoted to her the way Fergus was devoted to Marina. Her husband's burning hunger for her body thrilled her. But she wanted more, so much more.

Would she and Hamish ever enjoy that almost spiritual connection she saw linking the other couple? She reminded herself to be patient. They'd been reconciled only a few weeks. She had time to stake out her place in his soul.

Hamish looked thoughtful. "I don't need another blasted picture of me, but I do want to talk to you about painting Emily."

Marina smiled. "*Andiamo*. We can discuss this while we dance."

Fergus extended his hand toward Emily. "Shall we, lassie?"

They whirled off into the throng, while the clansfolk, who considered these London dances complete drivel, drifted away to investigate the free-flowing ale and whisky and the long tables groaning with food. There was wine and champagne, too, but the locals scorned those as too much in the English taste as well, it seemed.

"How are ye liking my homeland?" Fergus asked, once they'd found the rhythm and circled the ballroom like it was second nature.

"It's beautiful," Emily said, hoping she wasn't blushing. So far her time in Scotland had mostly been a series of explosive encounters in the laird's bed or wherever the laird and his lady could find the privacy to pursue their passion.

"Ye and Hamish must come to Achnasheen for Christmas. Marina would like that."

"I would, too."

He studied her with sharp green eyes that didn't miss much. "It's bonny to see ye two getting on so well."

"I like Marina."

"So do I. But I was talking about ye and Hamish."

"Oh," she said, suddenly wishing that she'd put Fergus off and danced with Hamish after all. She wasn't ready to confide in the autocratic Laird of Achnasheen.

"When I was down in London, I heard the talk about how the marriage came about. Despite the two of ye putting up a brave face, it was clear that neither of ye was overjoyed to be shackled to the other."

Emily frowned as apprehension began to coil in her stomach. This suddenly felt like an ambush – and one she wasn't prepared for, here where she was supposed to be amongst friends. "Fergus, it's a party. It's not the occasion for looking back on older, sadder days."

"But it's a braw chance for me to speak to ye alone."

She stumbled, but he caught her without effort. "You really don't have to."

So her instincts were right. This was indeed an ambush. Her heart sank to her knees, and she braced for what was to come.

His stubborn jaw hardened and out of the corner of her eye, Emily caught Marina sending them a concerned glance. Emily summoned a smile but wasn't sure it was as convincing as it might have been.

"Och, I do. There are two men in this world who are like brothers to me, and one of them is the man ye married. Hamish gives the impression that life comes easily and nothing pierces his confidence, but it's no' true. I hope ye ken the damage you can do to him. The damage you've already done, by God. I hope ye dinnae intend to do more damage."

Emily stiffened and missed another step. The attack took her by surprise and stung even sharper because there was more than a shred of truth in it.

"I care for my husband," she said tautly, wondering how much talk it would cause if she marched away from the laird's best friend in the middle of a dance.

She now understood why Fergus had insisted on the first waltz. Most dances involved changing partners or dancing in a group. The waltz, blast it, meant she was with one partner for the duration.

Astonishment vied with hurt that this man harbored such a low opinion of her. She'd hoped that she was making some headway in claiming her place at Hamish's side. This unwelcome conversation was a painful reminder that she still had a long way to go.

Again Fergus corrected her stumble and sent her a straight look that wasn't far off a glare. "I'm no' sure ye do. He spent most of the last year slinking around Glen Lyon like a whipped dog."

She hid a wince. The picture was a little too vivid to bear. She hated to think of Hamish unhappy. She hated even more to think that she'd been the cause. "He's back to king of the beasts tonight."

"Aye, and that's just how I'd like him to stay."

"Would you indeed?" she asked with rising resentment. "You know none of this is your business."

"It is, if I make ye see that you can hurt him."

"I have no intention of hurting him," she said hotly. Guilt and injured feelings created a rancid stew inside her.

"I hope ye mean that."

"I do, not that it's any of your concern. Please take me back to him right now."

The formidable jaw above the snowy white jabot firmed until it was like rock. "I havenae finished."

"Yes, you have."

Fergus ignored her and short of making a scene here where she was so keen to create a good impression, she was trapped until the end of the waltz. At least Fergus kept his voice low. So far, the scolding remained a secret from the rest of the ballroom.

"It takes more than a bonny face and a patronizing smile to fit in here in the Highlands. Life can be hard in these glens, and the people deserve better than a temporary lady who means to bolt back to London and her society friends the moment things get difficult. Hamish always said he'd marry a good Scots lass, right from the very first day I met him. From what I've seen so far, he'd be better off if he had."

Emily's lips flattened, and her question emerged with a bite. "So now you're saying I'm the wrong wife for him because I'm English?"

The ghastly truth was that Fergus could be right. His criticism sliced straight through to so many of her insecurities. In her earlier, more naïve days, she'd given little thought to the fact that Hamish was Scots and she wasn't. But that was before she'd seen him on his home ground and realized how rooted he was in the rich soil of Glen Lyon. The Hamish she knew in London was a thin veneer over the man she encountered here, the man who was Scottish to his marrow.

When he proposed, he'd mentioned his disappointed hopes of taking a Scottish bride. At the time, she'd dismissed his remarks as yet another complaint against a marriage he didn't want. But then she'd learned how his upbringing left him feeling like he didn't belong in Glen Lyon and she'd discovered how he longed to be recognized as a true Scotsman.

As if Fergus heard her troubled thoughts, he went on. "I'm saying that he's always had trouble finding his place here, because he sounds like a Sassenach and because he spent so much time in London."

"He can hardly advance through the ranks of science hidden away in these hills," she snapped.

"Aye, that's true. But he cannae make a place for himself as chieftain of his clan if he's off chasing a flighty London lassie who has neither his best interests at heart nor those of his people."

"You're not being fair. You don't know me." She felt sick as she stared into his uncompromising expression. Did everyone here despise her as featherbrained and selfish and...*English*?

"I ken what I've seen."

"Then you haven't seen enough. And I can't help being English."

"No, you can't, but if your heart's in it, ye can try to overcome that handicap."

Her heart was in it. More than this presumptuous Scot could ever know. "I don't view it as a handicap," she said, ice dripping from each word. Her pride revolted at the idea of him knowing that his cruel remarks hit their target. "And I repeat that this is none of your business."

The urge to break away strengthened, but people other than Marina had started to stare at them. Fergus's displeasure and her chagrin were becoming more difficult to hide under a social smile.

"It is, if I have to watch my best friend suffer the way he has this last year."

"We're together now," she forced out, through lips that felt frozen. She kept moving, but her feet felt like lead and the cheerful music mocked her futile hopes of finding a place at Glen Lyon.

Haughty auburn eyebrows expressed skepticism. "Aye, but for how long? Do ye mean to give him a few weeks of hope, then run off back to Mayfair? Or do ye mean to stay and do your best to understand him and his home and his kin? Glen Lyon needs a lady, no' a gawking tourist who finds the quaint locals an amusing diversion before she resumes her city pleasures."

If Emily hadn't been so angry and wounded, she'd laugh at that. This last year might have been hard on Hamish – and that wasn't altogether her fault – but nor had it been easy for her.

Fergus had picked up the impression somewhere that she'd abandoned a life jammed with feverish gaiety to follow Hamish up here. Whereas she'd been as lonely in Bloomsbury as he'd been sulking in his peel tower.

Probably lonelier. After all, he'd had his clan within reach.

"You've overstepped the mark, sir. I'm not going to make a scene because that would distress Hamish and while you may not believe it, that would suit neither you nor me." Inside she might be cringing, but her voice emerged flat and steady. "If you call yourself any kind of gentleman, you'll take me back to him this minute."

The frown Fergus directed at her was ferocious. If she wasn't feeling so heartsick, she might be frightened. "Ye need to hear me out."

She pushed back against the hand on her waist. "No, I don't."

"What the devil is going on here?" Hamish growled behind her.

"Hamish..." Emily struggled to sound as if she and Fergus hadn't just been at daggers drawn.

She plastered a smile on her face, as she stopped moving and turned to him. Hamish looked ready to explode. Marina hovered beside him, her dark eyes troubled as they flickered between Hamish and Fergus.

Fergus was Hamish's best friend and while right now, she'd dearly love to pummel some of the Scots arrogance out of the man, she couldn't be the cause of a rift. Fergus's accusations had pierced to her soul, but he'd spoken out of genuine love and concern for Hamish. She couldn't hate him for that.

"What the hell have you been saying to my wife, you carrot-haired bastard?"

"Nothing," she said, cursing the betraying quiver in her voice. She met Marina's frown and gave a small shake of her head. She'd had enough of airing her dirty linen in public. This brought back memories of that hideous evening in London, when she stumbled in from a rainstorm to face an almighty scandal. "There's nothing to worry about, Hamish. You're interrupting the dance."

He ignored her and glared at Fergus. "It looks like something to me. She's gone as white as a sheet. If you've upset her, Mackinnon, you and I will have a score to settle."

"Hamish, not here," Emily said in an urgent tone.

So far her husband had kept his voice down, but a six-foot-five man seething with fury was sure to attract attention, however discreet he tried to be. More and more heads turned in their direction, and the couples around them had stopped dancing to observe the storm gathering around the laird and his new wife.

"I was giving your lady some well-meant advice on how to handle ye." Fergus's voice was steady and self-confident. Emily had a suspicion that Fergus would sound self-confident standing naked in the middle of a hurricane.

"Giving her a lecture, more like," Hamish grated out. He lunged forward and pushed Fergus away from Emily, then he turned to her. "Are you all right?"

Emily was relieved to feel Hamish's arm go around her waist, and she sagged in his hold. After that vile exchange with Fergus, she dearly needed the reassurance of his touch. "Hamish, you're making a mountain out of a molehill. Don't spoil the party."

"Bloody Fergus, he always thinks he knows best. Whatever he said to you, ignore it."

"*Tesoro*, what have you done?" Marina asked, and the endearment sounded more impatient than loving, however much she might love her husband. "I said that you were better off leaving well enough alone."

Fergus's color had risen, and he subjected his wife to a furious glare down the long blade of his nose. "I did what I thought best."

Marina sighed. "And created a disaster."

"I want Emily to understand what she's cost Hamish. We all ken they married under duress. Now they've lived apart for months. I dinnae want his heart broken a second time, when she decides to flit back to England again."

Emily's "As if I'd leave him flat!" coincided with Hamish's outraged, "You can leave my heart out of it, chum. It's in very good hands right now, and I'll thank you to keep that damned big beak well away from my business."

Marina caught Fergus's arm. "*Amore mio*, you should know better than to interfere. Every marriage is a world unto itself. You can't hope to understand what happens between Emily and Hamish."

"I willnae have Hamish hurt," Fergus said stubbornly.

"What in blazes sort of fragile blossom do you think I am, you overbearing sod?" Hamish asked with searing heat. "I don't need you to protect me."

"He doesn't need protecting from me either," Emily said in a rush. "It's true – Hamish and I did start out badly, but we're finding our way now."

Hamish's grip on her waist firmed. "Yes, we are."

When Fergus leveled a penetrating green gaze on him, some of the aggression leached from his tall frame. "Och, then that's all I need to hear."

"You didn't need to hear anything," Hamish snapped and swept a forbidding glance around the circle of eager onlookers. "I'm hoping you've all heard enough, too."

Their audience looked discomfited and most of them turned away. The band had continued to play throughout. As the whispers faded, the sweet silly tune of the waltz drifted through the room. Except it turned out that something else was going on that Emily hadn't noticed while she fended off Fergus's criticism.

Fighting the urge to burst into tears, Emily turned her head toward where a scuffle had broken out over near the supper tables. She craned to see, but there were too many people in the way. "What is it?"

"God knows," Hamish said, with what she thought was justified annoyance. This had been such a joyous gathering. Now it threatened to turn into a debacle.

"Och, I will speak. A Douglas is born a free man with a right to an opinion, God damn ye." The voice was loud and belligerent, and slurred enough to hint at the liberal application of spirits.

"That's all I bloody need, Wee Rory opening his big mouth," Hamish growled.

As the music ended on a discordant clash of notes, a flurry of protest rose from the corner of the room. Above the hubbub, the tirade was clearly audible. "We've got to put up with a damn Sassenach laird, who's fool enough to think he's a good Scotsman. Now he brings us a bloody useless

Englishwoman as the Lady of Glen Lyon. Soon there willnae be room for a true Highlander to breathe in this glen. It will be nothing better than a wee England."

A storm of shushing followed, but the hectoring voice rose above the scandalized outcry. "No good Douglas will ever serve under the English. We should rise up and—"

"Shut your mouth, Wee Rory," Big Billy said, pushing his way through the crowd to the troublemaker. "Nobody wants to hear ye."

"I willnae shut my mouth, ye thick-witted yin. I'm only saying what every true Scotsman here tonight feels but is too chicken-hearted to say. Well, nobody ever called Rory Douglas a coward."

"Aye, but they often called him a ruddy great fool," a man called out.

Emily was cringing in Hamish's hold. She didn't dare to look at Fergus and Marina, for fear of seeing pity in their eyes. Pity – and the knowledge that while the man might be a drunken boor, he spoke the unwelcome truth.

Hamish released her and drew himself up to his full daunting height. "That's enough."

The crowd parted, and Emily found herself staring at a wiry old man with a bald head fringed in a scruff of untidy ginger curls. His face was flushed bright red, and he clutched a tankard in one hand.

"Do I smell the stink of a Sassenach?" the man asked, weaving on his feet.

"No, it's the stink of a man who can't hold his liquor or mind his manners." Hamish glared around the crowd, but this time nobody shifted away. Emily couldn't blame them. This was turning into the sort of evening that enlivened fireside tales for years.

Her husband released her and strode down the room to confront the drunken lout. "You will apologize to my wife for your rudeness. You call yourself a true Highlander, Rory Douglas, yet you treat a guest, and a lady at that, with rank discourtesy. I'm ashamed to call myself your kinsman."

"Aye, I'm a true Highlander, Glen Lyon. Truer than you'll ever be, with your London ways and your braying English tongue."

Big Billy bunched his fists. "Do ye want a beating, man?"

"Leave it, Billy," Hamish said with unexpected composure. "I can handle him."

"Och, no' from where I'm standing. It takes an army of Sassenachs to best a good Highlander, ye great fannybaws."

The crowd reacted with horror. Emily realized that the unfamiliar insult must be excessively offensive.

It might be funny to watch diminutive Rory facing down her powerful husband. Except Emily was sure that Rory was only saying what the other people in this room felt but kept to themselves. Now there was the added danger of Hamish losing his formidable temper. If he did, violence would follow. She couldn't bear to think of anyone getting hurt on her account.

"In that case, it's lucky I'm a good Highlander. Apologize to my wife, then go home and sleep off the whisky."

"I'll never humble myself to that English bitch. The besom can go to hell, or she can go back across the border where she belongs. No' that I can see much difference between hell and England."

There was an appalled gasp from the crowd, and all eyes fixed on Hamish. Even from behind him, Emily saw his muscles bunch ready for mayhem.

It was too much. First Fergus, now this. For one wretched moment, she stared at her husband's broad back, then with a broken cry, she picked up her skirts and fled the ballroom. Nobody tried to stop her. Everyone was too focused on the clash between Rory and Hamish.

CHAPTER TWENTY-EIGHT

"*Y*ou will speak of my wife with respect, or you will find somewhere new to practice your carpentry, Rory," Hamish said in an implacable voice.

All the guests turned to him aghast. Banishment from the clan was the worst punishment a laird could inflict.

"You think you're such a big man in the glens, Glen Lyon," Rory said, clearly too intoxicated to realize the dangerous line he crossed.

"Aye, I'm a big man, Rory. Big enough to know you've had too much to drink and there's no good to be had from you tonight." He glanced at Billy. "Take him home, and make sure he stays there. He'll have a devil of a head tomorrow and hopefully a pennyworth of the sense he was born with."

"I'm no' a bairn to be sent to bed with a smack on the bum and no supper. I willnae gae home, and I willnae apologize," Rory said, swinging at Hamish and missing by a mile.

"Glen Lyon, he'll think better of his temper in the morning," Big Billy said, grabbing Rory in one brawny hand and keeping him a safe distance from Hamish.

"Aye, he will. And we can decide his future when he's not half-pickled."

"You might get someone else to do your dirty work for ye, you bloody English bastard, but I willnae be silenced."

Hamish scowled at his troublesome kinsman. "Once you're no longer in my house, you can make as much noise as you want." His voice hardened. "But you will apologize to Lady Glen Lyon, and you will swear your loyalty to my wife and to me, or I'll have you off this estate faster than a hawk flies at a rabbit. On that you have my word as a proud Scotsman."

At last, his deadly serious tone penetrated Rory's alcoholic haze, and the man drooped in Billy's hold. "Glen Lyon..."

"Take him away," Hamish said wearily.

He faced the packed room and summoned a cheerful tone. "The surprise entertainment has come to an end. Apologies for the interruption to our revels." He waved to the band, who lifted their instruments and began to play. "Now let's get back to having a good time. It's not a real party at Lyon House unless the guests dance until dawn."

The jolly reel the musicians chose helped to ease the fraught atmosphere. With surprising speed, the chatter and laughter rose again. Rory's tantrum mightn't be forgotten, but it wasn't going to ruin the rest of the celebration.

Hamish looked around for Emily. Last he'd seen her, she'd been with Fergus and Marina and he'd been all set to knock his best friend's block off. He caught sight of rich red hair over the dancers and made his way through the crowd.

Marina came forward with a concerned expression. Hamish summoned a smile. "Don't worry. I'm not going to challenge Fergus to pistols at ten paces."

"*Porca miseria*, I'm so cross with him, I don't think I'd mind if you shot him. But that's not it. It's Emily."

Hamish stopped stone still. Foreboding as sharp and heavy as an ax crashed down upon him. "What is it?" He looked past Marina to where Fergus stood watching them with a stern expression. "If Fergus said anything more to upset her, I will damn well shoot him."

Fergus stepped closer, and Hamish realized that the sternness was worry. "She's no' here, Hamish."

"Where is she?"

Marina made a helpless gesture. "When Rory started that stupid outburst, she ran out. I wanted to follow her, but Fergus said—"

Now he wished he'd given Rory the beating he deserved. "I think Fergus has said quite enough for one night," Hamish retorted, his resentment stirring anew. "Which way did she go?"

Marina pointed to the door leading back into the rest of the house. At least Emily wasn't out in the cold. With October's arrival, the mild weather had become a memory, and now it had started to rain. "That way." She paused. "She looked upset."

"Thank you."

"Hamish, I probably havenae helped," Fergus began, looking uncomfortable. Apologies never came easily from the managing ass, although since his marriage, at least he was prepared to make amends now and again.

Hamish shot him an angry look. "Probably?"

"Hamish, he meant well," Marina said.

"What does that matter?" Hamish sighed. He was too worried about Emily to hang about arguing with this arrogant bastard who he used to call a friend. "Hell, what do I care? Right now, you and your unsolicited and uninformed opinions can go to blazes, Fergus. I need to find my wife."

Without another word, he strode out of the ballroom and entered the hall. He brushed off the guests who approached him and collected a lamp. He cursed the fact that Lyon House was so large. It would be quicker if he asked Diarmid and Fergus to help. They knew the house almost as well as he did. But he had no idea where the Mactavishes were, and he didn't trust himself to be civil to Fergus.

Hamish conducted a swift search of the ground floor, interrupting a couple of lovers' trysts but finding no trace of Emily. He checked down in the kitchens, but nobody in that hive of activity had seen the lady of the house.

Unless Emily had run outside, and as it was bucketing down, he doubted that she had, she must be upstairs. Their rooms were the most obvious place for her to take a wounded heart.

But when he went up, she wasn't in their suite. Guests staying over for the ceilidh were using the other bedrooms. She wouldn't seek refuge where she might be interrupted.

Would she venture as far as the servants' rooms in the attic? Surely not.

With every moment, his turmoil worsened. He was sickly aware that this latest mess was all his fault. He should have let Emily find her feet as Lady Glen Lyon, before he threw her to the wolves that were his friends and neighbors and kinfolk. How he cursed his impulse to show his lovely wife off to the world. He'd have been better off keeping her to himself.

What the devil would he do if Emily decided to go back to London? What if she decided that she didn't like Scotland and the Scots – and one Scot in particular, the boneheaded dolt she'd so reluctantly married?

Nausea soured his stomach at the thought of losing her now, after these golden, glorious days. If she went, he'd follow her south. He wouldn't stay here without her. But if she decided that she'd had enough of him as well as his country, she'd break his heart.

His mood growing grimmer by the minute, he kept searching. Finally he reached the gallery, stretching ahead dark and silent.

"Emily?" he called as he started down the long room.

He advanced a few more steps, but he already knew she wasn't here. The painted eyes of his ancestors stared down at him in disapproval. He'd brought the world's most marvelous woman into the Douglas family, and now it looked like he was about to lose her.

Perhaps Rory was right, and he was a disgrace to the clan.

His shoulders slumping, he turned to go back downstairs. Then he stopped.

What a fool he was. Hamish knew just where Emily was. Confound it, he should have guessed from the first.

If she was as upset as he feared she was, she'd want to be alone. There was one place in all this huge house where that was guaranteed.

Sure of himself at last, Hamish strode down the length of the gallery until he reached Granny Phyllis's cabinet of curiosities. There he paused, sucked in a deep breath, warned himself not to muck this up, and opened the door.

"Emily?" he asked softly, as he stepped into the dark, confined space. He told himself he had to prevail, because the alternative to prevailing didn't bear thinking about.

There was no answer, but he knew in his bones she was here. He'd reached such a state of intimacy with his wife that he could feel her presence.

When he raised the lamp, golden light reached every corner. His wife was sitting hunched on the chaise longue.

"This is where you are." Relief flooded Hamish, made his knees wobble. His voice cracked with the force of his emotion. His shaking hand made the light waver eerily across the shelves of treasures. "I've been searching the whole house for you."

She cringed away, and her response emerged thick with tears. "Well, now you've found me, you can go away again."

He struggled to control his urge to grab her up in his arms and kiss her. It was an effort to stay where he was, but everything about her screamed not to touch her. "No gentleman worth his salt would leave a lady crying and all alone."

"I'm not crying. I never cry."

"Not often, anyway." He ventured closer and set the lamp on the floor. "I was worried sick about you when your father died. It was as if you were frozen."

"Leave me alone, Hamish," she said, keeping her head down. The pearls in her rich dark hair glinted in the lamplight, and her slender hands twined in her lap.

"I can't do that." Carefully, as if she were a wild bird and his slightest move could frighten her into flight, he sat beside her. "I hate to see you so unhappy. What in Hades did Fergus say to you?"

With a trembling hand, Emily raised a crumpled handkerchief to wipe her cheeks. "Just a few home truths that I should have kept in mind."

"I'll kill him," Hamish said grimly, his hands fisting on his knees. "I'll cut out his liver and roast it over a campfire."

"No, he was right." At last, she raised her gaze to meet his. His heart clenched in guilt and misery and pity. His stalwart Emily had been crying her eyes out. "And I was wrong. Because I forgot."

For pity's sake, he was only human. He couldn't keep his distance any longer. He dared to catch her hand in his. "Forgot what, sweetheart?"

She tried to pull away but gave up before it turned into a genuine effort. "Don't call me that."

Just the touch of her hand was enough to soothe his burgeoning alarm, but he wasn't sanguine enough to think that he'd even started to solve this problem. "Why not? You are my sweetheart."

"No, I'm not."

He gave a dismissive grunt. "What the devil do you think you are, then?"

"I'm..." She sucked in an audible breath then spoke in a broken rush. "I'm the woman you had to marry. The woman who can never be what you want, no matter how hard I try."

What the hell? How on earth could a smart woman believe that was true? He was appalled that she still felt so insecure. Didn't she know yet what she meant to him?

His gut knotted with regret and apprehension, as he struggled to keep his voice even. "If you think back over the last three weeks, you'll know that's arrant nonsense."

She went back to staring into her lap. "You're making the best of a bad bargain."

"That's rubbish, Emily. I couldn't want you more than I do."

When she looked at him, the despair in her eyes stabbed him to the soul. "You're a kind man, Hamish. It took me far too long to see that. You were kind to Papa. You've been kind to me."

He frowned in confusion. That should be a compliment, but it didn't sound like one. More was going on here than hurt feelings after a few rude remarks from Fergus and Rory. Much more. Hamish had a hideous inkling that if he mishandled the next few minutes, the consequences would be disastrous. "There's nothing wrong with being kind."

"No, it's wonderful." Her smile threatened to break his heart. It was so utterly without hope. "You're wonderful."

"What..." Amazement stole his ability to put words together. He'd never imagined her saying that to him. She'd told him the things he did to her were wonderful, but she'd never extended the praise to him in general.

"But kindness isn't enough. Especially when I'll always be the wrong woman for you."

"Emily?" He'd been worried when she ran from the ballroom, and that worry had deepened as he searched the house. But hearing those words, panic welled up to choke him. She couldn't mean it. She couldn't. He wouldn't let it be true. "You're talking as if you're going to leave me."

A fraught pause. "It might be easier."

The devil it would.

"By God, I won't let you go." Hamish surged to his feet and glared down at her. Fear such as he'd never felt in his entire life chilled his blood to ice. "Why would you want to leave me? That makes no sense. You've been happy these last few weeks. I know you have. Stop speaking in riddles. Whatever

Fergus said to you, it isn't true. Pay no attention. I'll ban him from the house."

She stared up at him in astonishment. "He's your best friend."

"If he's turned you against me, he can go to blazes."

"You'd do that for me?"

He sighed and ran his hand through his hair. "Don't you know I'd shift every star in the heavens for you, woman? I love you."

For too fleeting a moment, her eyes turned brilliant with happiness. Then before he could be sure of what he saw, the skin tightened over the bones of her face and she went back to looking like something out of a Greek tragedy.

With an incoherent cry, she staggered to her feet and retreated behind the chaise longue. "But I'm not Scottish."

He set out after her, but stopped bewildered when he registered what she'd said. "What the deuce did you say?"

She wrung her hands in distress, and fresh tears glittered on her pale cheeks. "I'm not Scottish."

God give him strength. He growled deep in his throat. "Was that what Fergus told you? That you don't belong here? That you don't belong with me?"

One trembling hand made a despondent gesture, and her tone turned dull and flat. "It's not just Fergus. You told me about feeling like an outsider here because people think you're English. When you proposed, you said you'd prefer a Scottish bride, and—"

"I don't want a Scottish bride. I want the bloody bride I've got – even if right now I fear for her wits."

"And Rory—"

"Rory is a blasted raving idiot. What he says isn't worth a tinker's damn, even when he's sober."

Impatience churned in Hamish's stomach. Impatience and powerful, overwhelming love for this confused, brilliant, magnificent woman. Right now, he wasn't sure whether he wanted to shake his wife or kiss her. Probably both. He came around the chaise longue and caught her wrist in an implacable grasp. "If you hate living in Scotland, we'll move back to London."

She stood shaking in his grasp, as her great hazel eyes searched his face. "But you love Scotland."

"Not as much as I love you."

He saw the precise moment she believed him. Thank the Lord for that, at least.

"You mean that?"

He slid his arms around her waist and pulled her against him. The scents of smoky jasmine and Emily filled his head, the fragrance of paradise. "Of course I damn well mean that."

He kissed her, expecting to meet resistance, but she responded with immediate ardor. Her lips were voracious, and she made that soft hum of pleasure that always got him stirred up.

She flung her arms around his neck, pressing so close that he thought she was trying to climb inside his skin. Hamish didn't mind. He liked her frantic response. It soothed the terror that had struck him down when he found her, the even worse terror when she'd talked about leaving him. For a few horrendous seconds tonight, he'd feared he might lose her. He never wanted to go through that again as long as he lived.

When they finally drew apart, his head was swimming. He stared down into her face. She didn't look nearly so woebegone. In fact, if he took the optimistic view, he might say she looked transported with happiness, despite the tearstains marking her cheeks.

"You used to think I was the greatest pest in the world," Emily said, regarding him with such wonder in her eyes that he felt like a hero.

He settled his hands at her waist and kissed her again, fast and possessive. "Now you just drive me mad with lust."

A shaky but gloriously joyful smile curved her lips. "I had no idea you loved me."

He frowned. "How could I help loving you? You've had me in a spin for years. I was at least half in love with you when we got married. I've most definitely been head over heels since you turned up on my doorstep and lost your mind in that fit of jealousy. It turns out that I've lost my mind, too."

"I'll never call myself clever again – of course you love me." She sounded like she made a great scientific discovery – and in the last place she ever expected to find it.

"I told you I do."

"This just shows what a complete state I've been in. I've been so blind. I swear, my brain hasn't worked since I got to Scotland. I should have seen what you felt. How did I miss seeing it?" She shook her head, still looking as if he'd tossed her world upside down. Self-disgust turned down her lips. "In your whole life, you've never had an emotion that you didn't broadcast for fifty miles. For weeks, you've been showing me that you love me."

He was glad that she believed he loved her. At least that should stop her scurrying back to London. But he needed more than a one-sided declaration. He needed Emily to offer some hope that she might one day return his feelings. His voice flattened. "Now all I need to do is make you love me."

"But I do love you. So very much." Before he could process that miraculous statement, she rose on her toes and kissed him quickly. He could never think straight when she kissed him. "I've been in love with you for a long time, too. I was certainly in love with you by the time I chased you down in your lonely tower."

"You were?" For the second time in half an hour, his voice cracked with emotion. These past few weeks, he thought he'd been happy. Discovering that Emily loved him back showed him that he'd only tasted the beginnings of joy.

"I was."

A great wave of elation swelled inside him, until he was smiling like a lunatic. It might be incredible, it was certainly undeserved, but this gorgeous woman loved him as much as he loved her. They'd come through all their tribulations to find safe harbor at last. He could hardly believe it. Yet he must because when he looked into her beautiful eyes, they shone gold with an adoration he never imagined he'd see there.

He swallowed to shift the poignant emotion constricting his throat. "I call that a very happy coincidence indeed."

Emily smiled back and rose on her toes for a more leisurely kiss. This time, their lips met with a heady mixture of passion and tenderness. The kiss made a silent promise for a lifetime of love ahead.

With visible reluctance, she shifted far enough away to speak. "I don't hate Scotland, even if Scotland hates me. I'm happy to stay in Glen Lyon with you."

"Scotland doesn't hate you, you lovely, misguided creature. Once Scotland knows you, it will love you almost as much as I do. If anyone doubts your place here with me, they can jump off the top of Ben Nevis, for all I'm concerned."

"Even if Scotland does hate me, I can bear it as long as you love me and I love you. You don't have to give up your home for me. You don't have to give up your best friend. Fergus wasn't as tactful as he could be, but he just wanted to make sure that I had no plans to run off to London."

"Fergus should mind his own damn business. He sometimes forgets that I'm no longer the ten-year-old boy he rescued in the mountains and that now we're men, the four-year age gap doesn't mean a farthing."

With a sweetness that made Hamish's heart cramp with love, Emily stroked his cheek. "I wonder if he guessed you loved me and was just trying to save you from more heartache."

He shifted with discomfort. "Men don't think like that, my love. He'd be more likely to punch me in the head and tell me to stop moping."

"Hmm," she said, clearly unconvinced. Then she looked horrified. "I didn't even ask – what on earth happened to Rory?"

An unimpressed grunt escaped him. "I sent the foul-mouthed buffoon home in one piece. He has orders to come to terms with us as the Laird and Lady of Glen Lyon or pack up his tools and leave."

Puzzlement drew her eyebrows together. "But you were angry with him."

"I'm still angry. He's always been a nasty drunk. He's a dashed good carpenter, though, which is why I put up with him. But tonight he went too far." When she didn't speak, he frowned. "What is it?"

This time, she smiled at him as if he was sunrise on a chilly morning. "Hamish, my darling, I'm proud of you. I'm proud of myself for marrying you. Despite all my fears, it turned out that I married a reasonable man. Who would have dreamed it?"

He liked hearing she was proud of him. He particularly liked it when she called him her darling.

But he was still confused. "What on earth are you wittering on about, you daft lassie?"

Her smile widened further. "You didn't lose your temper."

"No, although if I had, that clodhopping brute would have deserved it. But however angry I was, I knew it would reflect badly on you if I gave him the thrashing he asked for. You wouldn't like it if I started snapping and snarling like an angry bear in front of all our friends and neighbors."

Emily cupped his jaw with a tenderness he felt to the soles of his feet. "Now I really do believe you love me. A year ago, you would have run amok. You wouldn't have given a fig who you inconvenienced."

With a theatrical sigh, he drew her closer, reveling in how willingly she snuggled up to him. "You've turned me into a mere shadow of my former self, you wicked girl. You'd better have plans to make it up to me."

Her low laugh played sensual music up and down his spine. "That can be arranged." She drew away to cast a lingering glance at the chaise longue. His blood lit to flame as she leveled those lovely eyes on him, lovely eyes bright with an unmistakable message. "In fact, there's no time like the present. Do you think our guests will miss us if we're absent for an hour or so?"

His laugh rang with triumph as he caught her up and kissed her with all the love overflowing from his heart. "To Hades with them if they do. Why should I care, when I have my beautiful English bride in my arms?"

Hamish's English bride gave a very unscientific giggle and surrendered to his passionate kiss with wholehearted delight.

Author's Note

Sadly, Hamish Douglas, Laird of Glen Lyon, is not credited as the discoverer of Saturn's moon, Hyperion. Hyperion was identified in 1848, twenty-five years after the events in *The Highlander's English Bride*, by William Lassell in England and by William Cranch Bond and George Phillips Bond in the United States.

ABOUT THE AUTHOR

Australian Anna Campbell has written 11 multi award-winning historical romances for Avon HarperCollins and Grand Central Publishing. As an independently published author, she's released more than 30 bestselling stories. Right now, she is working on a new series called A Scandal in Mayfair, set amidst the glamour and sensuality of Regency London. Anna has won numerous awards for her stories, including RT Book Reviews Reviewers Choice, the Booksellers Best, the Golden Quill (three times), the Heart of Excellence (twice), the Write Touch, the Aspen Gold (twice), and the Australian Romance Readers' favorite historical romance (five times).

Anna loves to hear from her readers. You can find her at:

Website: www.annacampbell.com

facebook.com/AnnaCampbellFans

twitter.comAnnaCampbellOz

bookbub.com/authors/anna-campbell

The Laird's Willful Lass:
The Lairds Most Likely Book 1

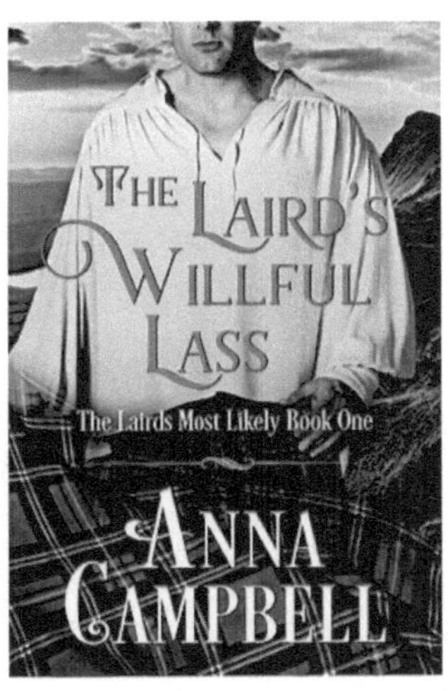

***An untamed man as immovable as a
Highland mountain...***

Fergus Mackinnon, autocratic Laird of Achnasheen,
likes to be in charge. When he was little more than
a lad, he became master of his Scottish estate, and
he's learned to rely on his unfailing judgment. So
has everyone else in his corner of the world. He sees
no reason for his bride—when he finds her—to be
any different.

***A headstrong woman from the warm and
passionate south...***

Marina Lucchetti knows all about fighting her way
through a wall of masculine arrogance. In her
native Florence, she's become a successful artist, no
easy feat for a woman. Now a commission to paint a

series of Highland scenes promises to spread her fame far and wide. When a carriage accident strands her at Achnasheen for a few weeks, it's a mixed blessing. The magnificent landscape offers everything her artistic soul could desire. If only she can resist the impulse to smash her easel across the laird's obstinate head.

When two fiery souls come together, a conflagration flares.

Marina is Fergus's worst nightmare—a woman who defies a man's guidance. Fergus challenges everything Marina believes about a woman's right to choose her path. No two people could be less suited. But when irresistible passion enters the equation, good sense soon jumps into the loch.

Will the desire between Fergus and Marina blaze hot, then fade to ashes? Or will the imperious laird and his willful lass discover that their differences aren't insurmountable after all, but the spice that will flavor a lifetime of happiness?

The Laird's Christmas Kiss:
The Lairds Most Likely Book 2

Down with love!

Ever since she was fifteen, shy wallflower Elspeth
Douglas has pined in vain for the attentions of
dashing Brody Girvan, Laird of Invermackie. But
the rakish Highlander doesn't even know she's
alive. Now she's twenty, she realizes that she'll
never be happy until she stops loving her brother's
handsome friend. When family and friends gather
at Achnasheen Castle for Christmas, she intends to
show the world that she's all grown up, and grown
out of silly crushes on gorgeous Scotsmen. So take
that, my gallant laddie!

Girls just want to have fun...

Except it turns out that Brody isn't singing from the
same Christmas carol sheet. Elspeth decides she's

not interested in him anymore, just as he decides
he's very interested indeed. In fact, now he looks
more closely, his friend Hamish's sister is pretty
and funny and forthright – and just the lassie to
share his Highland estate. Convincing his little
wren of his romantic intentions is difficult enough,
even before she undergoes a makeover and
becomes the belle of Achnasheen. For once in his
life, dissolute Brody is burdened with honorable
intentions, while the lady he pursues is set on
flirtation with no strings attached.

Deck the halls with mistletoe!

With interfering friends and a crate of imported
mistletoe thrown into the mix, the stage is set for a
house party rife with secrets, clandestine kisses,
misunderstandings, heartache, scandal, and love
triumphant.

The Highlander's Lost Lady:
The Lairds Most Likely Book 3

A Highlander as brave and strong as a knight of old...

When Diarmid Mactavish, Laird of Invertavey, discovers a mysterious woman washed up on his land after a wild storm, he takes her in and tries to find her family. But even as forbidden dreams of sensual fulfillment torment him, he's convinced that this beautiful lassie isn't what she seems. And if there's one thing Diarmid despises, it's a liar.

A mother willing to do anything to save her daughter...

Widow Fiona Grant has risked everything to break free of her clan and rescue her adolescent daughter from a forced marriage. But before her quest has barely begun, disaster strikes. She escapes her brutish kinsmen, only to be shipwrecked on Mactavish territory where she falls into her enemies' hands. For centuries, a murderous feud has raged between the Mactavishes and the Grants, so how can she trust her darkly handsome host?

Now a twisted Highland road leads to danger and passion...and irresistible love. But is love strong enough to banish the past's long shadows and offer these wary allies all that their hearts desire?

The Highlander's Defiant Captive:
The Lairds Most Likely Book 4

Peace in the glens means war in the bedchamber!

Scotland. 1699. In a time of heroes, the greatest hero of all is Callum Mackinnon, Laird of Achnasheen. Brave, reckless, canny, and handsome enough to turn any lassie weak at the knees, Callum is a legend in the wild corner of the Highlands where he rules. Now the young laird is determined to choose a new path for his clan and end the violent feud with the Drummonds, a conflict that has painted the glens red with blood for centuries. This means taking Bonny Mhairi Drummond, the Rose of Bruard, as his wife. When negotiations with her pig-headed father break down, Callum seizes matters into his own hands and kidnaps the fairest maiden in Scotland, swearing to make her his own.

Bonny Mhairi is the adored only child of Clan

Drummond's doughty chieftain and she's inherited all her father's courage and stubbornness. Not to mention his undying hatred for anyone called Mackinnon. When the Mackinnon chieftain steals her away from her home and vows to woo her into accepting him as her husband, she swears that she'll never consent to be his bride. But trapped inside her foe's castle, Mhairi finds it hard to cling to old certainties. She detests her arrogant jailer, even as he sparks a fierce, forbidden hunger in her soul.

Loving the enemy...

As Callum and Mhairi wage their passionate war of hearts, danger, treachery and desire circle closer and closer. When her father's army masses at the gates of Achnasheen, will Mhairi prove herself a Drummond now and forever? Or will new allegiances trump ancient hatred, as the desperate laird battles to win the lass he loves more than his life?

The Highlander's Christmas Quest: The Lairds Most Likely Book 5

She's found the man for her, but he has no plans to stay on her island. Perhaps it's time to try a little sabotage!

Scotland. 1725. The moment she sees handsome Dougal Drummond, Kirsty Macbain tumbles headlong into love. A chance storm a few days before Christmas has blown the gallant Highlander off-course to her father's isle of Askaval, but once he's repaired his boat, Dougal is determined to continue on his way. His bright blue eyes are firmly fixed on valiant deeds and a distant horizon. What does he care for a smart-mouthed, independent lassie who forms no part of his plans for his future?

Kirsty is convinced that if only she can keep Dougal on Askaval, he'll see how perfect they are together. With his boat out of action, he's trapped in her company. Some surreptitious midnight destruction with a drill and a hammer might help true love to win out. On the other hand, if Dougal discovers what she's been up to, there will be the devil to pay.

Will this madcap Christmas deliver Kirsty's heart's desire – or will her scheming see Dougal sailing away to a life without her?

The Highlander's English Bride:
The Lairds Most Likely Book 6

An impossible pairing...

Hamish Douglas, the mercurial Laird of Glen Lyon, has never got along with independent, smart-mouthed Emily Baylor. Which wouldn't matter if this brilliant Scottish astronomer didn't move in the same scientific circles as Emily and if her famous father wasn't his mentor. But when Emily looks likely to derail the event which will make Hamish's career, he loses his temper with the pretty miss and his recklessness leaves her reputation in ruins.

A marriage made in scandal...

Emily has always thought her father's spectacular protégé was far too arrogant for his own good. But what is she to do when the only way she can save her good name in society is to wed the unruly laird? Reluctantly she accepts Hamish's proposal, but only on the condition that their union remains chaste. That shouldn't be a problem; they've never been friends, let alone potential lovers – except that after they marry, Hamish reveals unexpected depths and a host of admirable qualities, and he's so awfully handsome, and now the swaggering rogue admits that he desires her...

From the ballrooms of London to the grandeur of the western Highlands, a battle royal rages between these two strong-willed combatants. Neither plans to yield an inch – but are these smart people smart enough to see that sometimes the greatest victory lies in mutual surrender?

The Highlander's Forbidden Mistress: The Lairds Most Likely Book 7

A week to be wicked...

Widowed Selina Martin faces another marriage founded on duty, not love. When notorious libertine Lord Bruard invites her to his isolated hunting lodge, he promises discretion – and seven days of hedonistic pleasure before she weds her boorish fiancé. All her life, Selina has done the right thing, but this no-strings-attached chance to discover the handsome rake's sensual secrets is irresistible. She'll surrender to her wicked fantasies, seize some brief happiness, then knuckle down to a loveless union. What could possibly go wrong?

In a lifetime of seduction, Brock Drummond, the dashing Earl of Bruard, has never wanted a woman the way he wants demure widow Selina Martin. When Selina agrees to become his temporary lover, he soon falls captive to an enchantment unlike any other. He sets out to slake his white hot desire until only ashes remain, but as each day of forbidden delight passes, the idea of saying goodbye to his ardent mistress becomes more and more unbearable.

When scandal explodes around them and threatens to destroy Selina, Brock is the only person she can turn to. After so short a time, can she trust a man whose name is a byword for depravity?

Will this sizzling liaison prove a mere affair to remember? Or will their week of passion spark a lifetime of happiness for the widow and her dissolute Scottish earl?

The Highlander's Christmas Countess:
The Lairds Most Likely Book 8

The new stableboy has a secret!

Kit Laing is a genius with Glen Lyon's horses and a favorite with his employer's family, but he isn't all he seems. In fact, the shy stablehand isn't a he at all. Kit is actually Christabel Urquhart, Countess of Appin, on the run from a greedy, violent stepbrother with designs on her fortune.

And the laird's handsome nephew has worked out just what it is.

Quentin MacNab, the dashing heir to Cannich, has had his suspicions about the new stable lad from the first. Kit is far too pretty to be a boy – and far too well spoken to be a servant.

Now passion and danger combine to create a Yuletide like no other.

When a snowstorm traps Kit and Quentin overnight in an isolated hut, the discovery of her true identity sparks a rushed marriage to stave off a scandal. But can the Christmas Countess learn to trust her charming new husband's promises of protection? Or will their fragile alliance fall victim to the evil forces assailing her?

The Highlander's Rescued Maiden: The Lairds Most Likely Book 9

The myth of Fair Ellen of the Isles.

Across the Highlands, people recount the legend of a beautiful lassie in a tower, locked away from her clamorous suitors by a tyrannical father. Any person of sense dismisses the story as a fairy tale, no more substantial than a wisp of Scottish mist.

Rogue or hero? Or a little bit of both?

Dashing Highlander Will Mackinnon is a devil with the ladies, disinclined to fall for such romantic nonsense. But one day, his storm-tossed boat washes ashore at a rocky island dominated by a stone tower. Inside the tower, he discovers lovely, gallant Ellen Cameron and a passion that eclipses anything he's experienced before in his reckless life.

Danger and desire...

This brave adventurer vows to rescue the captive maiden and make her his own forever. But dark shadows gather about the lovers and threaten to destroy all their hopes for happiness. Will has found the love of a lifetime – but will it end up costing him his life?

The Highlander's Christmas Lassie:
The Lairds Most Likely Book 10

Young love torn apart.

As teenagers, Malcolm Innes and Rhona Macleod fell passionately in love. But Malcom's parents were horrified to think of the aristocratic heir to Dun Carron marrying a humble crofter's daughter. Desperate to crush the affair, they locked Malcolm up and exiled Rhona to London where she disappears. But Malcolm is faithful and stubborn and devotes his life to searching for his beloved and the child she was carrying when they were cruelly separated.

A chance to mend two shattered lives.

On a snowy Christmas Eve, Rhona opens the door of her isolated farmhouse to find the man she never thought to see again, the man who betrayed her. When she was pregnant with his son, Malcolm abandoned her to find her way alone in a cold, heartless world. Now she discovers that her long-held hatred is based on lies and that he's been true to her. Yet surely after all these years, it's too late to awaken the love that once united them.

As Christmas Eve turns into Christmas Day, Malcolm and Rhona discover that their mutual desire has never died. Will this Yuletide reunion lead to a lifetime together? Or has old tragedy ruptured their bond forever?